Also by Ray Anderson
The Trail
Sierra

To—
CHRISTINE, JEFF, and STEVE

ACKNOWLEDGMENTS

SEVERAL BOOKS HELPED ME understand water wars and water rights, in particular *Water Wars: Privatization, Pollution, and Profit* by Vandana Shiva and *Cadillac Desert: The American West and Its Disappearing Water* by Marc Reisner. Other helpful books were *Where the Waters Divide* by Karen Berger and Daniel R. Smith and *The Big Thirst: The Secret Life and Turbulent Future of Water* by Charles Fishman.

I'm also indebted to the late Tony Hillerman, whose novels gave me understanding of American Indian culture. Two in particular opened my eyes: *A Thief of Time* and *Sacred Clowns*.

Yogi's CDT Handbook (February 2007), by Jackie McDonnell, was helpful in confirming my own journal notes. *The Divide* is a novel, but I relied on my daily postings. The plot, of course, is made up, and I took some liberties with Ute culture.

Thanks to Richard "Gus" Borgeson for providing tips on background and setting, and my thanks to Alan Kennedy who read three separate drafts of the manuscript. Thanks also to Linda Santoro, John Lovett, Bill Humberd Susan Trausch, Virginia Young, and many others who gave me advice and support. Finally, a big thankyou to my wife, Nancy, who has been in my corner since day one.

THE DIVIDE

RAY ANDERSON

TURNER PUBLISHING COMPANY

(the Continental Divide Trail map should be on this page. I sent a suggested map previously, from Internet public domain. If approved, I need to write in names and places on it, which occur in the novel.)

CHAPTER ONE

Central Colorado, west of the Divide
September 2007

DON REARDON PULLED HIS compound bow and aimed. Between heartbeats, he let the arrow fly. Forty yards away, the doe went down. Satisfaction rippled through him—he'd now have protein for another several weeks. What Reardon liked about bowhunting was the stealth, the efficiency with purpose. Without the accompanying sound of a gunshot, not a soul knew.

The camouflaged, bearded, six-foot mountaineer had built his own cabin in an unlikely spot. He was a mile away from water in an understory of aspen and pine blowdowns, far from any trail. The Continental Divide Trail, known as the CDT, was closest at over a mile beyond the stream, Reardon's water source that was often visited by wildlife. The creek bend, where he dragged the doe to, was so hidden that one could only find it by following the sound of roiling water. He came here to hunt and had never been disappointed. Animals would cover any tracks Reardon might make, but he'd never seen any human within two miles of his small cabin.

It hadn't taken him long to build the twenty-by-ten-foot structure. Alee of wind, braced and protected by blowdowns and debris, which absorbed storm and snow, Reardon had stuffed muddied mosses into cracks and the occasional small hole. He remembered what his father had once told him—climate is what you expect; weather is what you get. He did pack in brass hinges, screws, and a battery-powered drill to fix a door he'd fashioned onto an ax-shaved and sunken aspen trunk. He'd already brought in an old-time bucksaw, the kind one person pulls back and forth with two hands. He'd spent a lot of time finding a spot where he could use trees for the corner posts of his cabin. Two trees were already in position. For the other two corners, Reardon cut off sturdy limbs from a large oak, dug holes with an entrenching shovel he'd bought at an Army-Navy store, and sunk them himself. At the same store outside of Denver, he also bought an extra mess kit, three canteens, camo, boots, extra pairs of wool socks, and a waterproof bag, which he used as a case for his down pillow, one of the few items of domestic luxury he allowed himself.

Reardon pulled the arrow out of the doe, and after checking the feathers and running them several times across his forehead above closed eyes, he washed the arrow tip and shank in the stream. His father had taught him how to bowhunt and gut game. Reardon thought back to the day he asked his father why he rubbed arrow feathers across his temple. He remembered the relaxed smile of his father and his words: "Son, when you chalk up a kill, give simple mental respect back to the animal. It's never personal." Reardon stiffened as he remembered his father's suicide three weeks later. He'd hung himself from a garage rafter.

Back at his cabin, Reardon cleaned, dressed, and salted the animal. He attended to his diary, and later that afternoon, as the sun banked west, he removed a short cedar floorboard and took out the three-ringed binder holding what he'd requested from Butane: a report titled *Explosives and Demolition*. Butane, a military-trained demo expert, had prepared it privately for Reardon.

"Son, don't make the mistakes I did. Get the facts. Insist on the details." His father's words kept him company. After an hour of study, he restored the binder to its hidden spot. He looked forward to his next ritual. He picked up his Quest Storm compound and a quiver of extra arrows. Before sundown every day, good weather and bad, he practiced shots. He stepped as quiet as the Ute did a hundred years ago, and after a quarter mile, stopped. He turned to face a sugar pine at fifty yards, the kind of pine that drops cones the length of a large man's shoe. He steadied the quiver and held the bow beside him. He closed his eyes and counted the seconds as they passed. On ten, Reardon drew out an arrow, nocked it, pulled, and let the arrow fly. His count stopped at twelve. Two seconds. He'd done it quicker most times, but this shot looked good. He went to the tree. Near perfect. The arrow stuck the tree inside the newest bar coaster he'd attached to it. His next shot was half a second quicker, but he missed the cardboard coaster by a quarter inch. He took eight more shots, all but one under two seconds by his count. Five stuck inside the coaster; three were within a half inch. A decent shoot, but Reardon knew he'd get better.

That night, he placed a birchbark bookmark in Butane's binder and closed it. He liked what he'd read and would finish it tomorrow. He remembered the day he'd discovered Butane lying in the ravine, his twisted and cracked glasses beside him. After a storm with sleet and fifty-mile-an-hour winds had passed through, Reardon had taken a walk to check his perimeter, and after satisfying himself that his immediate environs were in order, he trekked farther on to the ravine that he knew would be flooded. From a distance, he saw him: a high-cheeked American Indian, unconscious with a busted leg. Reardon went to work. Drawing from the first responder course he'd taken and all he'd learned from his dad, Reardon removed the soaked, icy shirt, and being the same size and build as the victim, Reardon undressed and gave him his own shirt, still warm from his back. He revived the man, Paul Christo—he was wearing army dog tags—got him rehydrated, and set his leg. When Christo stabilized two days later, Reardon covered him with an extra wool blanket and went out to retrieve his drag, which he'd made from willow switches and limbs to haul deer and game. It was time to hunt.

After some success and another meal of cooked protein, Christo, no longer delirious, showed Reardon a look of thanks and love with grateful brown eyes. It was at that instant Reardon knew he'd be able to convert Christo to a supporter of his cause. He knew because he'd had a premonition straight from Christo's love-locked eyes that Christo swung both ways. Reardon actually hoped this was true; if so, Reardon would own him. Since Christo had served as a demolitions expert, Reardon gave him the trail name Butane.

CHAPTER TWO

AS BUTANE IMPROVED, Reardon probed into his past. The former army sergeant with a demolitions MOS was twenty-eight, one year older than himself.

"Were both your parents American Indian?" Reardon asked.

"My mother is a full-blooded Ute. My father, so I'm told, was a half-breed."

Reardon stared at him.

"He vamoosed before I was born."

"I see. Perhaps you'd like to know more about him."

It was awhile before he responded. "I learned only a few years ago that he was with a government agency that relocated tribes and"—Butane made air quotes—"looked after their welfare."

"That's how your mother met him?"

"In a manner of speaking. But, I'm told, he raped her and took off."

Reardon leaned over and patted Butane's bandages surrounding hickory splints, the leg hung in traction by ropes from the ceiling of the rustic cabin. He'd tried patching Butane's glasses but had given up. The fire hissed from the damp hickory and soft pine, but the small room was warm. A few sparks flew across the bandages, but Butane didn't seem to mind. Reardon had explained how he was going to reset the leg, and Butane gave him advice, explaining that he'd seen it done twice on the reservation. Butane confirmed that in both instances no trip was made to a hospital or clinic, just to a reservation "doctor of all maladies."

"Well, that must have been a shock, about your mother," Reardon said.

Butane shifted his eyes to the open hearth, which was fronted by burnt stones.

"My mother didn't tell me this. She's mentally deficient. Always has been."

"Is she on the reservation?"

"She's cared for there but will die within the next year or two."

"How do you know?"

"The doctor of all maladies—what most people refer to as the medicine man."

"Do you see her?"

"Rarely. And I need to make sure she doesn't see me." Butane trained his eyes back on Reardon. "I, apparently, bring back bad memories."

"I'm sorry, Butane."

"It's okay. My mother's older cousin brought me up and looked out for me. Now he's gone too."

"What happened to him?"

"Cirrhosis of the liver."

Reardon said nothing as he adjusted logs next to the hearth and dropped in another hunk of pine.

Butane sighed and closed his eyes. Several minutes elapsed as Reardon watched him. Finally, Butane recovered his voice. "When he died, I joined up."

"You served your country, Butane."

"Lot of good it's done for my people!"

"Are you sorry you served? Understand, I'm not bothered either way."

"I learned how to blow things up."

"I'm listening."

"One black lieutenant tried to patronize me, but unless you were an officer, most minorities were treated like shit." Butane shifted his good leg. "What's your story again? Your father went bankrupt. Something about a promise?"

"He started building a dude ranch—it was his dream, and he'd been promised a loan from the bank. There was some red tape and a delay, but the banker said he'd get the loan. My father hired men and began the project in Dillon where we lived. He paid them out of his own pocket, figuring the loan would be in soon.

"Out of the blue the banker says he can't get him the loan because more water is going to be diverted east of the Divide. 'Build your ranch over there in the Front Range,' he says, 'and you'll get your loan.'

"My father told him he'd already poured a foundation and was studding up. He couldn't stop now and wouldn't think of relocating his family east of the Divide."

Reardon's face burned red.

"How long after this was it that you found him?"

"He went bankrupt in four months. I was fourteen."

Not a word was said for the next twenty minutes. Twice a coyote howled. The third time, Butane pretended to spit and studied a spiderweb in a corner where the wall met the hand-planked ceiling.

And then Butane spoke. "My clan could have followed the main tribe to western Colorado. Could have also gone to our other reservation north of the Arizona border."

"Why didn't they?"

"Wasn't always about water. Gold and silver were discovered on Ute lands, the US government finagled agreements and made up new treaties, and we lost territory. My clan split off because Running Waters's grandfather refused to move. But the government considered us hundred or so as stragglers and pushed us near to where we are now, out of the way. We didn't fight back—how could we? We holed up and are still there."

"Any regrets?" Reardon asked.

Butane hesitated. "My little reservation wouldn't admit it. We are too stubborn. But the last straw was the Indian Reorganization Act of 1934. The white government bastards had to finally acknowledge the other Ute tribes but ignored our clan."

THAT NIGHT, REARDON MADE notes in his diary. He was sure of one thing: Butane was not happy with how American Indians were treated in his country—if he had a country. Reardon saw new possibility. This was the opening he'd been waiting for.

CHAPTER THREE

Mexico-US border—Antelope Wells, NM
Eight months later, May 2008

KARL BERGMAN STARED at the map, while his dog, Blazer, lay beside him. He kept his finger on the southern terminus of the Continental Divide Trail at the Mexican border and peered behind him. Several strands of horizontal barbed wires separated him from Mexico. It was 6:45 a.m. and getting hotter by the minute.

He'd gotten a hitch from a bowlegged Mexican straight out of *Viva Zapata*. The mustached man didn't speak any English other than a few words. He'd pointed to Bergman's backpack at the roadside restaurant in Deming, New Mexico, and said, "CDT, *sí*?"

"Yes, CDT."

"I take you—twenty-fi dollar, *sí*?"

They'd settled on the twenty-dollar bill Bergman had in his wallet. Bergman showed that there was nothing else as he widened the wallet's money pocket. He didn't reach for the other bills hidden in his pack.

They had jounced south on 81, Blazer in the bed of the rusted pickup, to music from a Spanish radio station that had too few mandolins and lots of trumpets and horns. Every so often, Señor Zapata would sing a few words, smile, and look at Bergman with a grin. At Antelope Wells, the southernmost point of the Continental Divide Trail, Blazer jumped over the tailgate as Bergman exited the passenger side. "*Adiós*," Bergman said as the truck bounced back up 81.

Now he tapped the border town on his map again and glanced northeast. Some thirty miles away was Crazy Cook Monument, the most popular of three legitimate starting points of the Continental Divide Trail.

Bergman was a pure long-distance hiker. He would contend that a bona fide CDT thru-hiker, one who intended to hike in one season the full 3,100-plus miles north to Canada, would begin the trek north from the bottom of New Mexico's bootheel, here at Antelope Wells.

The next afternoon, after trudging dusty dirt roads by countless cacti, sage, and spindly cholla, the hiker and dog arrived at Crazy Cook Monument. Someone had pushed the yard-high stone obelisk off its base, and it lay on its side in the sand next to a scrabbly creosote bush. Bergman tried to right the monument and gave up. Etched in the granite base were the words "The Trail Unites Us." Blazer sniffed at a lizard parked on a rock next to the base. The budding yellow flowers of the creosote bush offered hope, Bergman decided. He squinted at flat, desolate lands stretching in all directions. He was in the middle of nowhere as he watched a fiery sun slant to the west. For the first time today, the temperature was a tolerable and welcome eighty-one degrees, but there wasn't the slightest breeze. This didn't bother Bergman, who bent down and removed Blazer's wide-mouthed Nalgene water bottle from the dog's belt and held it for him so he could drink. Bergman was on a personal quest to be a triple-crown long-distance thru-hiker. While he hadn't encountered such arid desolation on the Appalachian Trail, he'd seen desert on the Pacific Crest Trail. He'd been through areas like this before. He again was hiking under the trail name Awol. Long-distance hikers used the convention of trail names, and Absent Without Leave, AWOL, suited the former army captain and had served him well.

What mattered to Awol was the destination, the goal. The accumulation of hiked miles over the next six months would give him a sense of accomplishment and the needed solitude to clear his head. The trek would stitch up old wounds and hopefully work on some fresh ones too. Awol had been flattened by a recent tragedy he felt responsible for, but out here, what mattered most was paying attention to his maps and putting one foot in front of the other. Added to this was the acute sense of adventure he felt whenever he began a long-distance hike. He hoped he could get through this one with no interruptions.

After Blazer finished drinking, Awol returned the bottle to the carrier, which hung over Blazer's back and was tied under his stomach. As Awol drank from his own bottle, he watched his animal, a Belgian

Malinois with some German shepherd, sniff the granite marker. He and Linda shared the animal as parents share custody of their children. He and Linda had separated three months ago, but they were friendly and cooperative. One week she had Blazer; he took him the following week. The dog didn't seem to mind and grew accustomed to the arrangement. But it was a given that Awol always took Blazer with him on hikes.

The water tasted good in the heat, and the windless air was dry. One thing that steadied Awol was that he had his affairs in order, and he could enjoy this last leg of hiking's triple crown. His business partner, Tommy, Linda's brother, had known for over a year about his CDT itch. The CDT is the acknowledged "king of trails," Awol had told him. The backbone of the Rocky Mountains from Mexico to Canada. They had both prepared for his six-month gap in their kitchen-bathroom remodeling business. Awol had worked extra hard to line up new jobs, and their crew had plenty of work for the rest of the year. He didn't accept that his marriage to Linda was finished. It didn't look good, but he would try to focus on the present. He had plenty of time for thinking and planning over the next five to six months.

CHAPTER FOUR

BRUCE HENDRICKS UNDERSTOOD this was the chance of a lifetime. The question was how to turn the advantage in his favor. Colorado's Front Range, which contained the urban corridor of Fort Collins, Greeley, Boulder, Denver, Colorado Springs, and Pueblo, was home to 85 percent of the state's population. It was the place to be, east of the Continental Divide, the place where important people came to live beside fancy pools and big lawns. Forty-four years ago, Hendricks's father scraped together every dime he had to buy eight hundred acres of prime property in the Front Range near Denver. Twenty years ago, while at the bank, Hendricks got his Colorado realty license by taking an evening course. Thirteen years ago, his father died, and having no siblings, the land was his. Then the Wharton-educated banker-realtor did something smart: he didn't sell or develop the acreage; he held on. The valuable land had increased in value eleven times over since his father had bought it, and recent news about the booming housing market made Hendricks understand the time was ripe to make millions.

Water. That was and would be the problem. The fact that Hendricks had three years left on his term as a Denver Water commissioner helped but guaranteed him nothing. Even as a newly elected VP of Denver Water, it would take all his moxie to deal with the Colorado Water Conservation Board. Water was becoming scarcer by the day. Blame it on global warming, droughts, more people, unending forest fires, whatever—man's number one resource for life on planet Earth was dwindling. More water was needed to satisfy the needs of the ever-developing Front Range, including Hendricks's eight hundred acres. No water meant no development, which in turn meant his land would become worthless if the water issue wasn't solved. There used to be a simple solution: divert more water from west of the Divide to the thirsty, expanding east. But this water was also needed by the Ute tribe for a planned casino with ski resort, bundled with their other development plans west of the Divide. West of the Divide, the Rockies provided natural trails for the skier, and with the addition of a huge casino and housing developments, and the predicted rise in numbers of people settling in the area, there was less chance for diverting additional water to the east, under the mountains. Hendricks cringed at the thought.

The reservoirs were drying up like many of the lakes. Lake Mead, the largest reservoir in the United States, situated on the Colorado River, was a prime example. All around Lake Mead were cracked and lined sand beds that until a few years ago had held water. Over 65 percent of the water for the Front Range was diverted west to east by tunnels drilled under the mountains of Rocky Mountain National Park. Hendricks saw red tape and water wars looming on the horizon. He had to act if he wanted his land developed. Aside from regular homesteads, he envisioned a retirement community with assisted living and a hospital.

Hendricks always wore a suit and tie to his office in Denver. A few took it as a cultural insult, but the pudgy Hendricks didn't mind. He wore the suit and tie in an effort to be taken seriously, an attempt at class. Besides, he didn't look good in a cowboy hat, buckles, and boots. He was the second-largest realtor in the Front Range. The largest was going through a painful transition: Two sons and a sister had buried their father, the sole owner of the brokerage, three months ago after his fatal heart attack. He died intestate. The state courts were having a field day. The two sons didn't get along, and each hoped to buy the other out. The daughter wanted nothing to do with the business. Just like that, Hendricks Holdings was now poised as the top dog in greater Denver. Before going to his office, Hendricks made a routine stop at a tobacco shop to buy his usual bag of candy.

Hendricks almost felt like whistling as he took an express elevator to his twenty-third-floor corner suite in downtown Denver. But it would be out of character for him, and he'd be cursed if anyone knew how he gloated. He couldn't believe how the stars had aligned in his favor, provided he could solve one problem: water.

CHAPTER FIVE

SENATOR RICHARD RODRIGUEZ, in his Denver office, eyed the American Indian like someone trying not to look intimidated.

"You follow?" the Ute asked.

Smooth. Just be smooth, Rodriguez thought to himself. The senator blinked like he'd thought of something, got up from behind his polished oak desk, and ambled to his matching credenza. He glanced back at the man sitting in front of his desk. He hadn't moved. Rodriguez would use alcohol. The Indian might take it as an insult, but it was worth a try.

"Can I get you something?" Rodriguez asked.

The man said nothing and didn't move. *Smooth*, Rodriguez told himself again. *Stay calm.* He poured two fingers of Scotch over ice and returned to his seat. He sat down before the man and froze. He hadn't noticed that in the time he'd gotten his drink, the Ute had laid an elk horn–handled knife with an eight-inch blade pointed right at him on the desk, a few inches from his belly.

"I don't drink when I'm at work," the Ute said.

Rodriguez frowned at the weapon and looked at him again, but not with indifference. This Indian's father was a full-blown Ute who'd been kicked off the reservation by his own kind. Rodriguez didn't know the details, but he knew that he'd raped a half-breed in Denver. The chief had told him to keep that a secret because the man in front of him as well as the minions on the reservation had been told a different story. The man facing him wasn't even a full-blooded Ute. Despite the senator's power, despite his rank, the senator owed his success to the tribe. They had supported his initial run in local politics after getting him started on the board of Denver Water. He'd been grateful but wanted to cut loose now that he'd developed his own cronies and network in Washington. And he wanted to look good to all the voters along the Front Range.

"My chief has given me instructions to *not* give you an offer you can't refuse," the man said. "As a matter of fact, he doesn't want me to make you any kind of offer at all."

Rodriguez touched his nose and took another sip. The man watching him through wire-rimmed glasses was sometimes called Angry Bear on the reservation. Off the reservation, he was known as Paul Christo.

"I'm going to have a chaw," Christo said. "Unless you want spittle on your desk, you might want to bring me a cup of some sort."

Rodriguez said nothing and dared another sip. Was he overdoing it? But he was a Colorado senator. He had connections east of the Divide. That's where the real future was. Always had been. He was tired of being reminded of past favors from the tribe. And he'd gifted them cash, an investment, for their new casino. He noticed the tremor in his hand as he replaced the glass on his desk, and when the man smiled, Rodriguez knew that he'd seen it too.

"Now, then," Christo said, fixing a wad in his cheek, "shall we get down to business?"

"I expected you to come here with a formal request. Written on proper forms."

"I could have come to your prim and proper office in DC to do that. You should know that this special request is private."

Seeing no way out, Rodriguez fetched a coffee cup for spittle and lit up a Havana. Christo with his fringed leather vest looked more like a trapper or old-time western tobacco salesman than a modern-day Indian from a reservation. The bleached pants looked like treated buckskin. He belonged on his horse, out on the range.

"What you're asking is next to impossible. For starters, I'm not the only senator whose constituents need water. There are water shortages everywhere."

Christo spit into the cup and reached over the desk for his knife. The edge appeared razor sharp and glinted in the sunlight shining in from the office window. He cleaned his fingernails.

"Mr. Christo, my vacation home is here in Denver. Doesn't it occur to you that Washington would make a connection?"

The man stifled a yawn. "We see it as a matter of paperwork with perhaps some discreet nudges here and there."

"Discreet nudges! To who?"

"Now, don't get yourself worked up, Senator. You are the savvy politician and powerful senator. That's how you got on the fast track—with a few discreet nudges from Chief Running Waters, remember?"

"Why didn't your clan go south and move into the main Ute tribe down there?"

"And where would you be now, had we done so?"

"I can't do it."

"Senator, let me stop you right there." The young man's countenance reddened as he pointed his buck knife at him. One tobacco-wadded cheek was ready to pop. "We may grease the skids to help you, but you will do this. Or would you rather I tell my chief you have refused?"

The senator looked with disbelieving eyes at the gimpy twenty-eight-year-old mixed-breed nobody. How in the hell could this Indian, this aide to the chief, tell him what to do? But Rodriguez was up for reelection. His relationship with the tribe had always been in the shadows. The Ute chief kept their mutual gifts quiet. If the tribe leaked information about his unfortunate past, there would be a scandal. He knew the chief wouldn't lower himself to come to him, but to send this half-baked ranchero? The senator seethed.

That night, Senator Rodriguez, a self-made man who had resurrected himself from a border barrio, whose big mistake was joining Gamblers Anonymous after it was too late, packed his briefcase with legal documents and minutiae referencing Colorado's water rights along and under the Continental Divide. If he had to initiate a paper trail, he would be sure it was initiated in Washington.

That afternoon, Paul Christo reported to Chief Running Waters. He drove through puddles of melting snow and negotiated dizzying hairpin turns up to an eight-thousand-foot-high arête. On the western end was a fancy, plushly landscaped A-frame with an extra-large front window. The ski chalet was built to spec and was offered as a second home, one of many planned, for the wealthy in the proposed Rocky Mountain High

Casino and Resort complex. The casino was the dream of the impov-
erished Ute Indian tribe and would resemble the Mohegan Sun casino
in Connecticut, but bigger. Added to the casino were plans for a huge
year-round resort offering skiing, kayaking, fishing, hunting, boating,
and hiking.

"Welcome to Rocky Mountain High," Chief Running Waters said as
Paul removed his vest and neck scarf.

"Tea or hot chocolate?" one of the chief's aides asked.

"Tea for now, hot chocolate later."

The chief took a cup of tea and sat in front of his fieldstone fireplace, which ran up to the beamed cathedral ceiling. He watched Paul's
contented face absorb the fireplace and its warmth. He saw him turn
to the winter-sports-themed watercolors hanging on the tongue-and-
groove knotty pine walls. Paintings of skiers, hikers, kayakers. Paul, a
decent-looking mixed-breed, was one of the toughest Indians the chief
knew. He'd known Paul's father and the woman he'd raped. He'd run him
off the reservation for good when Paul's real mother, a half-breed government clerk in the Indian Affairs office, died giving birth to her bastard
son. Running Waters called upon his own niece, a slow girl, but one who
could raise the boy. As chief, he instructed everyone to keep the true story
quiet. For a Ute to rape a white person off the reservation, even if she
was part Indian, was a serious matter, and the chief had to make several
payoffs and promises to smother the truth. The reservation had enough
problems without a rape investigation. To this day, Paul Christo thought
his father was a civilian half-breed who'd raped his Indian "mother." The
reservation witnessed the boy's tenacity, and Paul became a champion
wrestler in high school. The chief had also recognized his smarts and
was instrumental in getting him accepted to the University of Colorado. The one thing that was hard to deal with was his attitude. He was
moody and sensitive. He graduated with a major in history. He had no
money and couldn't get a job. The chief made him a personal aide, but he
rebelled and joined the army. He came back from Afghanistan and shut
down. Medicine Man, the reservation's eldest, had no solution other than
that he should embrace nature and the land. So Paul thru-hiked the Continental Divide Trail, damn near killed himself in Colorado while hiking
in a storm, and now he was here. The chief's aide yet again.

The chief had instructed Paul to act as an enforcer if necessary.

"I had to show him my buck knife," Paul said.

Running Waters smiled. "We expected that would happen eventually. Did he get the message?"

"Yeah, I think so."

"Did he light up a cigar?"

"Yep."

"Okay. He got the message."

CHAPTER SIX

AWOL WAS AFRAID TO LOOK, but he lifted up a sleeve and noted eighty-eight on his chronometer. He'd guessed ninety degrees, judging by the heat he felt pushing up through the rubber soles of his trail shoes. He squinted toward the shimmering mesa in the distance and questioned how cowboys and westerners covered this land in leather boots. He didn't think he'd make it through these drylands by nightfall, but he'd give it his best shot. The parched, cracked earth was a parquet of irregular stepping-stones of caked sand. Blazer was fine, and he suspected that was because the dog sensed another hiking quest in his master. Right now, Awol needed to pay attention and not get lost. Getting lost was a way of life for most CDT thru-hikers. First, the trail wasn't officially complete; second, it was poorly marked; third, there were few people on it, less than a hundred thru-hikers in season. Awol hadn't seen a soul.

The ocotillo cactus was in bloom, and Awol thought about rubbing the pinkish-red leaves of one taller than him, he at five foot ten, but kept on walking. Cactus and sage stretched everywhere. He neared more ocotillo blooms and thought about Linda and how she loved flowers. Strangely, the separation was not the result of one of his unpredictable bouts of drinking. Nor did it emerge from one of his moods and subsequent withdrawal, which could last for days. After dinner one night, during a cup of coffee, Linda had surprised him.

"This might be a good time to talk about us, Karl."

He looked up at her. "What's on your mind?"

"I think we should separate for a while."

"What? Why?"

"I'm not myself lately, though I know it's not all your fault. You carry too much inside you, and it starts to crowd out everything else. I feel like I'm walking on eggshells. You are ready to blow again. I can sense it."

"It takes time to process things. Look, I gave the PTSD counseling thing a go, but I have to work through these things myself."

"Yes, you gave it a go. And I appreciate you keeping that promise."

"So what's the problem? I haven't had a drink in almost a month."

Linda didn't explain. She stiffened and said she wanted to separate. For a while, for good, she didn't know. "I've reached this decision after a lot of thought, Karl. I'm sorry. Please understand that I can't keep living like this." It was decided. Right then. Right there.

Awol knew the reason, of course. His son, Gregory, had committed suicide six months ago, and it had knocked him off his sobriety—and everything else. About to graduate from high school, the eternally quiet boy had jumped from a tenth-floor balcony. *Why?* Bergman felt responsible. After the divorce, thirteen years ago, his ex-wife had left Massachusetts with his two sons for California. Two years ago, Awol had seen Gregory, but it was a brief and ineffectual visit—he couldn't reach him. It was so much easier to connect with his other son, Kenny. A year later, he'd seen Gregory again when he and Kenny attended Awol's celebration of renewing his marriage vows plus a year of sobriety. Again, the boy was distant and skulked around like a recluse. Awol was the cause of the divorce, and he blamed himself for Gregory's suicide. It was like someone had turned on a switch in Awol's brain. Since Gregory's demise, he'd been on and off the bottle and broached his own thoughts of suicide.

After Linda's bombshell and plea, Awol moved out the next week into a small house five miles away. He tried to look casual when Linda told him it was available but needed some work. *Damn,* he'd thought. *She had it planned.* She let him keep the dog the first week.

Awol realized as he stopped for water and a quick break under a Joshua tree that he wouldn't be leaving the drylands until tomorrow. This heat was as bad as he'd experienced in the Gulf during Desert Storm. He was beat, and Blazer didn't seem to mind his master taking an extended break. That night under a hammock moon, Awol convinced himself that things were going to be fine. He always stabilized whenever he hiked, and he did so now. The booze was out of his system, and out here he craved water instead. He had frightful memories, but there were those people who said he'd come a long way. And a few, like his other son, Kenny, considered him a hero. Now a graduate student in biochemistry at Stanford, Kenny would always make Awol smile. Years later, Awol would think back to this moment here in the desert. He told himself he was a good man. He was trying to overcome some terrible shit. Here in the drylands, of all places, he convinced himself he was on the right track to redemption.

Asleep under twinkling stars, this former army officer, experienced thru-hiker, and outdoorsman could not have known that his life would be upended once again. Though becalmed and dreaming serenely as a breeze feathered the night air, he would soon be walking into a human hornet's nest.

CHAPTER SEVEN

"**W**HICH TUNNEL ARE WE GOING to blow?" Butane asked.

Reardon squinted at Butane, who had brought him up to date with his dealings as aide to the reservation chief. As with most people Reardon had met in his twenty-seven years, the man in front of him masked his true self. Butane was blunt and feisty on the outside but quiet within. All show to cover his bisexuality, which Butane had admitted to. And which Reardon despised. He hated gays; he hated bisexuals more. In his mind, bisexuals robbed from both worlds.

"Don't know yet. Might be three of them, or two, or . . . who knows?"

"Three? May I ask which three you have in mind?"

"I ask you, what main tunnels deliver water to the Front Range?"

"Okay. I know the Adams does. And the Moffat."

Reardon stared at him like he was disappointed. "That all?"

"Well, cut me some slack here. I know about the Adams because the Old Ute Trail swings up in that area."

"Think Dillon Reservoir."

"The Roberts."

"As I said, all three, maybe two, could be one, and we use the others as a diversion."

Butane angled his head and looked away. Reardon had seen this pose from him before; Butane was thinking. Reardon heard the soft thump of a squirrel moving on the roof. He'd seen three up there the other day and considered them family—unless he needed quick and easy protein. He heard other slight thumps and looked up, his eyes tracking their movements across his roof.

"Gonna have to do lots of research here," Butane said.

"Right. Dig in and get me another binder like this"—Reardon held up the explosives binder—"on those three tunnels."

"Then what?"

"I'm working up my own notes. We will compare." He knew Butane liked the "we" part.

Butane smiled. "Okay, boss."

A week later, Butane came by. It was clear from the look on his face that Butane had missed him, his remote cabin, his affection. Reardon let him in and offered him a seat on his handcrafted stool.

"I haven't finished working up the tunnels yet," Butane said, peeking up with ardent eyes, hands folded as if about to pray.

Reardon looked to a half-hidden patch of loosestrife and other invasive weeds beyond the open door. "Why are you here?" He stared at the purple flowers.

The silence had become uncomfortable. Reardon didn't move.

Butane asked, "What did you mean last time by a diversion?"

"Ah," Reardon said, sitting across from him on his mattress pad. He pointed to his battery-powered radio. "I follow the news. There's been chatter. This is post nine-eleven, and we need to accept that word of our plan could leak out."

"Not if we—"

Reardon held up a hand. "You don't understand me. If it happens, we'd have to have alternate plans. What I'm implying is, we let our own diversion leak out."

Butane looked at him and smiled. "We could use one of the dams as a diversion."

Reardon looked pleased. "I've thought about that. We don't want to leak a particular tunnel diversion for obvious reasons. A dam points to other dams, and no one expects a tunnel."

"A dam would be the more obvious to blow because it's easier," Butane said.

"Exactly."

"How do we leak a diversion that's connected to a dam?"

"That's the puzzle that keeps me awake at night. It has to be done just right."

Both were quiet for several minutes.

"I've got a busted peace pipe I took from my mother," Butane said. "Maybe . . . Down in Cuba, New Mexico . . ."

CHAPTER EIGHT

NEAR HACHITA, NEW MEXICO, forty-four miles north of the border, Awol sat on an abandoned white porcelain toilet outside in the sun. The toilet didn't function other than it was a prankster's idea of a seat with a backrest. Awol took it and pondered the desolation as he sat under a hand-painted rest area sign banged into a weatherworn aspen. Blazer curled himself behind the toilet in a patch of shade. Awol worried about water. This was worse than southern California on the PCT. He hadn't seen one hiker. The signage was marginal. He'd hoped some trail angel, those anonymous souls that looked out for hikers, would have left water, but from what he could tell, hardly anyone came out here—no tracks, nada.

Everything was sere. No sign of water, and the few puddles he'd seen were fly-strewn and full of feces. But the guidebook mentioned working windmills, and Awol looked to the one he was headed to a mile away. He could see what he assumed were cattle near it. That morning he had been checked by Border Patrol. The cream-and-green-striped vehicle pulled up behind him. They'd asked some questions about his plans, and he wished now he'd confirmed water availability.

Awol was relieved after he filled his water bottles at the spigot driven by the windmill. The vanes spun slowly, but the water looked decent. Plus, he treated it with Aquamira, as always. Waiting the required time while the chemicals did their job, he watched Blazer lap from his bowl.

Awol drank the heavenly fluid. Now that his head was clearer, Awol pondered what he would say to his ex-wife, Gloria. He owed her a call. Years ago, he hiked in leather boots. Gloria hadn't been happy about that. She was vegan and not only eschewed eating meat, she argued that no one should wear leather from dead animals. He tried to explain the reasons hikers and outdoorsmen chose leather, but she wouldn't relent. In those hiking days, he met neophytes in their buffed new leathers who hobbled from blisters. That always happened when boots weren't broken in. He'd always packed extra bandages for those weekend leather-boot hikers with oozing sores.

Awol picked an exercise spot. He'd missed his routine yesterday and didn't want to get sloppy. He started with a hundred crunches, with a short breather at fifty. Next, Awol, who maintained the same 180-pound weight as he did his senior year in high school, counted push-ups. "Ten, twenty, thirty, forty." He stopped in the arms-extended position and leaned side to side before continuing, "fifty, sixty, seventy, seventy-five."

That evening, on the outskirts of Hachita, his cell showed three bars.

"Is that you, Karl?"

"Yes, Gloria, I've been meaning to call you. How are you?"

Silence. "Well, it's now six months since I lost my Gregory—"

"Our Gregory," Awol said, wincing at his pettiness. "Gloria, forgive me. Yes, more your Gregory. After all, he's been—"

"Okay. Okay." She muffled a sob.

"Do you know why, Gloria? What made him do it?"

"I don't know."

"Gloria. Please be honest. Did his suicide have anything to do with me?"

"I don't know. You have to stop asking me this."

It wasn't what Awol wanted to hear, and he choked up.

"I've separated from Linda."

"Okay. Sorry."

"How have you been bearing up?"

"Not good."

"Kenny okay?"

"He broke up with Jill."

"I'm sorry to hear that. He sounded okay when I talked to him a couple of weeks ago. I might have forgotten to ask about Jill. I'll call him."

"Karl, you've—I'm sorry, but you've gotten me all worked up again."

"What can I say, Gloria, except that Gregory . . . I can't let it go. I feel responsible."

Silence.

"I should have tried seeing him again that time in California at his school," Awol continued.

She was crying. Awol had made a mess of things with what he'd hoped would be a helpful call.

"Gloria?"

"I have to go."

"Please don't hang up on me. I feel like this was partly my fault with Gregory. Kenny became my hero on the PCT. Did Gregory feel left out? Is that why?"

"I don't know, Karl. I don't know."

And so it went for a few more rounds. The more Awol tried to come to some kind of resolution, the higher the tension mounted, until Gloria hung up. Awol felt furious with himself. He was a hiking hero twice over for accomplishments in bringing down a killer on the Appalachian and a drug cartel on the Pacific Crest Trail, but right now, sitting on top of his sleeping bag, he felt like a failure in every sense. He'd give anything to have another chance to connect with his son Gregory and save him.

Awol didn't thank his maker for the lack of means to temptation. He wanted beer. He looked around him and, of course, didn't see a way. Ten minutes later he lay on top of his bag looking at stars. Stars upon stars. *Gregory. Gregory. Oh, Gregory, my boy.*

CHAPTER NINE

TWO DAYS AND TWENTY-EIGHT MILES later, in Separ, New Mexico, Awol witnessed a confrontation at the trading post. He could see two men hollering at each other, and as he neared the store, they pummeled each other while a gaggle of onlookers stood around. No one did anything; no one said anything. Both men became bloodied, and as one began to beat and overpower the other and grab his throat, a big man charged out of the store and pulled him off.

"You take my water again, I will kill you!" the stronger fighter yelled.

The beaten man sat on the ground and spat blood. Awol couldn't decide if he spat in insolence or because he had to get blood out of his mouth. The yeller picked up his sombrero, looked at the assembled group, and hollered, "*Ladrón*," pointing to the beaten man and ambling to his battered pickup. The loser crawled to his hat, and after he sat and put it on, the act seemed to revive him, and he got up. Awol thought the guy started to smile but then realized he was checking his teeth.

He was Hispanic and looked to be in his forties. "Should be enough water for everybody. I got way more cattle than he's got. Am I supposed to let them die?"

One of the onlookers folded his arms across his chest. "Pedro, I've known you for twenty years, and I told you half a dozen times you got no right to divert water to your herd. Serves you right."

"We ain't none of us going to have water if we don't get those bastards in Denver to give us back our river. Them's the ones who oughta be shot!"

Another man in suspendered overalls rubbed his chin, seeming to ponder this. "The rules is the rules," he said. "We all got the same problem with water that you do."

"I got the most cattle," he yelled back, spitting out more blood. "They ain't overgrown kangaroo rats." He looked up at the sun as if that's whose fault it was. "We got no lakes anymore. Where am I supposed to get my water?"

"Sell off your herd, Pedro, and move north to the Great Lakes," the first man said.

"Fuck you," Pedro said as he lurched to a dirt bike. He got himself onto it and roared off.

BACK ON THE CDT, Awol walked by cacti. He'd read that the saguaros, with their creamy white flowers, survived because of their thick water-storing trunks. These fleshy water hoarders, as opposed to man, conserved their water, not wasting a drop. They stood their ground with attitude. He hiked by a leafless plant, the thorny horsetail, with its woody stem covered by thorns and prickers. A moment later, he noticed that desert cockleburs from some plant had stuck to his pants, and he fussed to knock them off his thighs with his poles. He looked at underbrush he didn't recognize but picked out prickly pear cacti, barrel cacti that looked like oblong green pumpkins with thorns, yucca, and agave, with its sword-shaped, spiny-margined leaves. He noted a small hole in one of the saguaros and remembered reading that Gila woodpeckers will peck the hole and nest there. These plants did all right under harsh conditions. The white man had become pampered and, unlike American Indians he'd read about, ignored requirements of nature and abused the land—the lands he'd kicked the Indians off of.

Awol tramped through dry arroyos that looked decayed in the soft sandstone. Drawing close to another cactus, Blazer barked and scrunched down near the red prickly pears. Awol couldn't believe it. A turtle had been nibbling on one of the pears and had stuck his head back into its shell as Blazer sniffed around it. They watched it crawl away. That afternoon, Awol spied a vulture circling above him. He could make out the wrinkled head of the large bird and saw the sunlight beam through its wings. He felt disconnected and looked forward to Colorado, Wyoming, and Montana, to white-trunked aspens and the green leaves of spring.

That night, after picking off the rest of the desert cockleburs attached to his sleeping pad, Awol camped under the stars and thought about the brawl in Separ. He looked up the kangaroo rat in the fauna portion of his guide. They were desert rats that slept all day in a deep burrow and didn't drink water. They got needed moisture from seeds and plants gathered at night. He remembered the declining shores of Lake Mead during his hike of the Pacific Crest Trail two years ago and heard it had gotten worse. From what he'd read, glaciers were melting at a faster rate, and global warming was now considered a fact. Awol didn't see how people survived the heat and droughts here, and he couldn't wait to break into forest and stream. Water availability had consumed him every hour of every day since he'd started this hike. That's why there were no trail angels out here providing water for hikers. Water was scarce. Water was needed by the locals who lived and farmed here. Something else to put up with. Two men fought not over a loved one, not over insult, not over broken promises, but over water.

ANOTHER FORTY-FIVE MILES and three days later, Awol breached the out-skirts of Silver City, 118 miles north of the border. For one of the few times in his hiking life, he had blisters, one on the sole of each foot. He knew the cause—sweaty socks and the lack of extra water to clean his feet. The sand was hot, and he remembered the scene from the movie *10* with Dudley Moore. Moore finds himself on a beach, and trying to look nonchalant but poised, he walks across a sun-starched strip toward the ocean. The sand heats the bottoms of his bare feet more and more with each step so that he begins to walk briskly, and soon he has to trot, and then he winces as he has to run because his feet are on fire and it is too late to turn back. He imagines gorgeous beachside ladies laughing at him as the cool waves seem forever out of reach. Here in arid southern New Mexico, the heat driven up through Awol's shoes and socks had caused discomfort and irritation all afternoon. He would have to take a zero day in Silver City if he was to preserve his feet.

At the Gila ranger station, the ranger stunned him when he warned of no water between Bear Creek and Sapillo Creek. *Christ.* The ranger pointed to a map and told Awol how to reroute.

"This water situation," Awol said, "is it always this bad?"

"Over the last ten years, it's gotten worse. This year is the driest and hottest I've seen."

"The few puddles I've found are infected—feces, dead bugs. I'm not sure my Aquamira can treat that contamination."

"Bleach is better because it's stronger, but you gotta be real careful with bleach. It'll gut you."

Awol looked around, not expecting to see free water but hoping.

"Relax, I'll give you enough to get you to Highway 35, but here's my question: Why not hitch up to the woodlands where you have better water availability?"

"I've a mind to, but I'm thru-hiking and trying to become a triple crowner."

The ranger smiled. "You thru-hikers are all nuts."

THE RANGER HAD FOUND AWOL a cheap place to stay. The so-called proprietor of the shed-like shack couldn't speak English, but he could count money, and for fifteen dollars Awol had a cot in the one-room shack. He was given a five-gallon plastic pail, and with charade-like animation, the hunched Latino indicated it would be the extent of the water offered. Awol looked at the lopsided sink. The stopper worked, so he had a sink bath after washing his blistered feet. He saved enough water to drink and to resupply and for his evening and breakfast meals.

After a meal of ramen mixed with rice and a long drink of water, he called his remaining child, Kenny.

"Hey, Dad. You out of New Mexico yet?"

"I wish. I've got blisters from the heat."

"Really?"

"Listen, as one with a scientific mind, going for a PhD in biochemistry, how bad is global warming affecting water availability?"

"You mean for the planet or for us out here in the West?"

"Out here, for starters."

"Aside from global warming, we use too much H20. Seen Las Vegas?"

Awol thought about that.

"Three days ago, I saw a fistfight. Two grown men, forty-something. One accused the other of diverting water because he had more cattle."

"From what I'm hearing, it's going to get worse. Lake Mead is gonna be a desert someday."

Silence.

"Kenny, I've asked before; I need to ask you again. Be honest, please. Could I have contributed, inadvertently, to Gregory's suicide?"

"No, Dad, and you need to stop thinking about this. I wasn't that close to him, I'm ashamed to say. He withdrew from everyone. We were all stunned."

"Are you okay?"

"Yes. Although now I do think about him. Lots. Wish I had known what was going on with him."

"Well, I won't ask you the question anymore. It doesn't make it any easier for me if I didn't . . . God, Kenny, he must have been desperate."

He heard his son blow his nose. "We'll never know. Dad, I've got to hit the books."

"What happened with Jill?"

"So, Mom told you. You are a bundle of sunshine, Dad."

"Sorry. She still have her dog?"

"Oh yeah. Lulu is in her life. I stopped seeing Jill. Don't know why."

Awol knew why. After his brother's suicide, Kenny felt like Awol had felt, and that's when Awol stopped paying attention to Linda.

CHAPTER TEN

COLORADO'S WATER CONSERVATION BOARD was led by chairman Wayne Anderson. Hendricks didn't like Anderson because he was wishy-washy about granting more water east of the Divide. Hendricks's comfort was Anderson's jealousy. While Hendricks built his empire and his millions, he and Anderson grew further apart. Normally, Hendricks wouldn't care, but his proposed developments required extra water diverted—water the Indians would also need.

Hendricks had a big arrow in his quiver: Colorado's senator, Richard Rodriguez. The Ute tribe had ramped Rodriguez, his old schoolmate, into local politics, which Hendricks had supported, but now that he was one of the nation's senators, with a main address in DC, Rodriguez resented the hold the Indians had on him and drew closer to Hendricks for one big reason: Hendricks was rich and Rodriguez wasn't. Hendricks knew that Anderson respected Rodriguez. Hendricks figured if he had trouble getting more water diverted for his future properties, he would find a way to get Rodriguez to support him. Which meant Rodriguez would lean on Anderson.

Hendricks had one other arrow in his quiver, shorter and less used, but it could do the job. The wife of a fellow water board member, known as the Admiral, was a friend and an admirer of Hendricks. In his teens, Hendricks had dated "Admiral" Denley's wife. It was casual and included a few school dances and high school football games. They were both seniors and had parted amicably. Hendricks went east to Wharton, leaving Joan, who enrolled at the University of Denver. She majored in broadcast journalism and was a star reporter in the greater Denver area.

As far as Hendricks was concerned, the stars were aligned. He had placed his chips. He had learned over the years not to force issues. First, he didn't have the physical attributes of any type of enforcer. Second, he accepted that his voice was tinny and high and that, with his paunch, he looked out of shape as well as unconvincing. What he had, however, was patience and an instinct for knowing how to corral his forces. He aspired to the popular notion that the best offense was a good defense.

Hendricks went over this line of thought several times a day, and each time he did, he wolfed down junk food, as he did now. He crushed the empty bag of deep-fried kettle potato chips that he'd gotten Moe to stock for him. He pushed the bag to the bottom of the wastebasket in his office and drew out a king-sized Hershey's with almonds from the extreme rear of his middle drawer. He realized it was his last and made a mental note to restock. He pulled open a bottom drawer and felt an ample supply of Snickers underneath a notebook, but his peanut M&M's were getting low. He sighed. Every day he told himself he would go to Overeaters Anonymous again and get help. But he kept putting it off. He promised himself after extra water was diverted, he would seek help. He had to do something. Some of his acquaintances had alcohol problems. Hendricks didn't share that addiction. Only food—but junk food, sweets, foods rich in fats. At restaurants, he always ordered pastas with extra garlic bread, which he would saturate with extra cheese and oils. He was fond of casseroles, tapas, and dips, especially if the dips were made with hot melted cheese and accompanied by lots of corn chips. He was ashamed of his affliction. But the more he felt shame, the more he compulsively overate. It was a vicious cycle he knew all too well, he thought, as he reached in for the peanut M&M's.

He sensed his intercom before he heard it. "The senator, line one."

"Good afternoon, Senator."

"The same to you, Bruce."

"How's Vivian?"

"Yeah, listen—good, she's good. Need to swing by in a couple of days."

"Okay." Something was up. Rodriguez didn't sound right.

"I'll be coming by with someone from the tribe."

Well, there it was. Hendricks knew what was up. Those goddamned Utes still controlled him.

AFTER AN EARLIER THAN NORMAL TRIP to Moe's, Hendricks decided not to go back to the office. There was a water board meeting tonight, but Hendricks wasn't up for that either. He didn't want to hear about American Indian rights. He didn't want to look vulnerable to the Admiral and others, which was how he felt. He needed to think. He needed chow. He could almost see the Burger King sign from where he was standing. He hailed a taxi. In the cab he visualized a cheese Whopper with bacon and extra fries.

CHAPTER ELEVEN

AWOL LOOKED UP AT AN OCOTILLO plant that rose eight feet tall. Each of
the long, skinny stalks was capped with a crimson flower. He poled on
by barrel cacti tucked into surrounding thorns. Gray-green ubiquitous
sagebrush dotted the landscape in all directions. All the while, Awol paid
attention and confirmed his surroundings. He was a few miles north of
Silver City, New Mexico, 120 miles north of the border. Every time he
did move by a CDT post or some other marker, he tapped it with his pole
as though to say, I'm on top of this.

In one way, the constant need to confirm location and direction kept
Awol from personal problems. After he oriented himself, his mind drifted
to his son Gregory, Gloria, and Linda. This got him off course again,
physically as well as mentally. He compromised by thinking about water.
Availability. Rights. Disputes. The way things were headed, he was sure
it was going to get worse. Nothing he could do about it, but he tried to
understand it better. He made a note to read more about it and research
present efforts to desalinate, to waste less, to treat it as man's life resource.
Protecting the ozone would retard the losses of water, and as he considered this, he got lost again. After another map check, he found the proper
route once again.

Awol had one inviolable rule: before he took a break, before any
meal, and before he chose his campsite, he would always confirm his
location on a map and agree on the direction to head next. Up ahead,
Awol found the perfect confirmation, a CDT marker post. He stopped
right at the marker and followed his next rule, which had saved him

untold frustration and anger for many years. Being right-handed, when-ever he stopped, he always set his poles down to his right and pointed the pole tips in the direction to follow after he finished his break, camp, whatever. He'd heard all the familiar stories of people hiking the wrong way. They had become confused because without thinking they had off-packed and dropped their poles, went somewhere to void, took out a camera, walked somewhere else to take a picture, and sat down to snack, often facing the opposite direction, not realizing it because in many areas everything looked the same. Then they poled off in a different direction, which on the CDT, with various paths in some areas, was easy to do. If there were several paths, the mistake would compound, and soon you would be lost. At best, you could backtrack; at worst, you took a new compass heading and prayed.

Blazer picked a spot. Awol took out his reflecting umbrella and man-aged to get shade. First, he drank and rechecked his water—three full bottles left, and twelve miles to go for the day. He'd be fine. Studying the map, he thumbed a spot for camp that was near water. He bowled water for Blazer and after the dog lapped left the bowl in front of him. Awol decided the near noon was close enough for lunch and unpacked it right from the top of his food sack, where he'd placed it that morning. The efficiency of his methods settled Awol and gave him satisfaction. Things were in order as he rechecked his straps and buckles and brushed off some thistles and a few meandering ants from the backpack itself. He took out a small baggie of freeze-dried tuna and a plastic jar of Jif chunky peanut butter. He scooped half a spoon of tuna and dipped that into the plastic jar of peanut butter to fill the spoon. Thru-hikers can burn six thousand calories on any given day, and they are never fussy about how they eat. He chewed his mouthfuls slowly, letting all the nutrients dissolve before swallowing. He finished off lunch with a Clif Bar, his favorite energy bar and snack. Next, he mixed powdered Emergen-C into his bottle and drank again before taking out his maps. He faced north and studied the route ahead. In sunglasses, he squinted. Not one cloud to shadow sunbaked rock, sand, and scant vegetation.

That night he cowboy camped under an upside-down bowl of stars. No clouds, and with a sliver of moon that looked like a snow-covered sagging hammock, the heavens were rich with stars upon stars. He'd seen something like this before in the southern tip of California, where it was also flat. He kept his eyes moving for a shooting star. He had at least one wish he wanted to make, but he didn't see a single one that evening.

It was warm, but temperatures would drop during the night, and more than once in his desert experience Awol had had to snug up inside his sleeping bag. He wondered if he would have been better off starting his thru-hike in Montana and trekking north to south. Things weren't right down here. He accepted that whether in the Middle East or in the USA, desertlike conditions had always given him trouble. He'd acclimated, but these drylands, or badlands, or anything else you could call them, brought out the worst in people. If he were a cattle farmer here, he tried to predict how he would handle himself. Himself first? Would he empathize with American Indians? To Awol, the Indians looked mixed with Hispanic blood, and that led to thoughts about Spanish explorers and the Portuguese.

Before drifting off, the phrase *free-for-all* came to Awol's mind. He began to understand the true meaning of the term and realized *free-for-all* meant the opposite of *free for all*.

CHAPTER TWELVE

BRUCE HENDRICKS CIRCLED THE ENTRANCES to the office building's restaurant. He needed his fix. The senator claimed a tight schedule and had
requested a noon meeting. Normally he would sneak across the street,
round the corner, and duck into Moe's bakery to buy a half dozen of
"mixed," which Moe understood was two cream-filled chocolate donuts,
two éclairs, and two sugar-coated crullers. Going over there crunched
his time. Rodriguez would be here in—he glanced at his watch again—
twenty-five minutes. Hendricks wanted to avoid anyone he knew, and
as he scanned the back entrance to the office restaurant, he panicked.
Rodriguez was there. That perfect posture, as if a parent or a mentor had
told him years ago: *If you want to be successful, then look this way. Sit up
straight, firm up those shoulders!*

Hendricks went to Moe's anyway. "Moe, in a bit of a hurry today,
just gimme three cream-filled."

Hendricks grabbed the bag and tore into the restroom at Moe's.
He entered an empty stall and sat on the toilet without pulling down
his pants. One by one, he slobbered into the rich donuts and chewed.
He started to feel more in control but was in a muddle. Rodriguez had
been sitting at a table with someone who was a stranger to Hendricks, an
Indian. Their profiles had faced Hendricks, and he'd seen two coffee cups.
Hendricks shoved another donut into his mouth and wiped off cream
from his cheek, which he fingered back into his mouth. He panicked
again. The senator with an American Indian. He munched as someone
used the sink right in front of his stall. He was upset that he had to rush

his fix but felt saved now that he'd gotten some food. Once the meeting was over—he now had a glimmer of hope that it would go smoothly—he'd take the afternoon off and go to Chuck's Ribs by the lake. The person at the sink left, and he listened for the door to shut but heard new footsteps as someone else entered and took the stall beside him. *Shit.*

Once he was able to exit the bathroom without being seen, Hendricks stopped at a candy machine on the way back to his office—with over five minutes to spare—and shoved in some quarters. He stuffed the Snickers into his pants pocket but tore open a bag of peanut M&M's with his teeth. He took a utility elevator up to his floor and timed it so that the last handful of M&M's dropped into his throat as he made his way to his office. Before turning into the varnished mahogany-paneled corridor, he went into a private restroom to brush crumbs off his suit jacket and straighten his tie. He reached into his private cabinet above the sink, marked with an "H," and grabbed a bottle of Listerine. He took a mouthful and swigged it from cheek to cheek and spat it into the sink. He poured a couple of drops onto his fingers and wiped his lips and the ends of his mouth.

With a negative foreboding, he steeled himself for the meeting with Rodriguez. Hendricks accepted that his grade-school friend was more than an acquaintance, but less than a close friend. Rodriguez was here on business with a contrary agenda. Hendricks remembered first meeting him in second grade. He was from a dirt-poor family, but his hair was always combed. Rodriguez beat off a bully who enjoyed taunting Hendricks, and Hendricks began calling Richard Rodriguez "*El Patrón*" and invited him to come to play at his home. He always remembered the awestruck look on his face as he moved through Hendricks's house. He was invited to Rodriquez's home, but Hendricks's father didn't allow him to go anywhere near the slum barrio. Perhaps this was why their friendship didn't blossom. Hendricks supported him as senator and sent him congratulations on his victory, but their relationship remained cordial.

With a mixture of hope and relief, he looked forward to dinner at Chuck's Ribs right after the senator left.

"Richard, please step in. Good to see you, my old friend."

Rodriguez looked at him and smiled. "Thank you, Bruce. Let me introduce you to my associate, Paul Christo, from the reservation."

Hendricks shook the outstretched hand and looked up at the stranger he'd seen in the office coffee shop with Rodriguez. "A pleasure, Mr. Christo. Gentlemen, please sit down." After a few more pleasantries and a decline of drinks, Rodriguez stared at him. Hendricks felt the extra heel insert in each of his shoes, and he had his chair jacked to the top height.

"You look prosperous as always," Rodriguez said.

Hendricks smiled. "What makes you say that?"

"Looks like you've gained a few pounds. Must be that fine cuisine now that you are the biggest realtor in Denver."

Hendricks tried to suck in his stomach a pinch without making it look obvious. He wasn't sure how to take the word "biggest."

"Biggest as in the size of my business, you mean." He smiled.

"If I'd meant the other, I would have said fattest." Rodriguez smiled again.

Hendricks didn't like the tone and pushed a notepad to the side of his desk. "I see." He looked at the two of them. Christo said nothing, but his almost-too-quiet demeanor annoyed Hendricks. He stared past the two men at the picture of himself and Ginger on the credenza. It was taken a couple of years ago, on her twenty-first birthday. How she beamed. Right after, she'd told her father she was now old enough to tell him to go to hell. He wished she was here to mute this ominous meeting, but she was at lunch with her friend.

"So, Paul. It is Paul, right?"

"Yes."

"Do you work with my friend Richard here?"

"I do."

"I see. So. Gentlemen."

"We've noted that you are lobbying for more water for your Front Range," Rodriguez said.

"It's not *my* Front Range, Richard. It's the peoples'."

Rodriguez smiled. Paul continued to look straight at Hendricks. Rodriguez crossed a leg. "You sound like a politician. Are the people in Denver your constituents?"

"Hardly. The Front Range is attractive. Everyone loves living here."

"To borrow a phrase, 'I see.' What about all our friends and potential developers west of the Divide?"

As I suspected, Hendricks thought. *Rodriguez is out to limit water diverted east. Or*—

Rodriguez continued. "Many of the people in my department—*your* government, I might add—think too much water is already being diverted to you and your Front Range."

Hendricks ignored the innuendo of the pronoun.

"Richard, you know I wish nothing but the best for all homeowners west of the Divide. Is there a planned development in the works?"

"Bruce, you know a new ski resort and casino is in the works."

"Of course. I'd heard about it. Has it been approved?"

"Now, Bruce, would I make a visit here with my associate if it wasn't?"

"I hadn't heard . . . if . . ."

"You don't have to bet the come with this one, Bruce—you can bet the house on it. The casino is coming."

"I see."

Rodriguez and Christo stared at Hendricks until he flinched.

"What do you want from me?" Hendricks asked.

"So glad you asked," Rodriguez said. And for the first time, Christo smiled.

"Paul, are you a government employee?"

"I don't work for our national government, Mr. Hendricks."

"Whom *do* you work for?"

"Rocky Mountain High Resorts."

Hendricks began to understand. "Does that include the casino?"

"Of course."

Rodriguez took up the thread. "Bruce, look." He placed his hands palms up as though to say sorry to his old friend. "You and one other board member, the Admiral, are looking to give us a hard time on this water diversion thing."

Hendricks froze. He saw his committed millions of dollars going down the drain, his Front Range subdivision thwarted. All he wanted right now was to extricate himself from these two.

"To answer your first question, Bruce, I want you to sleep on this and meet us here," he placed a business card on Hendricks's desk, "at noon tomorrow so we can plan out some things—what we need from you, that kind of thing."

Hendricks stared at the senator.

Rodriguez smiled. "A neutral, casual setting is always best for this kind of discussion."

Hendricks looked down at the business card. *Chuck's Ribs—One is too many; a thousand aren't enough.*

CHAPTER THIRTEEN

"LET'S MAKE SURE WE'RE ON TRACK," Reardon said to Butane. It was after Butane and Rodriguez's meeting with Hendricks, and they had just finished a one-arm chin-up contest, which the wiry Butane won. They used the method of one hand on the overhead limb while the other hand squeezed and pulled on the open wrist. Butane reset his glasses, which had become askew. He didn't make a lot of money assisting the chief. Glasses now, contacts later.

They sat Indian style across from each other next to a wood-burning stove, Reardon's other luxury besides his pillow and short-wave radio. Outside it was in the low thirties; here next to the stove, it was in the high sixties. An intermittent breeze creaked the southwest corner post, one of two oak limbs Reardon had had to position. It wasn't as thick as the stunted pine-trunk corners and was the weaker of the two limbs. The small cabin shifted in the wind. Sometimes at night, during a storm, Reardon feared the limb would snap, but the other two mature posts tamed the young'uns.

"You work for—or, as you maintain, you aid your reservation chief."

"Right."

"You also, with the direction of your chief, interface with Senator Richard Rodriguez."

"Right."

"Why are we going to blow up a tunnel?"

Butane leaned forward. His bad leg forced him to stick it out straight in front of him. The other leg stayed the way it was. He removed his glasses as he always did to emphasize a point. This had seemed odd at first, but Reardon was so used to it, he couldn't imagine him being serious with glasses on.

"Because we both grew up west of the Divide and are sick and tired of more and more water being diverted east under the Divide."

"So that in itself justifies us blowing up a tunnel?"

"Why should more water go to the Front Range for rich people and all the easterners that always settle there?" He held his glasses for a second and then stuck them into his shirt pocket. "Those people kicked my people onto a fucked-up Indian reservation. Some white government bastard over there raped my mother!"

"That's not enough for you to commit one hundred percent. You are tied to a terrorist act and will be executed. You will also put the reservation in a bad light. All because you want to deny extra water to some people with big lawns. Nah, you don't convince me."

Reardon could see that Butane was agitated. Butane stuck the other foot out and placed his hand over the pocketed glasses as if over his heart. Reardon decided to go for the kill, and if Butane passed, Reardon would not have to vet him again.

"Butane, look at me. Listen to me. What's in this for you? You need to get out."

"You saved my life. I was a goner. I'd do anything for you." Reardon was the one person Butane could say this to because it was true. He was more humbled before him than he was before his chief.

Reardon watched him. Butane had a pleading look.

"Besides, I like to blow things up. I'm good at it."

"Tell me again why you won't tell your chief about our plan?"

"If it got out to the public that the chief allowed a tunnel to blow, that would be the end of us as a reservation. What if my chief said no?" Butane looked off into the distance like he saw through the cabin walls. "All this was Ute land."

"Butane. Is there another reason you would risk killing yourself for me?" Reardon watched the steady look in Butane's eyes as he waited for an answer.

"I've had girlfriends. I've fucked them. Lots of times. I mean . . ."

"What?"

"I love you."

Bingo, thought Reardon. "Well, Butane, I confess that I . . . I have something more than admiration and friendship for you."

He didn't flinch when Butane placed a palm on his knee. Reardon could feel the palm's warmth through his pant leg.

"I lost my father . . . he hung himself . . . didn't get a loan, because of water diverted . . ." He felt a squeeze, and then Butane rubbed the leg back and forth with his palm.

"I understand the personal stake you have in this," Butane said. "The bastards wrecked your family. And some government bastard wrecked mine. I feel your pain and your hatred. You have my total and complete support, Don. Always."

Reardon teared up, which was easy for him to do in this situation, but he was on an edge and couldn't overdo the moment. Reardon wiped away a tear. He put his palm over Butane's moving hand and held it in a slight squeeze.

"Thank you." He wiped a tear from his other eye. "But—and you must believe me, Butane—I can't let anything, including . . . us . . . interfere with this mission. Not until it's over." He squeezed harder. "Okay, Butane?"

Butane stared at him. His pupils were enlarged. Reardon reached over with his other hand and, placing it behind Butane's neck, pulled his face closer to him. Reardon looked right into his eyes. Reardon chose to make it heartfelt and used his given name: "When this is over, Paul, you and I can go away, together."

Paul drew closer, their lips a couple of inches apart. Reardon whispered, "Wait for me, Paul," and kissed him. To seal it.

THAT NIGHT, REARDON REMOVED his secret diary from under the removable floorboard and made notes. He was proud of himself. Butane was solid. He felt a tinge of pity for the poor bastard. He didn't mind kissing him; it was all about the mission. Reardon pondered a thought: *He won't make it anyway.*

CHAPTER FOURTEEN

LOST! AGAIN. AWOL WAS PISSED at himself for not paying closer attention to his maps and scribblings thereon, but, dammit, he'd never before hiked a trail that was so poorly posted. He'd read about this problem from studying online trail journals, where other thru-hikers in past years posted daily summaries. Awol, keen on preparation, had printed out the complete chronological postings of a CDT thru-hiker of last year, 2007, stuck it in a three-ringed binder, and read it word for word. A lot of map work, that hiker said, but Awol'd had no idea. He was on his way to Pie Town, New Mexico, which lay 290 miles north of Antelope Wells, where he'd started. By nature and from experience, Awol was good at orienting himself outdoors, but here on the CDT, if your mind wandered for one minute, you could veer off track and soon come upon other paths and trails without markers and spend a frustrating half hour or more retracing your steps to find that you hadn't missed a trail blaze—there wasn't any! Then out would come the GPS, another map, more curses.

Awol was thankful that he had heard of Jonathan Ley, who had plotted GPS waypoints or specific coordinates for the entire CDT and mapped them. Awol had sent for Ley's 2007 CD-ROM and had printed out every map, every waypoint. Awol separated the states—New Mexico, Colorado, Wyoming, Montana—with their accompanying waypoint maps into another three-ringed binder. But the binder stuffed with all the maps was two inches thick and weighed five pounds. Packing it was out of the question.

Because Awol had uploaded the "meat" into his new Garmin GPS, he was confident he could re-find himself in any situation, but it was a nuisance and against his nature to use the GPS as a crutch every five or ten minutes. Awol, stubborn, proud, and determined to sharpen his skills, put the damned GPS in the bottom of his pack—emergency only. He restudied this week's maps, which he kept in transparent Ziploc baggies, and took a compass bearing. He knew what he had to do. Observe, watch, take in the entire picture, pay attention.

The thru-hiker was one hundred miles north of Silver City, New Mexico, on the way to Snow Lake, when he stirred up a covey of quail, which must have stayed hidden until the last moment. Focused as he was, Awol jumped as they sprang up like miniature rockets in front of him. The cunning of wild birds and animals that blended into landscapes always surprised him. For them it was all about survival. Ten minutes later, he couldn't believe what he was seeing. He blinked his eyes several times, puzzled, and meandered over the rocky mesa to an abandoned, stripped, and rusted pickup. He struck the banged-up, bullet-ridden frame of the truck with his hiking pole, thinking he might get a jump on a lurking rattler. Nothing. *If this old tub could talk. What stories!*

He'd filled his water bottles back at Middle Fork Gila River but noted from his map a campground after Loco Mountain. His blisters had hardened and were becoming a nonissue; nevertheless, he planned on stopping for the night at the campground. The sun slanted into an orange-streaked sky, and the temperature had dropped to forty-nine degrees. This morning, he'd awakened to twenty-nine degrees with a layer of ice on his tent fly.

After Loco Mountain, while walking to the campground, he heard the cackle of wild turkey and, as he reached an ear to their distinct sound, saw a bobcat. It looked like a full-grown tom, which stared right at him from twenty yards. Awol stopped in his tracks. Neither made a move, and Awol wondered if wild turkey was on the cat's evening menu. The tom dipped its head but continued to eye Awol. The cackling had stopped. Awol waited the animal out, and the cat angled his head so that an ear was on Awol while the eyes remained on Awol. The head turned sharply back at Awol, daring him to make a move. The bobcat gave up, turned around, and walked away.

Dread overcame Awol. Something like this had happened to him once before. On an orienteering exercise in the army, items were hidden at locations noted on a hand-drawn map. The idea was to physically run the course and record what you discovered at the map points. Bergman had been leading and could have placed first in the exercise, but before the last map point, he'd scared up a bobcat in the Georgia forest. The cat sprang away but stopped by a tree to turn and watch him. Awol had looked at the map. The bobcat was at the last location, right at that tree. Bergman watched the cat, and then his army rival rushed by, scaring away the cat for good. At that time, Bergman also felt mounting dread—unexpected. Incomprehensible. He didn't go to the tree and left the location blank on his map. The next day, without explanation and refusing to answer questions, the instructor informed the class of military intelligence recruits at Fort Holabird, Maryland, that Lt. Stokely, yesterday's orienteering winner, had been discharged from the army. Awol never saw him again.

That afternoon's incident with the bobcat and immediate sense of dread, an ominous foreboding that hadn't subsided, kept Awol awake for much of the night. All his life, he had paid attention to signs and signals from nature. He could tell by the feel of a birch leaf in New England how soon it would fall. He refused to listen to a radio while hiking. He listened to and observed nature. The size of pinecones told him the age of trees. Rings and flutters of water in ponds always told a story. A Chinook wind changed temperatures; feathered breezes from a Santa Ana foretold weather and revealed secrets. And animals, unquestionably, communicated. What was the message? Awol knew one thing indisputably: turmoil lay ahead. He couldn't figure any details, but he could feel his nerves and tensions shifting.

CHAPTER FIFTEEN

"**W**HEN I TALK, YOU SAY I'M INTERRUPTING. When I don't talk, you say I'm not listening," she said.

Awol was on the phone with Linda in Pie Town, New Mexico, and one way or another, their recent conversations had deteriorated in this manner.

"I give up," he said. "No matter what I do, no matter how hard I try—"

"Give me a break, Karl. Look, I know you've been though a lot, but—"

"Can't you listen a minute?"

"Oh, so now I'm interrupting *and* not listening."

And so it went, childish, petty, neither gaining ground. She screamed, and he yelled and wanted to say nasty things back at her, so he shut down his phone. And, of course, Awol knew what he wanted to do next. He was four days from the bobcat, had divined nothing, and after descending into Chavez Canyon yesterday, had thought about getting drunk in Pie Town, a popular Continental Divide Trail hiking spot. He was sure the beer would settle him. A.A. would have reminded him that he was HALT: Hungry, Angry, Lonely, Tired. But Awol didn't care about that. He was worked up , and it wasn't just from Linda. For the first time he could remember on a hike, he felt vulnerable. He told himself the feeling would ebb after he reached the eleven-thousand-foot Mount Taylor, several days away, but for now, he could stand a drink.

With this thought in mind as he entered a grill in Pie Town, he first wanted sustenance. He was famished. A javelina or coyote— marmots?—something had raided his food bag two nights ago. This wasn't, so far as he knew, bear country, so he kept his food bagged but in the open whenever he cowboy camped. He had Blazer. He'd heard the scuffle and understood more than one animal wanted his food. In the end, unable to see in the dark, he'd heard them drag the entire bag away despite Blazer's yelping. In the morning, he couldn't find any trace of the black sack. All he had was the gorp he'd saved in his shell pocket.

The waitress, who was also the owner, quickly figured out Awol's mood. She'd watched him through a side window as he fed the dog and left a bowl of water for him outside.

"You need my special café con leche and one of my pies."

Awol didn't argue while she concocted the strong black coffee with hot milk.

She watched him take a sip of the coffee. "I got strawberry-rhubarb and a warm apple-pecan-crumb, which came out of the oven a few minutes ago."

"Gimme a piece of both," Awol said.

He had to admit the strong coffee was perfect.

She came back with two pie slices on one plate. "Do you always dessert yourself before the main meal?" She smiled at him. "Now, how's that coffee?"

"It's a keeper. You got eggs and pancakes?"

Two coffee refills later, feeling grounded, Awol had almost forgotten about a beer. He decided to come back later.

THAT EVENING AWOL FOUND HIMSELF back at the cafe, bringing Blazer in with him. A young man with acne so bad that his modest beard couldn't hide it was placing paper beer coasters along the bar.

"You got that café con leche?"

The bearded man looked up, startled. "Yeah, I can do that."

"Fix me up over here," Awol said, grabbing a chair at the table farthest away from the bar, next to the door he'd closed.

He had a feeling the waitress he'd overtipped earlier was on the premises. He heard rattles from a back room behind the meal counter, now closed. Ketchup and mustard containers were aligned next to napkin dispensers and salt and pepper shakers. The counter glistened and smelled Windex-y. The stools were upside down on the carpet.

Awol thumbed through old *National Geographic*s and some maps and trail guides he'd spotted on the shelf next to him. Blazer curled himself up under the table.

He was reading from one of the guides and noted that a CDT thruhiker will cross the Continental Divide about three thousand times by the time he gets to Canada. The number of times varied depending on the route taken through Wyoming. This was a big surprise. By the time he finished that article and one other on fauna and flora in New Mexico, he'd had enough of the dark roast coffee with hot milk. As he peeked at the bar, his waitress came over with a tray of mints.

"I want to thank you for the generous tip. That doesn't happen often around here."

"You're welcome. I—you had the right thing for me earlier, at the right time." He looked to the bar and back to the mints. He took one and stuck the chocolate quarter in his mouth. "And you may have brought me the right thing again. At the right time."

"I think I understand."

Awol knew that she did. "Care to join me?"

"Sure. Little Fox, bring me my tea," she said to the guy behind the counter.

"Guess you know I'm thru-hiking."

"You have that look. You're hungry and tired and not from around here."

She sipped from a straw sticking out of the plastic cup that Little Fox had brought out to her. "Where are you from?"

"Pennsylvania, originally. Now I live near Boston." Awol took another mint. "I've got . . . a son in California. He's a graduate student at Stanford."

"Impressive."

"What's with the water situation down here? People are fighting over it."

"Things have been building up for a long while. It's gonna get worse."

"Why?"

"The Colorado River used to supply us enough water down here. But there's the Front Range, Denver, and then the other side of the Divide, Vegas, California, LA. Almost all the water is diverted, and we get hardly anything."

"That's not right."

"Those not from around here don't care. The last time I went up to Denver, the Front Range, I couldn't believe the development, and from what I've been told, a lot more is coming up there."

"Have you seen Vegas?"

"It's disgusting, the water waste there. It's out of control."

She pushed the mints closer to Awol. "I'm seventy-five. The Colorado River used to be mighty, and it gushed where I lived as a young girl. The river was mighty due to the headwaters up in western Colorado. Now it's *behind*-waters, if you ask me."

Awol nodded.

"I'm told that reduced summer snowmelt deprives rivers and streams of water," she said.

"We might be able to desalinate the oceans."

"I wouldn't count on that. It won't happen in time to save us around here."

They talked a while longer about general things. The bar had gotten rowdy, and she paused to look at the goings-on.

"He's getting backed up over there. Looks like he could use some help," she said.

As they stood up, she to go and assist at the bar, Awol to be polite, she said, "You know, two years ago, we had a fella come through here, and after some drinks he told everyone right there at that bar that he was going to blow up some dam up north on the Colorado, the Granby Dam, I think it was. I remember him saying, 'We'll see how much the bastards can divert then.'"

CHAPTER SIXTEEN

GINGER AND HER TWO GIRLFRIENDS were at the Paradise Bar & Grill for their weekly night out. Her two friends, one divorced, the other separated, were kidding with Ginger about hooking up.

"Don't wait forever, is all I'm saying," said the divorcée.

"Yeah, yeah. Don't worry, I won't waste time hoping for Mr. Perfect. But I do have standards, you know." She sipped from an oversized strawberry margarita.

Forty minutes later, she was dancing with a high-cheeked, glasses-wearing man who intrigued her. He said little, but when he did speak, he gushed words in bursts. He wasn't comfortable and seemed as if playing a role, which mystified her. She liked mysteries.

"I don't come here often. I hate it when I have to shout to be heard," he said.

"I don't mind it. I get a release from hollering sometimes."

He looked at her and gave her a closed-lip smile. "You warm enough? The AC is working overtime here."

"I noticed that. I'm acclimated, thanks."

Another pursed-lip smile.

She took him to her table and introduced him to her friends as though to say, "See, I'm trying."

"You ladies want something? The pleasure is mine."

Her friends declined, and he came back with a strawberry margarita for Ginger.

"But what are you having?" she asked.

"What happened to your friends? Did I—?"

"Oh, don't worry about them. They baby me."

She saw his puzzled look. "They want me to hook up with someone. You didn't answer my question."

She could see that he was thinking again. "I have a routine that I pretty much stick to," he said.

"Like what?"

He reached for her napkin and applied an end to her sleeve where she'd spilled a bead of ice. She appreciated the gesture.

"You work out. I can see that. You can't have a drink?"

"I'll have a glass of red wine. Mostly I do vegetarian and stick to a regulated diet."

They said nothing for a while. He tried too hard to relax.

"What gym do you go to?" she asked.

"I have my own gym at my place. I've built it to serve my needs."

"Treadmills, weights, and all that?"

A lady banged a chair on the floor and he winced, jerking his head around. He stiffened, stayed quiet.

"Weights and isometrics are the cores of my routine. I hike all the time."

She rubbed her neck and drew a sip from her margarita.

"Would you like to see my gym sometime?"

"You hike around here?"

"Around here, and every few weeks or so I camp out and go long."

Ginger looked around the table at his muscular, long legs. "You run track in school?"

"No. I wrestled."

"Where?"

"University of Colorado." He smiled and showed her, for the first time, a modest grin. "You didn't answer my question."

"What's your name again?"

"Paul Christo."

THE NEXT MORNING, PAUL MET with Chief Running Waters.

"I've met the girl," Christo said.

"What did you learn?"

"Very little. This will take time."

The chief pondered. Said nothing.

"You are right," Christo said. "Hendricks and Rodriguez are tight."

"Which means Rodriguez can influence him."

"I'm not so sure. Hendricks is digging in. He wants our water."

"Hendricks is a problem. Find out his weak points. Learn all you can from his daughter."

CHAPTER SEVENTEEN

MORNING. BADLANDS—EL MALPAIS. Awol remembered reading that the expression "badlands" originally came from American Indian languages, alluding to the difficulty in traversing such country. But here, it was named by the explorer Coronado and referred to the lava beds that were under Awol's own two feet. By midday, these lava beds could reach 115 degrees Fahrenheit, and now, at 7 a.m., he felt the rising heat with each step around undulating mounds of mud, clay, and soft sandstone.

When Awol finished the nasty seven-mile stretch, his feet were fried and his tendons and ligaments overstretched from trying to maintain proper balance while crossing small gullies with each step. He sat down in the marginal shade of a paloverde tree, the hanging beige pods doing little to block the morning sun. Blazer sat right beside him, also glad to take a break. He worried over Blazer because the dog was acting crazy, like he was dizzy or something. Must be the heat, Awol figured. He dug out his phone and was glad to see three bars in the window. He called his son Kenny, who might be able to shed light on Blazer's condition.

"Dad? Where are you?"

"On the way to Grants, New Mexico. I'm about three hundred fifty miles north of the border, right on the CDT."

"How's Blazer?"

"Glad you asked. He's been acting funny, like he's drunk."

"Why do you say that?"

"He keeps rubbing his head into the ground and making god-awful sounds. Yesterday in a canyon—while walking along a plank, like he's done a thousand times before—he fell straight into the arroyo. Had to pull him out myself."

"Dad, listen to me. He's got something in his ear. He's losing his balance."

Awol began to understand. "Something crawl in there?"

"Yep. Bet's that what the problem is."

"Like what?"

"Probably a beetle bug of some kind."

THAT NIGHT, AWOL DID EVERYTHING he could to get Blazer to let him work on his ear, but the animal would have no part of it. Blazer shook his head when Awol reached for him and snapped at the Q-tip. Not a month on the trail and a situation that needed fixing.

Two days later, Awol managed to get a hitch north to Cuba, New Mexico. This village had the closest veterinarian office, according to locals.

The veterinarian spoke English and understood the problem as Awol explained it. The vet's diagnosis was the same as Kenny's: something was in the dog's ear, and the canal needed flushing to discharge the critter. The vet said that while he might be able to flush it out without anesthetizing the animal, the sure way to get the job done was to put Blazer under. Awol agreed but was told the vet couldn't do the procedure until he pulled stitches from Miss Muffin and prepared the cat for pickup. Awol left Blazer and took the opportunity to get a much-needed haircut.

No sooner had he sat in the barber chair than two amigos came into the shop and showered the proprietor with hugs and kisses. The Spanish was loud and animated. The boss, dreamy eyed, explained half in Spanish and half in English that he would be back in a few minutes. Awol was left in the shop alone. He picked up the newspaper and thumbed through. In the local news section, he caught a small headline: hiker sought. No picture, but the article went on to say that the hiker had made environmental threats involving a dam and was reported by another hiker to the police who in turn reported it to federal authorities. His alleged trail name was Bear. Okay, Awol thought, this mitigates the bobcat. It was a threat, but it was being handled. And Blazer would be fixed. He could relax. But Awol tore out the article from the paper. He had put the article in his shirt pocket and refolded the newspaper by the time the barber reentered his shop.

WHEN AWOL WENT BACK to the veterinarian, Blazer yipped in delight as he entered. He was sitting on the floor next to a chair like he was waiting to admit himself to the clinic.

"Hey, boy, how ya feeling?" Awol said as he fluffed the dog's ear.

The vet rounded a corner and came up to Awol. "See this?" He held up a two-inch square transparent bag. Awol peered at it and saw what looked like a tiny white worm down in the corner.

"That's larval eggs from a screwworm fly—some people say maggot. Last time I saw one of these was in a farmer's ear. He'd been loco and had walked into furniture for two days. His wife realized that he wasn't drunk after all."

"What do I owe you?"

"Forty-five."

Awol paid him. "Just saw in today's paper that a hiker is on the run. Government says he could be planning to blow up a dam. Know anything about that?"

"Are you with the government?"

"No. But I'm hiking up the CDT and was surprised by this."

"I haven't seen the article, but this isn't the first time I've heard these kinds of threats."

"What's going on, if you don't mind my asking?"

"Water is sacred down here. There is less and less of it. You can blame the government, but it all comes down to common sense."

"You mean individuals need to care more for water and use it wisely."

"Of course, there's that. But it's been a lack of vision all along. The California town of Mojave was built in a desert. That town is home for lots of people, and their water needs are looked after. But Vegas? Who the hell needs Vegas? We give them tons of unnecessary water to sustain corruption, vice, greed. Vegas flaunts their water twenty-four seven in gaudy fountains and displays, while down here and elsewhere the rivers and lakes are drying up."

"You do have a point, sir."

"Are you sure you aren't with the government?"

"Yes. I mean, I am *not* working for the government."

The vet eyed him and moved his lips as he considered. "Step into my office a moment. You can bring your dog."

Awol followed him into a well-lit ten-by-ten-foot office. Behind the vet's desk chair, there was a diploma on the wall. Awol sat in front of the desk, Blazer beside him. A sign on the desk that looked like a nameplate faced Awol. It read: Water Is NOT Just for Anyone! Awol looked up to see the vet watching him. Awol opted to wait him out and scanned the office. A large framed painting of a mesa in sunlight with buttes on the horizon was on the wall to his left. The wall to his right was all bookcases floor to ceiling. The upper shelves contained medical books and periodicals. A lower shelf contained an assortment of titles—*Understanding Water Rights and Conflicts*; *The Big Thirst*; *Water Wars: Privatization, Pollution, and Profit.*

"Looks like you're studying the problem," Awol offered.

"I am. It's become a passion for me."

"I get the feeling you aren't a native here."

"I was born in British Columbia. All my ancestors are from Canada. How I got here is a rather convoluted story I won't bore you with."

Awol had learned the wisdom of waiting out a person who has things to say but is trying to be coy about it. He turned in his seat and glanced out a window overlooking a birdfeeder.

"When I want to relax, I watch birds," the veterinarian said. "I don't bring cats in here. It's cruel to the cats as well as to the birds."

Awol nodded. "My wife is a birder."

The vet folded his arms across his chest and continued to look at Awol.

"You have something you want to tell me," Awol said.

The vet opened his top desk drawer and held out two pieces of wood. Awol took them and realized they were two halves of a broken Indian peace pipe.

"How did it break?" Awol asked as he mated one end with the other and inspected the bowl of the American Indian pipe.

"About a week ago, I received what you have in your hands in a box with no return address. And I fess up. I do know the feds are looking for someone."

Awol stiffened but said nothing.

"Have you heard about WINJA?"

"No, what's that?"

"It stands for 'water is not just for anyone,'" he said, pointing to his desk sign.

Awol nodded. "I see. So how did this pipe snap?"

"A typed note was in the box saying our government broke our pact with American Indians when water from lakes and reservoirs west of the Divide was diverted east. I received a phone call two days later and mentioned WINJA. I told him I supported his cause but would not assist or fund him."

"How did he come to contact you?"

"I've written several articles in local papers about water rights and the squandering of water for frivolous and foul purposes."

Awol looked down and fingered the broken pipe pieces. He handed the pieces back across the desk and absorbed the same uneasiness he'd felt since seeing the bobcat.

"Your hiker," the veterinarian said, "who said he's American Indian, claims that in addition to diverting water for frivolous purposes, we succeeded in driving off American Indians for good."

"I gather that he is upset about that."

"Very."

Awol looked at him and shrugged.

"What you don't understand is that others may be joining the cause," the vet said.

"A cause you support."

"But will not fund or assist."

"Assist?"

"I'm going to tell you something. But I won't admit that I told you, if it turns on me."

Awol waited while the vet put the broken peace pipe back into his desk.

"A dam is going to blow somewhere up in Colorado. I don't know when. I don't know where."

"Why are you telling me this?"

"One, you are headed there and will hike through the state. Two"—he hesitated for gravity and lowered his voice—"I told the suspected hiker I would be on the lookout for possible kindred spirits. WINJA is a movement I endorse. They intend to shake some sense into those water people up there. Not one person up in Denver responded to my articles. I will not step in the way if an example must be made."

"There has to be a better way to attract attention."

The doctor leaned over his desk. "Tell me."

"Contact the authorities. Our government."

"I have." The vet leaned back into his chair and smiled. "I talked to an aide for Senator Richard Rodriguez of Colorado. I explained the animosity and our movement."

"Did you mention the hiker?"

"This was before I'd heard about any hikers. The aide thanked me for the call and said he would look into the matter. Didn't hear a thing. I called him twice more and left messages with his secretary. Never called me back."

"Send him a formal letter."

The vet opened his drawer again and handed Awol an envelope. The return address was in Washington, DC. Awol removed a piece of stationery with a border at the top—From the office of the senator—which was followed by five typed words: *Thank you for contacting us.* Clipped behind this was a formal letter from the veterinarian. It outlined his concern about water rights being abused along Colorado's Front Range. It was well written and not dramatic. It deserved a better answer. Awol looked again at the five words. No name below them.

"See what I mean," the vet said as Awol restored the sheets to the envelope and handed it back.

"Yes."

"Stay alert up in Colorado."

"Any other hiker names I should know about?"

"I've said all I'm going to say. As you know, they all use trail names anyway."

"Give me a trail name."

The vet worked his lips again while placing the envelope back in his drawer. He stood up, signaling the meeting was over.

Awol and Blazer followed him outside to the reception area, which was now empty. Awol extended his hand, and the vet shook it.

"Thanks for fixing up my animal."

The veterinarian followed him to the door and reached down to pat Blazer's flushed ear, and then Awol and Blazer stepped outside. Before shutting the door, the doctor said, "I've heard of a hiker called Butane."

CHAPTER EIGHTEEN

AWOL WAS HIKING THROUGH Ojitos Canyon, hoping to make it to Ghost Ranch in northern New Mexico by nightfall. He was worn and putrid and looked forward to a couple of days of cleanup and rest at the popular hiker stop. Ojitos Canyon was sometimes referred to as the canyon of the ancients, and as he looked at the sand and sandstone that stretched to the fiery-colored canyon walls, he felt as if he were on a different planet. He pictured himself from a bird's-eye view and saw himself as a lost ant on two legs trudging alone and without purpose.

He hoped to meet other hikers at Ghost Ranch. He had questions, but more than anything, he needed others to mingle with, to converse with. He was surprised at this because a big reason he hiked was for the isolation and the time to "deal and heal" as he called it. But since starting at the bootheel, at the tip of New Mexico at the border, he'd seen few hikers and had not met one thru-hiker. Many thru-hikers were socially stingy like himself. They respected privacy and didn't yak and monopolize conversations. They listened and absorbed. He remembered a time on the AT when he'd started to set up at a campsite and two weekenders about his age came by with too many questions. Sure, they were being friendly and seemed generous, but Awol wasn't up for chitchat and meaningless conversation. He had smiled and packed up.

Awol was overwhelmed as he hiked along the Rio Chama to the Ghost Ranch Visitors Center on Highway 84. A highway is not what he had in mind, and he felt vulnerable hiking the final leg into Ghost Ranch as the moon rose. He could hear traffic and semis behind him and couldn't decide if he was ready for this much humanity at one time. For some reason, he thought about the American Indian rain dance. *The Indians might succeed in getting needed rain, but now there is danger of an overrun dam.*

Awol tented up at a campsite right next to the bathhouse. A shower was what he needed. The water didn't go past lukewarm, but that was fine. He'd saved shampoo and conditioner from a previous motel and used that to untangle and clean his hair. He breathed deeply while the water ran over his face. He started to feel revived. Eyes squinted shut, for a second he believed he was in paradise, that all was right with the world.

Two other hikers, a man and a woman in their mid to late twenties, he figured—hooked but not married, they said—adopted him for dinner at a picnic table near a fast-food area. The three sat down with hamburgers, hot dogs, fries, slaw, onion rings, and big ice-filled cups of Coke. Blazer, sitting by the long end of the table, was a hit with the pair as they fed him scraps. A few minutes later, two young men, one of whom Awol recognized from the information desk in the visitor center back at the highway, came out of a storage building and sat at another picnic table next to them. Both had cans of Coors Light. After one of them came over to pet Blazer, the dog rolled to his back.

"That's a nice-looking animal," the other said.

"Thanks. You've now met Blazer."

"Great name," the woman said. "Does he always hike with you?"

"Yes."

More dialogue ensued. The temperature had dropped to about fifty-five degrees, and her partner helped her adjust the fleece she'd put on.

"Any of you guys know how to do a rain dance?" Awol asked.

"Sure could have used a rain dance back in the drylands," her guy said.

"I'm Joe," one of the other drinkers piped up. "You all are headed to Ute country. They got a reservation up in Colorado."

"You from Colorado?" Awol asked Joe.

"I'm from the Cumbres Pass area, about eighty miles," he said, pointing north.

"That's the end of New Mexico," the girl said. "Except for the lack of water, I thought New Mexico was pretty."

"You study your history. When the first explorers came through here, this area was lush compared to now," the other drinker said.

"What the hell happened?" asked Awol.

Joe nodded after taking a sip. "That's a good question."

The guy put an arm around his girl. "Many Indians where we're heading?" he asked.

"There's a small reservation, west of the Divide," Joe said. They keep to themselves." He stepped over and they both sat by Awol, who moved down to give them room.

A conversation followed between the younger set as Awol went to Blazer with pats and murmurs and retrieved his water dish, which he set next to him.

". . . is all I'm saying," the woman finished talking as Awol stepped back to the group.

"Right, but what you don't understand is that the Utes were driven away, not once but several times," her partner responded.

She blinked.

"Water rights. Silver and gold. All that."

"Water? What's that about?" Awol asked.

"Oh, Jesus." The other drinker stood and laughed. "Don't get Joe started. Who wants what? I ain't buying, but I'll get it." He was headed to the snack bar.

"Coffee!" Awol barked. Too loud, he realized. "Sorry. I can't handle that." He pointed to the beer can on the table but looked away.

"Got ya covered," he said. He came back with a steaming cup of coffee, handed it to Awol, and added, "It's on me."

Awol listened to all the usual water complaints he'd become familiar with. He said nothing but nodded as Joe kept on talking. Awol sipped the weak coffee and refused to look at the cans of beer the guys hauled to their mouths. The lone woman worked the straw in her Coke and didn't say much while Joe held court.

"What will it be like here in fifty years?" Awol asked.

"Lots of scorpions, snakes, spiders, and kangaroo rats," Joe said. "And the mighty Colorado will be all but washed up."

"So why do I hear chatter about possible terrorist acts taking out dams?" Awol asked. "Seems counterintuitive. We all need water everywhere. What will blowing up a dam accomplish?"

Joe chose his words carefully. "It would cause devastation. But it could send a vital and lasting message to abusers of the resource."

"It doesn't make sense."

Joe looked at him. "Did Columbine make sense?"

"Hell no. That was different."

"How so?"

"The kid was off his rocker."

"Some of our government people might not be loco, but a shitload of them think they can take water any time they want for constituents that already have way more than others have. Is that right?"

Awol thought about his discussion with the veterinarian. "There's a cause, a group that's called . . ."

"WINJA."

"Right," Awol said. 'Water is not just for anyone!' You a member?"

"Why do you ask?"

Awol saw Joe's partner squirm up his mouth and dent his beer can with his thumb.

"Back down in Cuba, New Mexico, a veterinarian unhappy with existing water rights told me of the group."

"Okay," Joe said. "It so happens I am a member and I support the cause, but I will not participate in blowing up any dam." He looked at Blazer and back at Awol. "Okay?"

"Of course. So you've heard the chatter?"

"My friend, that so-called chatter has been going on for years. Every time somebody gets pissed over a water issue, that person mentions blowing up a dam."

Awol nodded. "That somebody could contaminate a reservoir."

"Yeah. But a big explosion is a lot more spectacular. No?"

The gal yawned and announced she was going to bed. She left with her partner, and Joe's friend got up to clear the table of beer cans and cups.

Joe got up and stuck out his hand to Awol. "Don't worry about it."

"What?" Awol shook Joe's hand.

Joe attempted a fist bump and walked away.

CHAPTER NINETEEN

TWO MOUNTAINS, SIX- AND EIGHT-THOUSAND FOOTERS, stood between him and camp. The mountains Awol was used to held firs and thick-trunked trees. Here the mountains' shoulders were spotted with much of the same rock and brush he'd walked through all day. He was east of Lumberton, New Mexico. He'd cross over into Colorado soon, possibly tomorrow.

In late afternoon, as he topped the second mountain, he was startled to see a snowflake, another, and soon more. Early June, and here was snow near the Colorado border. He would have to have Linda or Tom ship him his ice ax. He'd thought, stupidly, that if he didn't ask them to ship the ax as he neared Colorado, he wouldn't miss it. He looked at saplings of poplar and cottonwood, at wild shrubs of manzanita, the upside-down flowers looking like pink gumdrops. Would snow accelerate their growth? The land looked forlorn.

That night in his tent, the guidebook mentioned an Indian reservation—the Ute tribe—situated close to the Colorado-New Mexico border farther west. He wondered what the conditions were like there. He remembered the last time he'd been on an Indian reservation—the Mohawk tribe—in upstate New York. There hadn't been much to see except dilapidated mobile homes with rusted pickups beside them—unlike the huge Indian casinos of Foxwoods and Mohegan Sun in Connecticut. He and Linda had spent a weekend at Mohegan Sun, and the accommodations were extraordinary. So was the entire American Indian experience. Palatial gaming rooms, lots of shops, first-class entertainment. They'd missed a heavyweight boxing match but got to see Phyllis

Diller and a great band whose name escaped him. Those tribes appeared prosperous. He wondered about the Utes.

In the twenty-four-degree morning, the ground was covered with two inches of snow. Awol wondered about snow depth on top of the two mountains behind him as he put on liner socks and pulled on wool stockings over the liners. He looked south before poling north. The other day he and Blazer had gasped for water in ninety-five-degree heat. Maybe the planet *was* getting messed up.

THE NEXT DAY, AWOL WAS STUNNED with the change in weather. He'd been looking forward to Colorado and cooler climes. But this? It was snowing as he climbed Cumbres Pass, which was the gateway to Colorado from the CDT. He was poling through six to eight inches of snow, and it was June. Welcome to the Rockies. Blazer yipped and frolicked in the fluffy western snow. He admired the Malinois with shepherd-like ears. The animal adapted to anything and everything. He wondered if Blazer was as happy with eastern snow, which contained more moisture and packed to a harder consistency. His mind wandered to the difference between eastern alpine skiing versus the less icy western slopes, which held rich fields of easier-to-handle fluffed snow.

For the next few minutes, he reminisced of happier times skiing with first Gloria and then Linda on ski weekends in New Hampshire's White Mountains. He couldn't remember having a bad experience skiing with either of them and made a mental note to invite Linda . . . He stopped, taking the hiker's rest step: one foot inclined on the upgrade and stretch, switch legs, stretch again. *Nah, it's a new ballgame now. Have to ski on my own.*

At the top of Cumbres Pass it was cloudy, and although flurries swirled about him, he felt a breeze with a hint of warmth, but he'd worked up a sweat, so maybe he felt refreshed and warmer. As he did on every peak that required exertion, Awol got ready to snack. He took out his rubber pad, straight from his kayak at home, and after smacking snow off a stump with his gloves, put the rubber mat on the stump and sat down. His mouth watered in anticipation as he tore open a packet of cinnamon oatmeal and added cold water. He stirred it to a paste with a plastic spoon and took a mouthful. He swirled it around and swallowed while undoing Blazer's belly strap that held his bowl and the saddlebag. He took another spoon of oatmeal and got Blazer's Purina Dog Chow unpacked while Blazer waited patiently.

"There you go, boy, bon appétit."

The dog dug in as Awol finished the oatmeal packet and opened another. Oatmeal with cold water, for breakfast or lunch, had been a way of life for Awol on long-distance hikes. Why take time to fire up a stove just for hot water? He'd gotten the idea from a pack of Boy Scouts he'd seen on the Appalachian Trail in the middle of summer and decided from then on to boil water once a day for his evening meal.

Colorado. The skies had cleared before he finished snacking. He would have liked to linger. The flurries had stopped, but his temp gauge said forty-two, and he didn't want to get cold again and have to change out of sweaty clothes. By right, he should do that anyway—dehydration snuck up on a hiker. He should have taken his pack off, but at the last minute he opted to move on. The hastiness lingered in his thoughts, and he remembered how a retired priest had sweated himself into dehydration on the last hiking leg of his day, from the top of Mount Washington to the AMC Madison Hut. Awol, it turned out, may have been the last to see him alive. He remembered passing a man who appeared okay though he walked slowly. Late that afternoon a hiker blew through the door at Madison Hut, saying, "Emergency! Hiker down!" They found the former priest, in soaked clothes, dead, a half mile away. Awol always felt bad about that. Might he have helped him? Should he have stayed with him? *Forgive me.*

His two "zero days" at Ghost Ranch were beneficial. The hiking community got it right; a no-mileage day was a zero day, pure and simple. He was glad to have had them. He felt refreshed and clean for a change. Blazer seemed happier, judging by the way he darted to smell things on the path. Awol felt stable for other reasons. First, he'd stayed away from alcohol yet again. Each time it got easier. Second, he was able to use the guy and gal's computer to do some research on the internet. Awol told them the truth. "I'm interested in the *chatter*, and I'd like to learn more about where I'm headed and the Utes." He was able to draw up the "Hiker Sought" article he'd seen back in Cuba and found two similar articles, dated the same as the original. The government had no news other than the hiker was believed to be American Indian and ex-military. *That's interesting*, Awol thought.

After reading about the Utes in Colorado and how a separate tribe up near the Divide had broken away from the main reservation, he Googled WINJA. From what he could tell, the water defender organization was a small, underfunded group of left-wingers who demanded a voice for proper water usage. Their main mantra was *Water Is Not Just for Anyone!* There were a few American Indians in a photo of about thirty, but one picture showed modern-day Utes performing a rain dance. Information was spotty, and news coverage was nonexistent.

Awol thought about everything he'd learned and felt better prepared for what he expected ahead. He was convinced his unsteady nerves and the appearance of a bobcat after more than ten years were trying to tell him something. He looked north at the Colorado horizon and inhaled with his mouth open. He wished he knew what lay ahead. *Watch and wait*, he told himself.

CHAPTER TWENTY

IT WAS EARLY JULY, AND AWOL had been on the trail for two months. He'd hiked over a thousand miles, not counting all the times he'd gotten lost. He'd have to pick up the pace to finish before the snows of Glacier National Park in Montana shut him down. This last thought occupied him as he poled toward Silverthorne, Colorado, a popular resupply stop for trail hikers and outdoorsmen. The lower levels of the Copper Mountain ski area, with over a foot of snow, were behind him, and he poled along a bike trail that was flat, with a dusting of snow.

Awol took a well-earned zero day in Silverthorne. After watching the news—and with Blazer resting beside him, looking relaxed from a dip in the pond—Awol was irked by an alert from Homeland Security about possible terrorist attacks in the US. Whenever he heard something like this, he wondered if it was a planned annoyance, a scheduled ruse from the enemy. If this was true, our government wasted time, manpower, and money that could be used elsewhere—resources that could be used to deal with the water problem out here.

He went to the motel office for coffee. A lady with black braids peeked out at him from behind a curtain.

"Just need some joe," Awol said as he pushed the large round button on top of the silver airpot and placed a dollar in a black leather-covered tom-tom, relieved of a top. A few quarters sat at the bottom of the small drum.

She didn't reply and slipped back behind the curtain. She was American Indian. Awol scanned the brochures protruding from the stand by the coffee and noticed the one for Running Waters Trading Post. *WAM-PUM* it read, under the title. He assumed he was near the reservation and confirmed this from the brochure: Utes of Colorado. The brochure explained that a smaller clan of the Ute Mountain tribe had not relocated to southwest Colorado back in the nineteenth century but had remained in northern Colorado, west of the Divide. This particular offshoot had complained when they were shuffled west and had refused to follow the other Utes. Their home near the Divide looked small and was stuck in no-man's-land near Winter Park. That puzzled Awol, because from the map inside the brochure, it looked like ski country.

Curious, and tired from all the hiking, Awol had the perfect excuse to take another day off. He'd bargained with the motel manager, who said he could borrow his car for a few hours if he filled it with gas and pointed in the direction of a filling station. Awol fired up the dented Pontiac station wagon, and the gas needle sat on red. Awol shook his head and smiled. After gassing up, he got lost off of Route 40 and had to ask directions from a man retrieving mail from, presumably, his mailbox, although Awol didn't see a house nearby. He ended up having to backtrack a mile and take an unmarked gravel road.

An unsmiling attendant in a feathered headdress took the ten-dollar donation, opened a gate, and waved Awol through. Though Awol could see mountains nearby, this area was flat and the sun beamed upon it. He rode by a totem pole, which listed to the north. Upon closer look, it appeared that some totems were missing. The gravel road was full of potholes, and the right side of the road was next to a dirt-heaped arroyo of shallow water. The surroundings were quiet except for the *woof! woof!* of a large German shepherd tied to a post behind the gate. Blazer growled from the window as the mangy shepherd stood by a bowl, daring Blazer to come near it. The land looked deserted except for a handful of trailers off to the left. A mile later, Awol pulled into Running Waters Trading Post. One jeep, a muddied dirt bike, and two battered and rusted pickups sprinkled the parking area.

Awol stepped by a wooden gate that closed off a horse corral. What looked to him like two mustangs stood aside a mare and her colt. A potbellied Indian sat on a fence and watched Awol.

"Fifteen dollar and you can ride Tokyo, the horse on the left," he said.

Awol went over to him. The Indian sported one eagle feather attached to a baseball cap that read *Cleveland Indians*.

"Tokyo? That an Indian name?"

The Indian smiled through rotted teeth. Awol thought he must be having a chaw.

"One of my own kind fought in Korea. He married a girl from there who said she'd fled Tokyo after that first A-bomb dropped." He spat out his chaw. "Turned out she used him to get her ticket to the great and mighty USA. After a week here—he called her Tokyo—she disappeared, and two weeks later that horse was dropped off right where you are standing. A government man gave me a paper for the horse, some sort of receipt. All it said was, 'Thanks and love, Tokyo.'" He spat again.

"What happened to her husband?"

"Go ask Teepee," he said. "You'll find him inside next to the teepee."

Awol walked inside and met a withered Indian sitting in a wooden folding chair beside a teepee.

"You can ride my horse for twenty dollar," Teepee said.

"You must own the other mustang. Your compadre said I could ride Tokyo for fifteen."

"Ha!" another Indian with a newspaper said with a half grin. A vehicle pulled up and backfired. The newspaper dropped and the Indian swiveled his head and touched an ear as if in pain. "Jesus!"

A woman walked in. "Get that engine checked!" he said, cupping his ear. "Don't come here anymore until you fix that engine. Understood?"

She walked out while the Indian pulled on his ear, eyes closed.

"What can I do for you?" he said to Awol.

"Nothing, really. Going to look around. That okay?"

" 'kay." The Indian looked forlornly out the window, and something triggered in Awol.

"By any chance . . . No, sorry." Awol walked over to a shelf of peace pipes.

Awol figured the man rattling the paper was a vet. He had that look of desolation mixed with anger that he'd seen in others who served overseas like himself.

"Do you sell many peace pipes?"

"Ten percent off," Teepee said.

Awol wandered over to him. "That's quite a story about Tokyo."

He looked up and analyzed Awol's eyes. "You want to buy him?"

"Nah. I'm hiking through. Got all I can handle taking care of myself."

"You thru-hiking the CDT? Angry Bear over there hikes the CDT all the time."

"Angry Bear?"

The papers rattled. The man kept reading.

"Know why we call him Angry Bear?" Teepee showed his rictus. "He's sensitive, touchy."

Angry Bear ignored them but pulled on his ear again. Awol was certain the paper-reader listened closely. His ear was turned to them like a bobcat's.

"Be good to those horses," Awol said, and walked out. He felt eyes drilling his back.

CHAPTER TWENTY-ONE

Rocky Mountain National Park. One knew by the name what to expect, and one was rarely disappointed. Awol wasn't as he stood at nine thousand feet viewing spires of granite, snow-capped peaks, and slopes of evergreen and pine. Below him, twisted rivers flowed in ravines and rock-choked gulches. He inhaled forest-infused mountain air—Rocky Mountain highs—and felt boulder and granite under his weatherworn fingers. Awol closed his eyes and heard the lingering echoes of westward-ho pioneers, had visions of horses and weather-beaten men in ragged wide-brimmed hats, hunched over campfires and tin cups of coffee. Together these Westerners pushed into the frontier, together but alone, alone but together. Awol breathed in long and slow. Somewhere was the smell of woodsmoke wafting through spruce, hemlock, and pine. He opened his eyes.

That morning, Awol had emerged from a glade in a forest of spruce and oak. He'd hiked to this ridge and followed it up. On top of this escarpment, Awol saw the expanse before him and felt the history of Colorado and his country. Colorado, he knew from his reading, was the most mountainous of all the states. Over eleven hundred peaks rose to ten thousand feet, and the state had fifty-four peaks jutting beyond fourteen thousand feet. Rugged country.

Despite vague fears and the feeling of futility, wisdom seeped into Awol and gained a foothold. Viewing the panorama before him, he forgot about his predicament. He owed himself this moment with nature, on this king of trails, to sip from nature's chalice, which held an elixir of God-given beauty.

His eyes turned to a tor of rock surrounded by pines in a pattern like a monk's tonsure. The trees all looked about the same height, but as he looked closer, he noted that as the trees crept up the sides of the tor, they grew shorter. It dawned on him. The depth of soil decreased until the rocks took over. Of course. The depth of the soil decreased the higher and higher the tor went. Pines had taproots, and the roots would hit bottom shallower and shallower. As the soil decreased in depth, so did the growth of the trees.

Turning back north, as a wind brisked his profile, he squinted at serrated granite peaks as far as he could see. Due north, the direction Awol would head, the clarity of the distant expanse diminished, along with his joie de vivre. Awol was left with a mixed anxiety of despair and hope. He felt as useless as a speck and had no delusions. Except for Kenny in the coddled wings of university and Blazer beside him, Awol was alone. He scanned left into a canopy of sun-filled clouds inching east. He smelled evergreens and sucked in brisk air that would be shrill if those firs could sing. The long-toothed granite spires, not quite blocking the sun, stared at him, and Awol was reminded of a passage in Kazantzakis's *Zorba the Greek*. Zorba was staring at the ocean and at once became engulfed in total unending laughter. He couldn't stop laughing as he realized in the late sunset of his life that it didn't matter what happened to him—the waves would continue to comb the beach, and the tides would still ebb and flow. Awol felt that way now as he returned the granite spire's stares. It didn't matter what happened to him. He could be sacrificed. These spires, these mountains, would remain the same and continue their uninterrupted vigil.

Awol thought more about the settlers hauling their wares and family to the great West, about wagon trains being caught in the snow and pioneers freezing to death. He visualized the unfortunate Donner Party and their tragic route across the Sierra Nevada and shifted his eyes west.

Then he turned his head east. More spires but tinted with morning alpenglow. They also stared back at him, uncaring. Life goes on no matter what. Awol would not glance south this day. Nor would Blazer. Awol figured, what is one life for his country? Make it count.

CHAPTER TWENTY-TWO

AWOL INTENDED TO SURPRISE the hiker, but the hiker turned and looked right at him. He'd heard him coming the whole time. He was thin and high-cheeked, with black hair sticking out under a sweat-stained Broncos hat. He looked very fit. Awol was looking at the same person who had been reading the paper in the reservation wampum store.

"Good seeing you again. I'm Awol." They shook hands.

"Paul Christo. I remember you. You military?"

"Why?"

"Your trail name."

"Yeah. Was."

"You're an Easterner."

"Yes. Originally from Pennsylvania. How about you?"

"I live on the reservation where I was born."

Awol sat and removed his boots as if he were the most unconcerned person in the world. Blazer showed no concern and lay down.

"Do you hike often in Rocky Mountain National Park?" Awol asked.

"I do. You like it here?"

They were in the middle of the park, before the CDT turned northwest for several miles, then north again into Wyoming. "Very impressed."

They discussed the predicted stormy weather, which led to a discussion of gear. Soon they were quiet. Christo had decided to snack and ate tuna and cheese wrapped in tinfoil. As he proceeded down the sandwich roll, he kept unwrapping the foil.

The wind picked up, and a tree limb creaked. Christo's head leaned toward the sound. More trees swayed, and the creaks and snaps distracted the Indian. As acorns dropped and popped off a rock beside him, he jerked his feet away.

"Were you in the service? Awol asked.

"Afghanistan. Two tours."

Awol nodded. "Seen some shit, I bet."

Christo said nothing, but his eyes were vigilant.

Awol put his boots back on. Dark clouds shrouded the mountains behind him.

When the storm broke, it came on quickly. The first rip of lightning was followed by a crack of thunder. Christo jumped up and, while chewing, said to Awol, "Follow me."

A half mile later, bending into hysterical winds and pouring rain, Awol followed Christo off-trail onto a barely perceptible path. He wanted to get out his pack rain cover and shell, but the Indian waved him on.

"Don't stop. We're almost there," he said.

Awol followed Christo's moccasin tracks and noticed his gimp. Christo chanted Indian. *War chants?* For sure, he was hollering in Indian. Awol followed him into a rock-protected overhang. It reminded Awol of a movie scene where Neanderthals sat by their fire.

"Huh," Awol said. "Just what the medicine man ordered."

Christo smiled. "Too many Indian movies, white man, but I won't hold it against you."

It was Awol's turn to smile. "What were those chants?"

"For our protection. It alerts mountain lion, bear, cougar that we are coming."

"Was there more to it? You could have hollered anything to drive off animals."

"What you would have hollered could make an animal stand his ground. I invoked the Great Spirit."

Awol thought about that. The rain came full-on, lightning ripped, thunder cracked. Awol couldn't believe his good luck. He watched Christo, sitting Indian style, facing out, but with eyes closed, his hands over his ears. He was a sculpture.

Twenty minutes later, the storm lessened, and the rain-filled swale angling in front of the cave reduced its gush. Christo opened his eyes. He looked to Awol.

"Where'd you serve?"

"Desert Storm. One tour."

Christo nodded. Awol felt the silent connection.

A minute later, in the last gasps of the raging storm, a blast of wind kicked up. The ground beneath them quivered, and a tremendous crack peeled off behind them. The Indian covered his ears, jumped up, and fell to his knees, ears covered by his hands.

"Christ Jesus! In the name of the Great Spirit, make it stop!"

Awol watched him. Watched him rock back and forth, silent, eyes shut. Finally, he uncovered his ears but remained on his haunches. An aspen treetop now hung halfway down over the entrance.

A few minutes later, the Indian looked at Awol. "You'd figure after two tours in Afghanistan I'd be used to loud noises."

"What was your MOS?"

He laughed. He started to say something, laughed more, louder and longer. He threw some rocks outside the opening. One of them ricocheted off the aspen and bounced back near Awol.

"Demolition. They call me Butane."

CHAPTER TWENTY-THREE

BUTANE KNEW WHERE TO SEND the roses. He tried to think of the right note with the right tone. He settled on *Ginger, I wish to see you again. My gym is open. Paul,* and sent the flowers to the address corresponding to her phone number, which she'd given him.

TWO DAYS LATER HE CALLED AND left a message: "Hi, this is Paul. My gym is open."

That evening his phone chirped. "Hi, thank you for the beautiful roses."

"You're welcome. I'm glad you liked them."

"Don't know if I'm up for any gym yet, but maybe something else?"

"Can I pick you up for dinner this Friday? I don't want to interfere with your Saturday girls' night out."

BUTANE TOOK A CHANCE AND PICKED her up with his red Vespa Dragon double-seater. He'd bought it used after graduating from college, and though he rode it hard, he maintained it properly. He'd guessed right. She looked at him and smiled. Ginger, in blue capris, hoisted herself behind Butane and gathered her arms about his midsection.

Butane became aroused, as he knew he would. He had a job to do for his chief, and Butane wanted to look normal and, as a man, be normal.

So far, Ginger was making it easy. At the last second, feeling romantic, he decided to skip the bike stop hangout and take her to a candlelight dinner at Rojas by the lake. The twenty-minute ride was exhilarating. During a scenic section as they drew near the water, she briefly laid her head between his shoulders and squeezed her arms about him. The effect was more powerful to Butane than if she had outright muscled him tight or kissed his neck. It was the suggestion of intimacy, the future of unknowns that warmed his testicles as well as his heart.

He gave the waitress a wide-eyed look and pointed to a corner table. The waitress caught the implication and smiled at both of them. "The perfect spot for you two," she said.

"Let me use the man's pickup line," Ginger said. "Come here often?"

Butane smiled. He noted her blue eyes and the dilation of her pupils. He hoped that was due to more than adapting to candlelight. She looked happy and fresh—clean and the other type of fresh.

She deferred the wine to him, and he ordered a bottle of Estancia Cabernet Sauvignon. He told the waiter to give them a few minutes, and the waiter, offering a telling nod, withdrew.

Butane couldn't think of what to say. This happened to him with attractive women. He leaned in to say something. She watched him. Butane was tongue-tied as, up till now, he could always count on Ginger to converse. After a moment, they started to say something at the same time and both laughed.

"Here's to your mighty gym," Ginger said.

"Oh. Thanks. And here's to you, Ginger."

She ordered roast beef, and he ordered salmon with extra vegetables. They talked infrequently, but both were comfortable and ready for unknowns. Butane tried to focus on his objective for the chief but couldn't do it. She caught his glance to her breasts. She put down her fork, took a sip of wine while looking at him, said nothing, and resumed eating.

Butane did think of Reardon once but couldn't hold him in his thoughts either.

"Did you say you graduated in criminal justice at Denver?" he asked.

"Yep."

"Guess I'd better watch my step."

She smiled at him. "You don't have anything to hide, do you?"

"Let's hope not. No, I don't think so."

She smiled again as they nursed the last of the wine. He gave her the dessert menu, and though he said he didn't want any, she ordered flan with two spoons.

Before the dessert arrived, Ginger excused herself to go to the restroom. Butane stood as she left. He sat back down and tried to focus on what he should do next—get information. Gain a foothold. But he felt relaxed and content. He didn't want to spoil the moment. She returned, and he stood again, gave her a smile, and touched her chair. Little things, but he was conscious of a shift within him. There was no hurry here. He'd do a better job if he took his time.

Butane did, in fact, eat half of her flan and smiled while she admonished him. "Double the push-ups and pull-ups tomorrow," she said.

They talked about her time in college, his time at the University of Colorado. She smiled as he told her about his wrestling. "Guess I'd better watch *my* step," she said.

She pressed him about his tour in Afghanistan, but he didn't want to go there, and she backed off. "Yeah. We don't want to talk about that," she said.

On the way out, moving toward the Vespa, he walked her along the shore of the lake. There was a well-used path, and two other couples nodded to them as they walked by holding hands. Butane kept his hands beside him. Ginger did the same. Butane, used to the Great Spirit, got a mixture of signs that he couldn't untangle. His heart pumped faster. His groin was warm. He didn't want to rush and slowed his pace as he angled her back to his bike.

They enjoyed a pleasant ride back to her apartment. Ginger was discreet, and Butane appreciated that she didn't lay her head against his shoulders again or squeeze him. Butane liked her for making the right moves at the right time. It had been a perfect evening.

He took her to the door and pecked her cheek.

"Thanks, Paul. Sometime we'll see your gym."

THAT NIGHT, BUTANE DID NOT masturbate. He felt Reardon looking at him, but that wasn't the reason. He saved it and was ready for unknowns.

CHAPTER TWENTY-FOUR

HENDRICKS RETURNED TO HIS OFFICE right after meeting Senator Rodriguez at Chuck's Ribs. In a reverse kind of way, it bothered him that Rodriguez's associate, Paul, wasn't at their meeting. He wondered what Paul's real role was. He noted the sweat in his armpits and felt the shirt's dampness. He tried to look poised as he walked by Ginger, his out-of-wedlock daughter from his first marriage. But nothing fazed Ginger, which was why he'd hired her right after she'd graduated, magna, from the University of Denver.

"The Admiral called. He played the annoyance thing about your absence at the board last night. I told him to chill."

She always referred to Denley as "the Admiral" because he graduated from Annapolis Naval Academy and because, as she'd said, he tried too hard to take charge.

"All right, I'll call him. Anything else?"

She tilted her head, looking askance. "Might want to send a card to my mother. You missed her birthday."

"Right. Thank you, Ginger."

He headed for his office.

"Before you close the door on me and isolate yourself in your chamber, where did you hide the Rodriguez file?"

"I have it. I'm keeping it with me for a while."

She said nothing as she removed a stick of sugarless gum from a packet on her desk. Ever since she gave up smoking, she relied on gum, chewing constantly. She worked the gum quietly, which pleased her father, but when she was pissed, she would smack the gum with open mouth and blow tiny bubbles.

Hendricks closed his door but didn't lock it. Ginger was discreet and always knocked, but he was embarrassed that she knew he was a foodaholic. He'd noted some candy missing once, and she'd worked late the night before. But she'd kept it a secret, and nothing had been touched since. He went to his bottom drawer and reached behind the back divider. He pulled out a medium-sized bag of Cheetos.

Ten full minutes later, munching with eyes closed, he finished the bag. He tossed the bag into the ubiquitous circular file and placed scrap paper over his supposed secret. He wiped his mouth and reopened the bottom drawer to bring out an oversized Snickers and a bag of his favorite candy, peanut M&M's.

Hendricks didn't know what the fuck to do. He stood to make millions. Now he was being bribed to screw his own deal of a lifetime. Paul had to be Rodriguez's enforcer. Rodriguez had intimated as much at Chuck's Ribs. The image of all those ribs he'd eaten and now the junk food on top of it made him ill. Soon he would have to use his bathroom commode and stick a finger down his throat. He reached for the last of the M&M's.

He tried to understand why his old friend Rodriguez, a senator, would get involved with a resort west of the Divide. And casino. Why, of course: the compulsive gambler. The tribe had saved his ass, so Rodriguez could avoid a scandal. He hid the candy wrappers under the scrap paper on top of the Cheetos bag and wiped himself somewhat clean again. He took out a transparent plastic box of cinnamon Tic Tac breath mints from his top drawer and tipped it to his mouth, letting the contents slide in. As an extra cover, he took out a well-used bottle of Listerine and poured some drops on his fingers, which he used to wipe his lips and the ends of his mouth.

He swiveled one-eighty and after a minute of contemplation, fingers tapping the arms of his high-backed executive chair, reached into the side of his credenza to retrieve his untraceable cell. Time to call Joan, the Admiral's wife, and send her on a wild-goose chase. Who knows, maybe she would find a scoop.

CHAPTER TWENTY-FIVE

Butane and Ginger met weekly over the next month. He took her to a movie; a wrestling match at University of Colorado, where he introduced her to his former coach; and to a casino east of the Divide, where he watched her lose at slots and craps. Tonight, he told her he would show her his gym. But first he'd take her to the roadside hangout where he'd meant to on their first date. Butane smiled to himself: she'd be a tulip in a field of weeds. They rode in lane on his Vespa, and this time she did cling to him, squeezing at every turn. She frequented her head between his shoulders, and once he sensed a kiss on his neck but may have been mistaken. He did hear her whisper in his ear, "I feel safe with you."

Once they were sitting outside among tables of other noisy bikers and their women—the raucous laughter often rising to such a crescendo that Ginger or Butane would have to stop conversing for a moment until they could hear each other—she said, "How come I don't see you at the Paradise Bar & Grill anymore?" While waiting for the noise to die down, she reached across the table and placed her hand on top of his. A cycle revved and backfired; Butane jumped and crinkled his eyebrows.

"Someday you'll have to tell me about Afghanistan," she said.

Butane nodded but said nothing.

"The Paradise?" she asked.

"I don't want to interrupt you with your friends."

"You wouldn't be interrupting me. Besides, they'd like to see you."

Butane understood. Things were developing between them. Truth be known, Ginger made him feel special. He wanted her. He was falling in love.

"Okay, I'll come by. This Saturday?"

"Sure. We'll all be there."

They smiled, and he kissed his merlot with her sangria.

They both shared vegetable paella from a single plate. She'd deferred to his preference for vegetables. The evening temperatures were dropping into the mid-sixties, and he helped her pull on her sweater. He rolled down the sleeves of his checkered plaid shirt. A crescendo of laughter rose again, and he eyed her with a what-can-you-do look.

"Don't fret," she said, smiling with straight, white teeth, "we're not at the Ritz."

In this moment, Butane realized what he loved about her. She didn't bitch or complain. If she did, she had reason to and was blunt. But her normal demeanor was one of acceptance. The ghost of Don Reardon crept into his mind. Butane saw him weekly, but the last time, several days ago, Butane was agitated and twisted by loving feelings for the man who'd saved his life and who trusted him with their mutual mission. Reardon put on the brakes. "All in time, Butane. I haven't forgotten about us."

Butane hadn't been able to concentrate. He cheated on pull-ups, avoiding full extensions. Instead of one-handed push-ups, he did two-handed. His mission as outlined by the chief was no further along than before he first took Hendricks's daughter out. Part of Butane's mental muddle was that he couldn't and wouldn't dare tell Reardon. He knew that Reardon hated Hendricks, and if Reardon knew that he was dating his daughter, Reardon would feel betrayed—doubly betrayed. His chief was antsy. Butane had failed his chief. *What the fuck is happening to me?*

"Paul, did you hear me?"

"I'm sorry. What?"

"That guy to your right keeps looking at you."

Butane turned and at once recognized his old wrestling foe, John Ippolito. Butane stood up as Ippolito stood and raised a beer to Butane. Ippolito came over, and the two shook hands.

"Paul. I thought that was you."

"John. Good to see you. Meet Ginger Hendricks."

The table where all the over-the-top laughter had come from became as quiet as the empty chair that John had left there. The men all smoked cigars.

John smiled at Ginger. "My toughest match," he said, pointing to Paul.

"I'd like to say," Butane said, loud enough for the other table to hear, "I was sick that day, but no, you beat me fair and square."

The other table all raised their drinks to both of them then became absorbed in their own conversation once again.

"What's the occasion?" asked Ginger.

"I'm a father. Just had—I mean my wife had me—a son."

"That's great," Ginger said.

"Cheers all around. I'm happy for you," Paul said.

"I'm out of cigars. Sorry."

They talked briefly, and Paul's bad leg weakened when he heard John say to Ginger, "By any chance, are you the Hendricks whose father is on the Denver Water Board?"

"Yes, I'm his daughter."

"Wow. I'm on the board's wait list."

Ginger's looked surprised and responded, "They *are* looking for young blood."

After he left and Paul confirmed John's full name, she remembered it from water board correspondence.

THE GYM WASN'T MUCH TO LOOK AT, but she didn't mind, nor did she bat an eye at his trailer and the shabby reservation. This had been a test. She passed.

"Do a routine for me," she insisted, and then winked.

He jumped up and grabbed the pull-up bar extending the top width of the kitchen doorframe. He did ten full extensions.

He went to the mat. "You are aware that you have succeeded in arousing me."

She smiled as she pulled over one of two flimsy metal folding chairs, sat, and watched him do crunches. After thirty or so, he stopped and looked at her from the mat. He hadn't broken a sweat.

"Would you like to see the rest of the place?" They both laughed as he went to her.

They quieted as he placed a palm to the side of her cheek. She rose from the chair, and he kissed her sweetly on the lips.

"Can I make you coffee? Tea?" he asked.

"Maybe after," she said, and kissed him back.

A HALF HOUR LATER, SHE MADE him coffee and smiled as he took a sip and added cream.

He looked up at her. She hadn't added anything to her coffee and sipped it black from a University of Colorado mug.

"Well. That is robust coffee," he said.

"Aren't we dainty. Am I dating a wuss?"

He smiled and reached for a Splenda. "You are wild."

She took another sip. "Do you mind if I chew gum?"

"Not at all."

She didn't explain and chewed as they talked about anything and everything for the next four hours. In his cot that he used as a bed, she'd made him feel like a champion. Things within him were not resolved, but some tangles were undone. He was gratified that he could converse with Ginger and listen to her with both ears. She was a rare woman, and he was lucky. He wanted to tell her that he'd been at her office, seen her picture with Hendricks in her father's office. But it wasn't the time or the place to do that. And he knew he couldn't.

"Well, I'm sorry I've kept you up late. Let me take you back."

"Okay. I think that's best," she said.

At her door, he pecked her cheek. "Not much time left in the night for dreams," he said. "Let them be sweet."

"Aw, shucks," she said, pouting her lips, thrusting out a hip, and pulling some strands of hair across her eyes. She blew him a kiss.

CHAPTER TWENTY-SIX

Awol KNEW WHAT HE WOULD DO NEXT. As soon as he'd secured his room in Fraser, Colorado, he made tracks to the nearest tavern. He didn't have to ask where one was; instinct carried him. He would say it was in his DNA. He sat there with a schooner of Coors and noticed a good-looking woman walk behind him and take a stool, leaving an empty stool between them. She placed her purse on the empty stool and smiled at Awol. She ordered a red sangria. She wore lipstick and looked a touch American Indian with her high cheekbones. Two men sat at the far end of the bar. She stirred her drink with her straw and looked straight ahead into the mirror, which ran the length of the bar. Awol turned to where she was looking in the mirror and caught the slight smile before her eyes turned his way—she'd been watching him watch her.

Awol picked up his schooner and moved over to the empty stool. "May I join you?"

She removed her purse from the stool. Awol took the stool and looked into the mirror. He waved and she smiled.

"You work here?" he asked.

She faced him. "No. I know the bartender, so I come here."

"Oh. Guess I'll be on my best behavior."

The bartender caught that and smiled at Awol. He shuffled to the other end and grabbed a newspaper.

Awol looked at her profile. "Do you always study people using mirrors?"

She smiled wider and took a sip through the straw. "You passing through?"

"Yeah. I'm hiking the CDT. You know what that is?"

"Sure. I've done some small parts of the CDT."

"Nice. I'm thru-hiking. What sections did you do?"

"The Wind River Range area in Wyoming, and two years ago my husband took me up to Glacier."

"Glacier. I'm told that's an amazing park."

"It's beautiful. I liked all of Montana."

"You hike much of it?"

"No, but most of the hiking I did was in Montana."

"But I'm guessing you are from Colorado. No?"

"I'd done a few trails here before I met Sven. He was from Montana, so he took me there."

They both nursed their drinks for several minutes.

"May I ask what happened to Sven?"

"We split."

"Sorry."

That led to a long explanation that did not interest Awol. Awol fidgeted, seeming to fight his stool for the most comfortable perch. Truthfully, he had lascivious thoughts. He wanted to screw this attractive woman, and he was frustrated about the work it would take to get to that point. He didn't have the time when he could get drunk instead.

Finally, sensing she had spoken too much too soon, she quieted.

"Are you married?" she asked.

"Separated." Awol unconsciously rubbed his ring finger and looked at the telltale indentation where he'd removed his wedding band before beginning his trek up the CDT.

"What's so appealing about a thru-hike?"

"Right." He took a swallow of beer. "For me it's always been the keen sense of adventure at the start and the steady accomplishment of miles along the way."

"Don't you have problems out there with the weather? Supplies? Animals? I mean a week or two is one thing, but to go all the way . . ."

"Sure. I have good days and bad days. I get fed up with foul weather. Storms are dangerous. Yet I'm always wondering what's around the bend ahead, over that next hill, and what that mountain peak yonder will reveal."

He looked at her, took a slow, deep breath, and glanced at the bartender.

"Is something troubling you?"

He chuckled. "Kinda wish you hadn't asked."

She smiled and, seeming to understand, took a sip from her drink. "It's okay."

"You could join me on the trail for a few days," he said.

She put her hand on her cheek and took another sip, her face tilting sideways toward him. Her sucking from the straw made a bubbly sound, and Awol realized she was at the end of her drink. He was too.

"Can I get you another?"

"No, I have to go. But it was a pleasure to meet you." She smiled and slid off the stool.

Before going out the door, she whispered a few words to the bartender and patted his arm. After she left, the bartender poured another schooner of Coors and took it down to Awol.

"My name's Sam. Diana told me this is for you, on the house."

Awol thanked him and took a gulp. He felt conflicted because he knew he shouldn't be drinking, but if he was offered or given a drink, he had a hard time passing one up. He preferred to drink on his own terms and didn't like it if somebody else got involved. Nevertheless, he swallowed again, and seeing Sam move to the other end of the bar, he called him back.

"I may have been a bit forward to your friend Diana. I didn't introduce myself to her and didn't get her name. I asked her if she wanted to camp with me for a couple of days, this after I'd hardly met her, and I'm afraid I turned her off."

"I wouldn't worry about it." He lip-smiled and grabbed a glass a patron handed him.

Awol nodded and looked up at the TV. Baseball was on, but he paid no attention and didn't check to see who the teams were. Christ, where was his head. What the fuck was he gonna do here? Get drunk or not? He wanted to call Linda. He hesitated. Kenny seemed like an easier call. *Nah.* What was there to say to either?

He was halfway through a third drink when the local news came on. He heard something about the Denver Water Board and something about an expansion of the Moffat Tunnel. An official was at a televised town meeting and with a pointer showed the viewers mockups of the tunnel with planned improvements. "This restaged tunnel will increase water by 25 percent of its current output to the Front Range," he said. Years later, Awol would think back to this exact moment. Something had shifted inside him. He doesn't remember pouring the drink into the bar sink he could see from the mirror or easing off the stool or leaving a tip for the bartender. What he does remember is the heavy feeling in his gut that tragic events were going to unfold and that he had to get back on the Continental Divide Trail.

CHAPTER TWENTY-SEVEN

Bruce Hendricks could not believe his good luck. He was reminded of the cliché: Pinch me so I'm sure I'm awake. He pinched himself several times a day. Why? The housing market continued to explode. As he sold acre lots at increasingly higher sums, his bank, which was his former employer and on whose board he sat, kept giving loans to the lower-middle class and, in a few cases, the needy. Lately, Hendricks secured mortgages for buyers who put little money down—anyone could buy. And the more money Hendricks made from this seemingly unending source of wealth, the more he invested in the hidden schemes behind it.

Hendricks knew other banks in Denver were solid. All the big banks in America were doing the same things following the leads of the big financial houses in New York. Hendricks understood that for the rest of his days, his buyers would be paying back their loans, and Hendricks would become super rich.

Hendricks was so certain of this—after all, he wasn't the biggest realtor in Denver for nothing—that he decided to add frosting to his cake by investing all his cash and all his other profits into the same types of mortgages the great financial houses in New York did. He contacted a fellow Wharton classmate who worked at Lehman Brothers and got the inside scoop. Hendricks felt heady, rarefied, as he placed and received calls to and from NYC. After all, he wasn't an MBA graduate of Wharton for nothing.

The first hookup with his fellow Wharton graduate had been six months ago. His cake was already becoming enormous from icing, and with the housing market continuing to rocket, Hendricks decided to take the ultimate step. He would create his own financial fund and petition select customers. He would capitalize on the financial opportunity of ten lifetimes.

Hendricks set up Front Range Equities, FRE for short, and decided that he would only accept clients with an initial investment of $250,000. This he marketed as an *exclusive*. Hendricks would be honored to serve his clients' needs, admit them into the elite, and make them rich. To Hendricks, a million dollars was nothing anymore, and he looked down on a mere millionaire as a pauper. Hendricks checked his net worth three times a day; the last check bottomed him out at $331 million. Further, his intricate calculations, learned at Wharton and involving back-timed chronological formulae, revealed he could be a billionaire in two years at the outside. Worst-case scenario, proven with other abstruse marketing information and equations, Hendricks would have to settle with a net worth of $700 million within two years. Well, he could live with that.

Hendricks invited his elementary school acquaintance and most powerful contact, Senator Richard Rodriguez, to be his first client. Hendricks relished this opportunity to steer Rodriguez away from the casino-resort project. He'd sussed out from the Admiral's wife that Richard was tired of being in the clutches of the reservation. He wanted to break loose, and here was a way. He'd make his schoolmate rich and put him in Hendricks's corner for good. The invitation was simple: "Richard, Meet me for the opportunity of a lifetime. Bruce."

The senator had called and pressed him for details. "What are you up to now?"

"This is so hot, we need to converse privately."

———————

ON THE FLAGSTONE PATIO OF HENDRICKS'S chalet, bordered by trimmed eight-foot Rocky Mountain juniper shrubs, seated around a raised circular firepit wafting heat from lava rocks, after his butler had catered to their every need, Hendricks laid out his newest venture to Richard. Hendricks showed him his personal FRE profit statement since he'd started selling off lots and investing the proceeds.

"And you, Richard, are invited to join me."

"Must admit, Bruce, I've been envious of you. The plebes tell me I'm powerful, but I have little to show for it. Got three kids to educate."

"Understood, Richard. I'm envious of your fine family." Hendricks pushed out his wine glass, Spain's finest Rioja *tinto*, and their glasses kissed. "Richard, I submit to you that I will make you a rich man within two years."

"What do I have to do?"

"Invest a minimum of two hundred fifty thousand dollars into my Front Range Equities. I shall take five percent of all profits."

"Hmm. That much? Five percent?"

"Richard, would I fail my Colorado senator, an old classmate from E-4?"

"No."

"Richard, let's do this."

TWO DAYS LATER, AFTER SCROUNGING every last dollar he could beg, borrow, or steal, after selling stocks, selling a Murillo oil on canvas of his wife's, and pulling from the educational funds—under bank penalty—that he had set up for his children, Rodriguez left his house with an envelope, to the horror of his wife. Vivian hadn't reddened, which Richard had seen her do on several occasions, she purpled. He stood his ground, and after her rant, amplified by a thrown candlestick, knowing the right moment to speak and move to her, he did so, and this time she put a palm up. "Don't! Don't come near me. My grandfather gave me that painting. My thirteenth birthday, a teenager," was all she said.

At the Denver airport, Rodriguez met with Hendricks in the VIP lounge.

"Bruce, because of your success and our boyhood affiliation, I went out on a limb here." He handed Hendricks an envelope. "Now, dammit, make me rich."

Hendricks smiled as he tucked the envelope into his suit jacket. He extended his hand. "Old friend, you won't be sorry. We shall celebrate soon. And I'm sure we will get our water."

On the way back to his office, Hendricks took out the sealed envelope and looked at it. "Bruce, Your first partner. *Primar! El Patrón.*"

Hendricks tore open the envelope and saw a check for $250,000. He at once deposited the check and sent a gracious thank you to the senator's private email. The next day in his office, Hendricks warmed to the task and with the assistance of his Lehman-Wharton classmate spent a pleasant half hour portioning his first Front Range Equities client's investment among the newest arcane subprime mortgages and CDOs. Hendricks was too proud to ask what CDOs meant but read later that it stood for Collateralized Debt Obligations. *Interesting*, he thought. Hendricks relished the notion that he was on a superheated track for the chosen, those who, unlike pedestrian investors, were at the cutting edge of financial stardom. The financial arena in which Hendricks planted himself was not for the ordinary, the obtuse, the ignorant, those middling parasites who would be left in the dust. After all, Hendricks wasn't accepted into the inner circle of the biggest investment house in NYC for nothing.

CHAPTER TWENTY-EIGHT

"I'M COMING BY YOUR OFFICE tomorrow," Butane said.

"You are? What for?"

After Butane had completed his workout, he'd waited for his heartbeat to return to his resting rate so he could converse with Ginger on his cell. The chief had gotten demanding, and there was no way around the issue. Hendricks had declined their bribe.

"You know that I assist my reservation chief."

"I don't recall you telling me much about that."

"No. You're right. Anyway, I'll be coming by."

"What time? I've promised to take my mother on a birthday outing and have to leave late morning."

THE CHIEF SAID RODRIGUEZ couldn't make this trip; something had come up last minute and he'd had to stay in Washington. Butane dreaded calling on Hendricks. He loved Ginger. He fretted about Reardon. How could he pressure Hendricks? Butane accepted that the reservation and Reardon had to come first. And she wouldn't be there anyway. Time to show his true intent and do his job.

The next afternoon, Butane stepped into the outer office of Hendricks Realty. Letters painted on the door below the original sign read Front Range Equities. *That's new.* Inside, he felt relief followed by a foreboding made more pronounced by Ginger's chair pushed up to the desk, PC shut down, laptop missing.

Hendricks's office door was open, and he worked behind his desk.

"Come in," Hendricks said.

Butane said nothing as he sat down in the chair Rodriguez had used during their last office meeting.

"What can I do for you?" Hendricks said, looking at his folder.

"Although shaking my hand is not a requirement, I do ask that you treat me with respect. Look at me."

Hendricks looked up, surprised. Said nothing.

"That's better. Do you know why I am here?"

Hendricks closed the folder, sat back in his chair, and clasped his hands behind his neck. He said nothing.

Butane maintained eye contact; he was good at this. Hendricks finally blinked, at which time Butane smiled and nodded.

"Okay. I'll remind you again. You met our senator over a pile of ribs. It was his understanding that you were going to steer the water board away from any further eastern diversions. Correct?"

"That may have been his understanding—"

"Now, let me stop you right there. It wasn't maybe. He called my chief, and the senator made it very clear."

"As I told you and the senator before, I don't control the water board."

"That's why you are to steer them. You don't instruct them. You use your skills and steer them."

"All right. Look, I'll get with the senator on it."

"Uh-huh. Of course you will."

They maintained eye contact again, longer this time, until Hendricks blinked.

Butane didn't smile, nor did he nod. He remained rigid and drilled Hendricks with his eyes. "Does the name Reardon mean anything to you?"

Hendricks said nothing.

"There are ghosts," Butane said, leaning in to Hendricks. Butane's eyes were lasers. "The ghosts are not happy about the unfortunate demise, make that suicide, of Mr. Thomas Reardon."

Hendricks had his hands behind his neck again. Said nothing, but his face blanched.

"In a long-last tribute to Mr. Thomas Reardon, our Rocky Mountain High Casino and Resort will include a full-blown dude ranch, complete with horses, corrals, and trails for riders. Like the one he'd planned with you thirteen years ago this very month. We intend to build the biggest dude ranch in the West."

Butane got up. "Don't bother," he said to Hendricks, who hadn't moved. "I can find my way out. By the way, it's kind of hard to influence the water board if the vice president doesn't attend board meetings. My chief isn't happy about that, nor these foolish rumors of more water going east."

Butane glanced back once as he reached Hendricks's doorway. "The Utes aren't going to back down on this one, Mr. Hendricks. The tribe that was kicked into the mountains, that particular tribe that was shoved west of the Divide and abandoned all those years ago, is not going away."

SHE CALLED HIM.

"You've got a shitload of explaining to do!"

"I know. Listen—"

"No! You listen. You tell me in person."

She hung up.

It was late morning of the next day. He was sure she had drilled Hendricks about the meeting. He couldn't go to her office. He'd go to her apartment in the afternoon and wait for her.

But he didn't have to.

She pulled in to his place at noon. Her silver Toyota Camry careened to a stop. She wasted no time getting out and left the driver-side door open. He noted her blue pantsuit with long-sleeved matching top.

Butane stepped down from his mobile home as she drew up in front of him. She was smacking gum.

"I'm going to ask you to take off your glasses," she said.

He did as ordered and knew what was coming.

With every ounce of strength, Ginger slapped Paul across the face. It was colossal, and he felt it.

He fingered his glasses and looked at her. "I didn't think you would be . . . dainty."

Ginger's lower lip quivered but she rallied and in measured tones, mocking his own style of speaking, said, "Put your glasses back on."

He did as instructed.

"You think long and hard about what you want to tell me." She got back into the Toyota, slammed the door, and skidded off.

Butane, minutes after, went straight to her apartment and waited.

Four hours later, she pulled up behind his double-seater.

Butane doffed his Cleveland Indians baseball cap and pointed to his bike.

"Give me a few," she murmured without looking at him, leaving him standing there.

She came back ten minutes later in pants, a long-sleeve shirt, and a sweater. She'd removed her makeup and wore no hat. Not looking at him, she went to her seat first and gripped the sides. She remained that way, and Butane ran the bike slower and took the turns gently.

He took her to a small trailhead park. There was a privy and a sheltered map board showing trails, with side postings of flora and fauna common to the area. A small covered box held maps.

"I'm not up for a walk on any trail," she said. "Explain."

For the next twenty minutes, Paul explained everything he could. Indian plans. The senator. His instructions from his chief. He finished; she waited.

"Is that all you have to tell me?"

"I went to the Paradise with the purpose of meeting you."

That seemed to satisfy her as she looked away from his eyes. She sat for several minutes processing everything. Butane dared not speak another word. He'd said nothing about Reardon nor his father's suicide, surely caused by Hendricks. He would not tell her of that.

She got up and went to him. "We shall never speak of this again."

Their sex that night, back at her place, was more colossal than the slap across his face. She wanted to be on top, and he let her take charge, but at that right moment, while underneath, he spanked her rump. The more powerfully he palmed her ass, the more she loved it. She accepted that Paul had to reassert himself. Ginger again made him feel like a champion. In a way that lovers divine, he knew how much slap she would take from him and when to stop. They'd performed a secret ritual together that was more than a truce. It became for them locked in sex, a mutual embrace of an inviolable pact. An agreement that this was a new path for them. In thought, word, and deed, they were as one.

They said not one word after they finished. There was no need to. They lay on their backs, holding hands, under a single sheet. One of them would squeeze the other's hand, and there was a squeeze back. After more minutes passed, she kissed his cheek. He kissed her lips. He couldn't remember feeling so content.

THE NEXT DAY, DESPITE WHAT he'd done, despite the fact he'd put himself in the worst possible predicament, Butane was a happy man. He often played the tom-toms. He pulled them from the bottom of his one closet. He sat on his exercise mat and closed his eyes. It wasn't long before he was Buddy Rich on steroids. His ramped emotions—love, fear, love—propelled his wrists and fingers. He had no idea how he was going to extricate himself from this mess he'd created, but he did know that if he could go back in time, he would do the same all over again. Would he betray Don Reardon? He already had, but no, he would not give Don up. Yet he would stand by Ginger, always. Whatever happened to him, she was sacred. With these thoughts permeating his being, it was not until an hour later that he picked up his cell and saw two messages.

Teepee: *You need to get over here.*

Teepee: *Where are you? The chief's upset. Get here.*

So now it starts, he told himself, thinking of the probable consequences, including the possibility he'd been found out with Ginger. He looked at his barbells. He wanted to press, curl, hike up steep mountain trails. He felt his happiness seeping away and steeled himself. He knew he and Ginger had an inviolable pact, but couldn't he have had more time today to enjoy it?

CHAPTER TWENTY-NINE

SENATOR RODRIGUEZ LOOKED AT the fax again. The fax was from Hendricks, and he kept looking at the number at the bottom: $435,601. *This can't be right*, he said to himself. He looked at the date, which was the current day, and traced his finger to the column on the left. That date was three weeks ago, his initial investment, $250,000. "Get me Hendricks," he hollered into the intercom.

"Been waiting for you to call, Richard. How's things in our nation's capital?"

"Peachy. Bruce, am I reading this fax correctly?"

"You are. Congratulations."

"Christ. No bullshit with these numbers?"

"Richard, if I didn't know you, I'd be insulted. To borrow a phrase, 'You can take it to the bank.'"

"I congratulate us both, old friend. I'll be showing this to Vivian at dinner tonight."

"Good idea, and here's something to think about. I predict you will reach six hundred thousand in nine more working days. I'd think about making another investment."

"Hmm. I'll think about it, Richard. Fax me as soon as I reach the six hundred thousand. And I'd like to see some backup supporting the numbers. Not that I don't trust you. Please understand, it's—"

"Richard, I understand. If you want backup to the numbers, consider it done. But, seriously, take heed of my advice. As they say, make hay while the sun shines."

EIGHT WORKING DAYS LATER, the senator received another fax before leaving his office. He heard it coming, and as his secretary had finished for the day, he pulled it out of the machine himself. He had his $600,000 and about seven pages of backup to support it. *Damn!*

Over a candlelit dinner in Georgetown that night, he pulled out the newest fax.

"Take a look at this, my dear." He smiled and tipped his wine to her.

She studied the balance sheet and handed it back. "Well. This doesn't give me back my painting."

"I did wrong on that. Please, forgive me."

"This newfound source can't last forever, Richard. You be careful."

The next day Richard set to work. He sold his adored cabin cruiser to a friend who had told him he wanted first dibs. The senator got a loan from his bank. He sold everything possible, including a new set of Ping golf clubs. He raided the girls' education fund to the last penny and managed to get another loan from two more banks. He was a senator, and he played the part perfectly. "My secretary will forward the necessary documents," he'd said.

By the end of the week, he wired another check to Hendricks for $250,000. Hendricks beamed at the sum and sent him a text: *Gracias. You have made a wise move, El Patrón. Here's to us.*

But the senator had a plan, which he kept to himself. At two million, he would withdraw his investments and all his earnings. His wife was right. "Too good to be true" couldn't go on forever. Nothing could. Yes, he'd made a wise move. He would also be a wise man. Bruce would squawk, but he'd been helping Bruce's fund with his contributions. Besides, Bruce took 5 percent right off the top. Rodriguez knew a lot of people who would consider the rate itself a fortune—$50,000 on one million. The fact that Rodriguez needed Bruce Hendricks to succeed to secure his own fortune was a given. He would do everything he could to support FRE and get him his water. All Rodriguez thought about was two million dollars, being a *multi*millionaire. Before the limo pulled into Georgetown Baptist Church's parking lot, he told the driver to pick him up in one hour. Senator Rodriguez took a side entrance, went down a flight of stairs, and turned the corner to face a lighted room with a front table and chairs horseshoed around it. He entered and nodded or grunted to several hellos and settled in a back row for his weekly meeting of Gamblers Anonymous.

CHAPTER THIRTY

Diana could feel events coming together. She'd been waiting for over seven years for this chance, and now it was here. Her record as a special agent—Counterterrorism Division, FBI—was beyond reproach. Indeed, she'd wondered why it had taken this long to shake things up so she could move up to a level worthy of her skills and achievements. With the retirement of Emilio and the transfer of Frank, who, all knew, were both forced but offered in unctuous sincerity, she assumed she would break the glass ceiling and be promoted to assistant field director, Counterintelligence, in FBI's Denver headquarters. All she had to do was keep her head up, keep working diligently, and keep her intel reports current and sharp.

That would be easy, because she'd been the first to pick up new chatter about a homegrown plot to blow up a dam in Colorado. That threat, if carried out, would be catastrophic for the region, so the FBI's National Security Branch and the Department of Homeland Security were updated regularly. Diana took ownership of all dam-related files and made sure her name was on every bit of information regarding water threats in Colorado.

Diana's competition for the big step up was Special Agent Ronald Avery, a savvy politician who turned schmooze into an art form. She detested him, and because he knew it, he enjoyed yanking her chain. Like yesterday at the bi-daily recap for their pathetic field office director, Everett Watts.

"Diana, be kind enough to take notes for me and the group," Avery said as he tossed her a pen.

Diana didn't touch the Waterman as it slid across the table and came to a stop a few inches in front of her.

"No, wait." Avery threw up his hands. "Nobody can decipher your writing." His sneer was real, but there were some titters from the group, and her spineless director, Watts, chuckled. Oh, how she wanted to yank Avery's silk tie and pull his sleek puss in front of her.

That same night, she worked extra and called her sources, which included several park rangers. They had no new information but allowed that if an act of sabotage to the water supply were enacted, it was the worst possible time. The drought was the worst ever. It was sere, and the immediate concern was fire, which would draw on the already diminishing water.

"I've never seen it this bad," her head ranger said. "All rivers and streams are running shallow."

"So maybe a terrorist thinks to blow a dam won't be that catastrophic."

"Ever hear the phrase 'too much of a good thing'? If the Granby were to blow, the unchecked runoff would demolish gardens with their lack-of-water-weakened crops and make life miserable for thousands."

"Never mind all those that will drown."

"Of course. And, don't forget, firefighters need that water. If there is a forest fire nearby, how they gonna get water if it spills over the dam and floods homes?"

"I'm doing all I can to substantiate threats and prevent any disaster. Keep this confidential: I've vetted a thru-hiker on the CDT. I've asked my people to get this man involved."

"Does he look like a thru-hiker?"

"This is why you are to keep your lips sealed. He has lots of experience, former army officer, and he helped our government on another long-distance trail."

"I'll keep it in the vault. But I've got a sense that we're running behind here. Are we up to speed?"

"Gotta go. Call me with anything."

No, we're not up to speed, she thought. *Director Watts needs to get off his ass.* Diana had one last phone call to make that would do just that.

"Hi, Rachael?"

CHAPTER THIRTY-ONE

PAUL "BUTANE" CHRISTO SAT IN front of the chief, not at the chalet but in his cold and rancid office on the reservation. Chief Running Waters eyed him as he sipped diluted honey, molasses, and cinnamon from his usual "chief" mug. For the first time, Christo wasn't offered any. The chief's father's headdress sat on a shelf behind him. Next to it was a picture of the chief as a young boy holding a bow, standing with his father, who looked stern but dignified, his face etched with lines and creases. On the chief's desk, Christo could see plot folders, site maps, and a larger surveyor-drawn map. On a four-by-eight-foot rectangular table to his left was a scaled model of the proposed resort, complete with passageways, a lake, and a river with footbridge. The casino was a pentagonal construct with each floor built back to a fifth-story top. The top floor was glass enclosed. At the end of the table, an arrow pointed to "Dude Ranch," which Christo assumed would be modeled later.

"Tell me about your progress with the girl. I want to hear everything."

Christo told him almost everything. He told him he made love to her, but stopped it at that. The chief knew he was also attracted to men, or as the chief put it to him back in high school, "You don't catch how the wind blows. You will create your own weather."

At the end of his account, Christo said, "I don't believe Hendricks will ever accept any bribe from us. I asked her how he'd become so successful, and she said he played by the rules. In my opinion, he will ignore us and do whatever he can to divert more water to the Front Range."

"Should we make him an offer he can't refuse?" the chief asked.

Christo watched him sip from his cup, their eyes locked. Christo blinked.

"I don't think there is a way to buy his favor. We tried that."

The chief put his mug down and continued to eye him, but said nothing.

"The senator is the only one who can help us," Christo said.

"Think about that," the chief said. "You know as well as I that he and Hendricks are connected, all the way back to grade school."

"But the senator owes us more than he owes Hendricks."

"Who's spreading the nasty rumor?" The chief's eyes drilled Christo.

"What?"

"Who is spreading the nasty rumor?"

"Chief, I don't know what you mean."

"It will be on the news tonight. It appears that the tribe's casino will be Mafia run."

"What? I don't understand."

"Hendricks is on the water board with Admiral Denley, right?"

"Yes. But he's not a threat."

"I know that. You know who his wife is?"

"The reporter. Joan Denley. Channel Four News."

"She called me this morning. Wanted my reaction to the proposed Rocky Mountain High Casino being run by the Mafia."

"Jesus. I swear I haven't heard a thing about this, Chief."

Running Waters eyed him, and Christo blinked again. The chief took another sip from his mug and gazed out the window.

"She said it came from a reliable source."

"Who?"

"Know why you haven't heard anything?"

"Why?"

"I asked her if her source was Hendricks. She remained silent."

Christo understood and nodded.

"Hendricks has low-balled me and your tribe," the chief said. "He's spread this rumor. I'm sure of it."

"I believe you're right. I guess you have summoned me to confirm this with his daughter?"

"I've summoned you for a better idea."

LATE THAT NIGHT, HOURS AFTER the eight o'clock evening news on Channel 4, Hendricks was woken from his sleep by a pounding on his door. His ashen-faced valet handed him a note: *Be ready to take a personal call on your cell in ten minutes. Take this call first before doing anything, or you will regret it forever.*

"Who gave you this?" Hendricks demanded.

"There was no one there, sir. Whoever it was disappeared."

Too soon, Hendricks thought, he picked up his burring phone.

"It's two a.m. where I am, here in New York. Am I speaking to Mr. Bruce Hendricks?"

"Who is this?"

"I asked you a question. It would be very wise to answer me. Am I speaking with Bruce Hendricks?"

"Yes."

"Listen to me carefully. No one casts aspersions on the family. I had every right to have my man come in and blow your brains out instead of leaving a note. You have twenty-four hours to publicly retract your blasphemous rumor against the family, or I will sever your fucking head."

"But—"

"We will discuss water another time. Meanwhile, the clock is ticking."

Christo shut down his phone. He was scared and humiliated.

"Not bad," Chief Running Waters said. He looked at Teepee for his reaction and received a yellow-toothed smile.

Christo tried to look normal, but his heartbeat was pitter-patter. He'd done his best to disguise his voice and had taken time to write down and revise words. But he prayed that he wouldn't be found out.

As if the chief had read his mind, Running Waters said, "Even if Hendricks claims it was you, he does see you as Rodriguez's enforcer, right?" The chief eyed him. "Don't worry, Hendricks will retract his false accusation."

"Suppose he doesn't?"

"I will summon you again."

Christo shivered and knew that the chief saw it.

CHAPTER THIRTY-TWO

"**S**ACCO'S GOING TO CALL YOU. Says it's important."

"Well, of course it's important, Kenny, that's why I asked you to call *him*."

Awol knew what this meant. The government was planning to foil a terrorist. But he didn't understand why Sacco would call. He handled narcotics. This wasn't about drugs.

"Just remember," Awol said, "whatever comes down, don't think of coming out here. I'm removing myself from this, and you stay in school."

"Sacco said . . . well, I'll let him tell you."

That night Awol heard why Sacco was involved.

"Ya see, Awol, we are going to bring some people out there—don't fret, Kenny is out of it."

"Why did you call him?"

"Besides getting a fix on you, I wanted to run the idea by him. We'll always remember how you helped us on the PCT."

"Yeah, yeah. Almost lost my boy."

"He told me about Gregory. I didn't want to mention it. I'm truly sorry, Awol."

"Thanks. What can I do for you?"

"The FBI wants some agents out there to pose as undercover drug operatives. We'll drop the concern that there has been confiscation of hard drugs along the CDT in Colorado. That way the terrorists will think it's not about them."

"So you are working with another federal agency on this?"

"Right. The FBI's Joint Terrorism Task Force got hold of me on this one 'cause of my experience."

"The bombers will see through the undercover ruse."

"Possibly. But they will accept that it may not be a ruse. In any event, we need to get out there."

"Which led you to me."

"Yes, Awol. You can be an extra pair of eyes and ears for us. How's Blazer?"

"Doing fine. He's beside me taking a nap."

"Well, we sure put you and the dog through some shit, didn't we?"

"That you did. How will I recognize your people?"

"You won't. But I've told them about you and the dog. They know all about you."

"Figures. Anything else?"

"Okay. Expect somebody from the FBI to come out and meet you, geared up like a hiker."

"When's he coming?"

"Don't know, but you'll be contacted."

"How?"

"I'm sending you a special satellite radio and an emergency beacon, like last time. You can pick them up at the Cumbres Pass, Colorado, post office in two days."

"Cumbres Pass! That's almost back to the New Mexico border. Hell, I'm ready to break into Wyoming."

"Sorry."

"I'm heading north, ya know, like I'm sure Kenny told you. Christ."

"Awol, my good friend, if I may be so bold. We need you to stay in Colorado. At least for a while."

Silence. "Mail it to Buffalo Pass-Steamboat Springs, Colorado. I'll have to backtrack and hitch in."

———

THREE DAYS LATER, AWOL LOOKED at the yellow beacon contraption and stuffed it into the bottom of his pack. He put the satellite radio and his GPS on top of it, deciding to keep the radio off but to check it twice a day for any messages. He intended not to get into an emergency. Not this time. So why had he agreed to stay in Colorado? He couldn't answer that but knew he wouldn't forgive himself if he continued north and a catastrophe, which he might have helped prevent, befell the area. That's the way he was, ever since . . .

IT WAS NOW EARLY AUGUST, and he'd been on the trail for three months. He didn't think he could finish the CDT before the end of September, not with his agreement to help the FBI. But if there was one thing Awol had learned in all his years and miles of hiking, it was not to rush. The former army captain was goal driven but not stupid. He would not push himself into injury, and he would attempt to absorb and enjoy the hike of a life-time on this king of trails.

As the former army officer hiked through a vale that showed traces of a once-gushing stream, he had to admit that bringing out some under-cover agents posed as narcs was a good idea. They would shake something loose. At worst, they would raise the chatter and delay any terrorist plans, giving the feds time to prepare and counter. He'd heard all the rumors and had seen many articles about continuing battles for water rights. Threats of bombing a dam weren't something new, but the government took all threats seriously.

Awol's mind wandered. Thoughts about his ex-wife, his sons, his dear wife, Linda, whom he missed terribly, floated through his mind. The separation had been cordial. But he hadn't seen it coming. He loved her. He stopped by a purpled meadow of loosestrife and said a silent prayer for Gregory. Awol removed his hat while he closed his eyes. He replaced his hat and looked at the meadow and stream beyond, which stretched to the northwest, and counted four pronghorns, those swift antelopes distinguished by their forked horns. They were the fleetest of American mammals and reached forty miles an hour. Awol scanned mountain crags with his binoculars looking for bighorn sheep, the state animal, but didn't see any. The ragged peaks of granite spiked an ominous horizon to the northeast beyond the buttes—bad weather was coming; Awol could sense it. A combination of temperature, breeze, and gut feel told him a storm was heading right at him.

Within a half hour, Awol had put the cover over his pack and retrieved his shell. He vented the shell and put the hood up. He was ready. Before the storm hit, he'd avoided big trees and sought the refuge of granite and boulder. He sat on his rubber kayak pad in front of several boulders and watched the gathering streams of water, fed by a monsoon-like rain, flow by him. It was late morning, too soon to camp, so he stood and trudged on.

Thoughts about an ever-increasing onslaught from the heavens and how it would contribute to river flow—and if not stopped, how it would crumple a dam or flow right over it—kept his mind busy. Absurd, water is lacking; we need more of it. He'd read an article in a Colorado history book about how water is diverted through tunnels under the Continental Divide. He found it incredible that some of these tunnels had been blasted through mountain rock below ground and that one stretched for over ten miles. And there were lots of tunnels, one of them—was it the Moffat?—allowed passengers to travel through on a train!

CHAPTER THIRTY-THREE

"**B**RUCE! CALM DOWN. What in Christ's name are you talking about? It's three a.m., by the way."

"Richard, this Mafia guy, from the New York family, called me an hour ago, after his man pounded on my door and left a note."

"Tell me again what he said over the phone."

Hendricks told him.

"Okay, let me make a few calls, and I'll get to the bottom of it."

———

HENDRICKS HAD NOT BEEN ABLE to go back to sleep. He told his valet to make him omelets with extra bacon and a double dose of sharp cheddar cheese. He dismissed his valet and ate with a mug of coffee beside him. At seven in the morning, he considered calling Joan to retract but at the last second held off. He would wait for the senator's call.

After breakfast, on his way to his office, he had his valet drop him off at Moe's and dismissed him. "Call me if anything unusual transpires," he instructed. "Take no calls. Answer no knocks."

He ordered the usual and took it to go. He hid in his office and locked the door. Ginger wouldn't arrive for another forty-five minutes. He'd call Richard as soon as she walked in. Meanwhile he ate in isolation. He checked his drawers between bites and was comforted to see ample supplies. He decided that after finishing the bakery items, he'd go for his kettle-fried potato chips next. He didn't think further than that other than imagining chewing a Snickers, its chocolate and nuts and nougat coursing over his tongue and down his throat.

Hendricks knew he fucked up with the reporter, Joan. He'd thought the Mafia, if they hadn't already made an overture to the tribe, would appreciate the implication. *Christ. I blew it.*

Hendricks had moved from the chips and Snickers and was already on to Cheetos when he heard Ginger arrive. On his way to pushing the intercom, his cell chirped.

"Okay. Are you listening? None of my New York contacts know anything about this. They didn't even know about the rumor."

"What about out here? He has men in the area."

"That was my next question to them. I waited on my phone while my top contact checked with the family in Colorado. Nada."

"Well, who the fuck called me, Richard?"

"Let's think about this. Who doesn't want water diverted?"

"You and your tribe."

Silence.

"Okay. I'm sorry, Richard. The tribe. But don't forget what you and your cohort asked me—wait, could Christo be behind this?"

"It's got to be someone from the tribe. You have no idea of their pressure on me not to divert."

Hendricks perked up. "And the Mafia rumor gives their proposed casino a bad rap. But you've confirmed the Mafia has nothing to do with it." He felt better.

"That's right."

"There would be public outrage over a Mafia-run casino."

"So, Bruce, who spread the rumor?"

Hendricks played dumb but thought Richard knew. "I don't know, Richard, but this was a serious threat. No amateur could set it up."

"Never underestimate the tribe."

"What would you do if you were in my shoes right now, Richard?"

"Again, I've investigated the matter fully, and no one within the Mafia knows a thing about this. Bruce, you can take that to our bank."

HENDRICKS HAD SIX HOURS TO MAKE a decision. The number the caller, whoever he was, had called from was untraceable. He could discuss his predicament with Joan but didn't want her to overreact. He didn't want his name and implications in the news. But if someone from the tribe could send a man in the middle of the night to make such a threat, Hendricks felt *beyond* vulnerable. Two hours later, Hendricks decided to think about his situation somewhere else. He said a brief hello to Ginger in passing, telling her he was going for a walk. Hendricks exited the lobby, made a few rights and lefts and slid into the bakery from a back door. The workers were used to this, and the owner played dumb as soon as he got the nod from Hendricks. Hendricks took his usual bag of sweets and entered a restroom stall at the library down the street. He sighed over his food addiction. He decided that if he lived another full day, he would attend Overeaters Anonymous meetings yet again.

In the quiet of the handicapped library stall, a custard-filled chocolate éclair squished into his mouth, Hendricks thought it through. Rodriguez had bribed him at their meeting at Chuck's Ribs. A free chalet and $250,000 was his if he got the Denver Water Board to not divert water and to plan with the Colorado Water Conservation Board to keep more water in the west. At the time, Hendricks felt more than pressured. He felt warned. But now, with FRE investments, he'd pulled Rodriguez close to him, and the tribe was furious. They saw that Rodriguez had, in effect, been bought. And though they had originally set up Rodriguez at Denver Water, they could no longer threaten a senator. All the tribe's fingers pointed to Hendricks as the number one problem in getting more water. He was the tribe's obstacle. Hendricks convinced himself it was the tribe who had left the note and ten minutes later the tribe who had made a threat that also managed to mention water. *New York! Nice try.*

Hendricks saw through it now. He'd accomplished his objective with the rumor he'd planted. Already there was fallout about a "Mafia-run casino." He'd seen it in the morning's paper. He figured Joan was doing a follow-up to her scoop. Hendricks smiled, whipped cream from a sugar-coated confection smeared on his cheek. He was sure he'd get his water now. Who in his right mind would want to support a Mafia casino? Political suicide.

Hendricks brushed himself off and cleansed his face in the restroom. He proceeded to the library reference room and scanned the papers. He spotted a feature in *Barron's* detailing hedge funds and the new securities driving the real estate markets. He read it word for word and was fascinated with new opportunity. He stepped from the library into a late sunny morning and didn't check the time. Feeling heady, he hailed a cab, which he directed to Chuck's Ribs.

CHAPTER THIRTY-FOUR

"**R**ODRIGUEZ IS A HUMAN OIL SLICK."

Hendricks listened to Wayne Anderson, the Colorado Water Conservation Board chairman, rant on his speakerphone as he closed his office door. Ginger smacked her gum, never a good sign, as she burned him with a look. He figured she was on to him because of his warning about Paul. He'd told her that Paul was at odds with him over water issues and that he wished he'd fall under a bus. Suddenly, it hit him. She was in love with the prick. No longer an acquaintance. She loved him.

"Wayne, look, I can't deal with this right now. I'm not the one pressuring you."

"That's the problem. You and Rodriguez are tight, so why is *he* pressuring me?"

"I can't answer that."

"C'mon, Bruce, we all know you want more water. You didn't have to sic him on me."

"Tell him the board will approve, but we have to wait for the right moment."

"Approve?"

"Can the bullshit questions, Wayne. You got investments in the Front Range too."

"Bruce. You tell our senator that there is no guarantee."

"Dammit, Wayne, I told you I can't discuss this right now. I have another call on hold and two people outside my office waiting to see me."

"When can we discuss this?"

"I'll call you." Hendricks hung up. His heart was like a boxer's in the ring.

Over a month ago, he'd overheard Ginger say to one of her girl-friends on what he knew was her private cell, "Roses. Yes, he sent me roses." This was a first, but he didn't make anything of it; she always yammered with friends during the day. Yesterday, he noticed her studying a brochure—and could spell out VEGETARIAN backward on the titled top. She'd never been interested in anything like that before, so the idea had to be from someone new in her life.

Bakery aromas filled his nostrils. He wanted food and visualized oven-warmed oatmeal cookies filled with walnuts. Warmed apple and cherry tarts. His spirits lifted. Time for a break.

He walked to the bakery and placed his order. He watched the count-erman fold the waxed paper and separate the rich tarts from the cookies. He'd been trained on how to prepare goodies for Mr. Hendricks.

Ginger. He should have put it together because it connected to her saying over a month ago that she'd seen Paul at some bar or other and later, when she'd asked questions about him the day after he visited, he confided more that he should have. He didn't make the connection because, as he remembered now, she'd asked for the afternoon off to take his ex, her mother, on a birthday outing. He realized she'd improved her posture, no more slouching over her keyboard or holding her face with her hands. And had he sensed a tinge of rouge or lipstick the other day? *Where the fuck's Moe with my food? Wait, I'm at the counter.*

CHAPTER THIRTY-FIVE

BUTANE WAS PUMPED. Reardon had asked him to find out all he could about tunnels, diversions, dams, and water rights, and he took the assignment with gusto. Reardon preferred the written word—"It nails all thought," he'd said—and Butane took copious notes. But there was one thing that became the so-called elephant in the room: How does one person make it past security and descend down to the specific tunnel to set charges? Butane learned how the tunnels were made, where the weak links were, where to set the charges, what type of charge to use. He knew the flow rates by tunnel, the probable end results of particular demolitions, and other extraneous info, but how would he gain entrance to the tunnel itself, and how would he be able to get out if he was followed in?

Now he was about to learn from the doctor of all maladies himself.

"Medicine Man, I'm told you are eighty-eight years old. Is that true?"

The hunched Indian sat with his pipe, which looked older than he did. The medicine man said nothing as he puffed and studied Butane.

"Can I ask why you smoke that? Aren't you better off without it?"

The old Indian pointed to a curl of smoke ascending to the ceiling.

"What does that tell you?"

Butane looked up and had a feeling where this conversation would go. He'd been with his people most of his life. Nevertheless his own enthusiasm wasn't diminished.

"I'm not good at reading signs, Father." It was rare for one to refer to an elder this way, and he hoped Medicine Man would divine an ultimate purpose here.

The old Indian puffed again and studied the curl of smoke. He took out the pipe and pointed at the wisps. "That says you will have to improve or you will fail in your quest."

"What makes you think I have a quest, Father?"

"Why are you here? This is only the third time you have been in my tent."

"I remember one time. Why was I in the other time?"

"What are you looking for?"

"Were you around while the tunnels were built?"

"For two of them. My father was around for another."

"The Moffat?"

The doctor of all maladies held his pipe and stared at him.

Butane was fearful of proceeding. "Teepee said you had a map. There is a secret way to access the tunnel."

The Indian waited, and Butane felt cramped. He'd been too direct. The Indian looked away as he tapped his pipe upside down against a stone.

"Teepee says you have a map showing a secret entrance," Butane blurted.

"You learn a lot about explosives in Afghanistan?"

"Yes, Father, I did."

"Why should I give you a map? Will it help our people?" He opened a blackened pouch of elk skin and refilled his pipe.

Butane dove off the cliff. "Was Teepee wrong, Father? You don't have a map?"

"Teepee is wrong and correct. I don't have a map, but I have a map."

Butane felt his face flush red. He felt as if in a mental straightjacket. It was the height of ignorance and bad manners to show emotion in front of the reservation's oldest Indian. He stifled his words and looked down between his legs.

The medicine man relit his pipe, and as Butane watched the smoke curl from his lips, the answer came to him.

"The map is in your head."

The Indian nodded.

"Can you . . . Father . . . tell me . . . ?"

"I asked you two questions. You didn't answer either."

"I—we have been pushed around for generations, Father. We want to build a casino and resort. We want to develop our land, reservation land, and expand this development with homes, schools, a hospital. It can become a small town, eventually a city." He watched Medicine Man's stare. "This will help our people."

The Indian puffed. "Where will you get the necessary water?"

Butane had regained the cliff, and now he dove off it again. "We've been denied. What's worse, more water will divert east. There will be less for our people. Like I said, Father, we have been kicked around for generations. We need to send a strong message. We must act."

Medicine Man became quiet. He puffed and watched his smoke for several minutes.

"I must study the signs more," he said.

"What happens if you die? If you leave us, it will be too late."

The Indian moved his eyes over him. Butane understood that he was reading him like an ancient scroll.

"You doubt my map," he said, motioning to him with his pipe.

"No."

"Yes. You do."

For once Butane kept quiet.

"Do you remember where we buried the bones of this elk?" Father held up his tobacco pouch.

Butane nodded.

"Go there and listen to the winds. Come back to me after you find it."

"Find what, dear Father?"

"Go and listen. Observe. Study the signs."

CHAPTER THIRTY-SIX

AFTER A TURBULENT NIGHT of bizarre dreams—he dreamed he was in Afghanistan again working in a kind of people zoo that had mazes and stairways that went sideways, animals outside the zoo that moved in concentric circles and communicated with each other in Indian languages—Butane drove out to a secluded burial ground designated for sacred animals. He hadn't been here in twenty years, the last time as an adolescent during a ceremony for elk. At the time, he was not impressed with anything Indian and hated living on the reservation. The meaning of the burial ceremony escaped him now, but he remembered a dance around a bonfire with full-blooded Utes in native costumes.

He leaned his Vespa two-seater, with custom tires fit for mountain paths, against a shrub and looked around. A vague outline of the burial ground for animals remained. But the sixty-by-sixty-foot plot was overgrown with weeds and wildflowers. He examined hoof prints of elk, deer, and horse. What else could he find here? The plot backed up to boulders the size of Volkswagens, which supported a natural ramp up to an arête lost in sunlight.

Listen to the winds? There was no wind. *The fuck*, Butane thought. Medicine Man was becoming senile and had buried himself in riddles within riddles. He sat down Indian style and faced west, the morning sun behind him. He closed his eyes and heard eagle and hawk and coyote, but there was nothing on the wind but a vacuum of stillness. He watched and listened, and after getting impatient and upset, stomped around the cemetery, all the while looking for "come back to me after you find it." Twenty minutes later, he took off on the Vespa. He hadn't a clue.

He slept better that night, fewer dreams, and returned to the burial ground in the morning. This time, he decided he wouldn't leave until he found "it." But the more he listened and concentrated the more distant he became. He felt disconnected and for a few minutes felt delirious. Medicine Man was provoking him. Perhaps he was being set up to try and solve some type of riddle the father couldn't decipher himself. This was madness, and Butane spit on the graves and yanked out weeds. He chewed some strands of wild chicory and ate some of its blue petals as he'd seen his people do when they were agitated. An hour later, he couldn't stand it anymore and charged off. He wanted to drive straight to Medicine Man but accepted that he couldn't do that, for it would prevent any further help from him. This was his charge. If he didn't find something, it would be futile to try and get any type of map.

He returned the third day, this time in the afternoon to catch the Santa Ana, but the end result was the same: the winds gave up nothing. At dusk, forlorn, tired, angry, sullen, he left once again. He'd uncovered several buried arrowheads and tried to see a pattern as he noted the direction of the tips but had given up. He tried to create his own pattern giving direction with the four arrowheads and heard the terrible squawk of a hawk protecting her chicks from a predator. He tried to fathom something from the timing of the squawks with the making of his pattern but could see nothing and chalked it up to coincidence. He smelled and sensed smoke trails from the reservation meandering to the sky, and he went back to his trailer. He'd hoped to have new news for Reardon. They were looking for a breakthrough. He wished he hadn't told Reardon about the medicine man and what Teepee had said about a map.

On the fourth day, he returned to the burial ground at dusk. He'd dreamed of smoke and campfire the previous night. Thinking this a sign, he returned to the burial ground and decided to spend the night there. He spread out a horse blanket over a patch of open ground and rolled out his bedroll on top of it. He watched the near-full moon creep up in front of him. *Listen to the wind, watch, study the signs.* He relaxed as he built a small campfire for the night. He drank from a half-empty bottle of Wild Duck and fished through his bag of nuts, figs, and dates. He drew his knees up. He could hear distant calls from the reservation. There was a slight breeze. Despite his failure, he was at peace. He would find his own way to blow up the tunnel.

During the night, when he got up to void, he rekindled his campfire. He noticed that though the eastern breeze had stopped completely, the smoke from his fire continued to drift to the huge boulders to the west, behind him. That was odd because the boulders were so huge that they blocked his view, and if there was a breeze, wouldn't the smoke rise up straight and curve to the west? The smoke from his fire traveled horizontal to the boulders behind him. He retrieved his flashlight and walked over to the giant boulders, one the size of a Mack truck. His flashlight revealed nothing, but he sensed escaping air. He lit a match and grazed along the boulders. At one point, the match flickered and died. He relit another, and it flickered and died at the same spot. On instinct, he pulled at some roots growing from the rock and uncovered a hole that gaped larger under his flashlight. He remembered to take pictures for Reardon. He hollered into the hole and heard a distant echo.

Before dawn, Butane got to work. He removed more roots, and as he did, he felt a slab of rock shuffle. He pitched in a hand but could not shift the slab any farther. With the aid of a tire iron he kept in a tool bag bungeed to the Vespa, he pried the rock up and realized the compromised seam in the rock was half as tall as he was, and it started at ground level. Forty minutes later, after taking more pictures, he got it wide enough and crawled in.

CHAPTER THIRTY-SEVEN

"**A**LL I FOUND WAS ONE circular cave," Butane said. "I walked around inside. There was one small tunnel about the diameter of a basketball, if that, which led down at a sharp angle, but for any human, unless he was an undersized pygmy, entrance was out of the question."

It was dawn the day after Butane discovered the cave. Medicine Man was sipping from his buffalo-horn cup his daily drink of hot water, honey, and cinnamon. Today he had inserted a stem of bear root into his cup. The Utes used the plant to treat colds and upper respiratory ailments. He stirred the drink with the stem and sipped again. He set the cup down.

"You found one cave. Don't be discouraged."

"Are you suggesting that there are other caves?"

"There are, but you have the right one. What you haven't discovered is the other tunnel inside, and I don't mean a man-made tunnel."

"Father, if I may be bold. Can't you draw me a map?"

"I can. Before I do, I need to know, are you the only one who will descend to the man-made tunnel?"

"Yes." He didn't know for sure and hadn't outright lied.

"You alone will set the charges?"

"Yes. Why?"

"My study of signs during the time you left reveals that more people are involved. This complicates any and all outcomes."

"There is one other person. He is tangentially involved in the explosives aspect."

"You are talking like a government man. The Spirit knows. Whenever another person is involved in an act of revenge, it is total. Not 'tangential,' your fancy government word."

"But . . . okay . . . all I'm saying is that I will be the one setting charges in the tunnel."

"There are other signs. Spirit of animal."

Butane decided not to confirm his tramping of the burial ground, figuring the father already knew.

Father took another sip.

"Hand me an arrow."

Butane hopped up and pulled a homemade arrow from an ancient-looking quiver.

Medicine Man grabbed it with quicker-than-expected reflexes. "Pay attention." He drew a three-foot-diameter circle. "Show me your outside entrance."

Butane took the arrow. "Facing east, on the outside boulders, the entrance was about here." He stabbed the arrow tip into the dirt. "Behind brambles."

"The moon wasn't full, and you were facing east-northeast."

"Should that make a difference?"

"That little tunnel you found leads to a blocked entrance nearby. I memorized this. The moon was full and I was facing due east." He stabbed a new place and the arrow took hold in the dirt.

"But no one can enter that tunnel."

"I said pay attention. Do you think our forefathers would make it simple? Look where that arrow tip is placed."

"Just outside the circle."

"Which means?"

"There is another blocked entrance?"

"Yes. Take a four-foot length of mid-growth pine with you tomorrow. You know what to do."

"And that will be the correct entrance?"

"Yes, but there is one other thing."

Butane cradled his head in his hands. "What, Father?"

"You will be able to descend in this new entrance, but at the fork, go left for thirty arm lengths, measured shoulder to wrist. Look for a scored heart on rock with an arrow through it."

Butane waited. "And?"

"You will know what to do."

"Father, please."

"Trust me. I've become tired. Do not come to see me anymore."

"I hope I will satisfy your wishes, Father. May the Spirit be with you."

Medicine Man nodded, his eyes glazing into a trance.

CHAPTER THIRTY-EIGHT

Diana was so pissed that she wanted to shriek. She looked straight at her new boss, Ronald Avery, recently appointed assistant director, Counterterrorism, Denver Field Office, and pictured herself springing over his desk, bashing the top of her head into his nose, and jabbing her fingers into his eyes.

"As I say, Ms. Santos. It makes sense, you going out there." He looked up as he placed a memorandum to his outbox. "You've done some hiking, right?"

You bastard. That's how you toy with me? You're the big deal, and I've been passed over again. "Why don't you go one further and dump me on the Peraita case so you can kick me to the bottom?"

The assistant chief smiled and sat back in his chair. He folded his hands in front of him and rocked the chair slightly, like the nod he wanted to give with his head. "Diana. You know how it is. You've got to take the good with the bad."

His unctuous tone inflamed her all the more. "Bastard," she said under her breath.

He stopped nodding the chair, smiled. "Sometimes, Diana, you look more attractive when you keep your trap shut."

She stood up like a shot and glared at him. He took the folder that had been lying on his desk and held it out to her.

She snatched it and stormed out. She left the door wide open, knowing that he preferred to work behind closed doors.

After a trip to the ladies' room, where she attempted to calm herself, she marched to her desk. If any of the other agents noticed her countenance and demeanor, they didn't say anything. This wasn't the first time she'd felt like this. She looked at no one, put on her reading glasses, and pretended to study the file. Some minutes later, she realized she had the entire file upside down, but she didn't care and continued to hold it that way.

Diana repeated to herself that she was going to be the first woman to break the glass ceiling in Denver FBI counterterrorism. His job should have been hers. Her new boss had less time here, and she'd had more commendations than him. True, he was a former air force officer, but she was a few years older, and in her mind, she had more experience and energy. He'd gained some pounds around the middle, and she didn't see him work as hard. *What the fuck*, she told herself.

She rotated the file right-side up. She'd met this hiker, Awol, at a bar to assess him and assumed that she would get her own team and set up her own command. It was obvious Awol wanted to get into her pants, and she wasn't flattered. She reviewed his background again. He'd been in and out of scrapes since leaving the army, and from what she could understand, that is why he left the army in the first place. Something had happened in the army, but whatever it was, it'd been covered up. She put the file down and gazed out a window she could see from her doorway. She ignored the few nods and smiles from passersby, and when Rachael, her friend in the next cubicle, stuck her head around the doorway, asking if she'd like a mug of coffee, she declined with a shake. Diana said not a word about the restructuring; they all knew how bitter she felt. Her emotions were always written on her face. "Don't ever take up poker," her ex had said.

Avery had initiated the meeting with the hiker. She took it as a demotion and couldn't back out of it for any reason she could think of. She hated to leave her office and tormented herself about what would happen going out *to field*. Field and forest. The irony. A year ago, Rachael took leave to have her baby. Diana was shocked at how Avery had swiped her small side table, which held family pictures, and took it into his own office, claiming he needed it. He said he'd return it but didn't. Recently, Avery jumped ahead of the line to preempt a close and covered parking space before "Gentleman Jim," with twenty-nine years of government service, retired. When she met Jim under an umbrella he offered as he locked his car on a wet and raw day a week before his last day at work, she stared at him in puzzlement and fury. "Don't let it upset you, Diana. It's the little things that bring one down." Yeah, sure. She'd gone straight to Avery's desk fuming, eyes accusing. "What is it now, Diana, the weather got you down?"

That night, Diana, a cascade of thoughts—*could've, would've, should've*—plunging through her mind, bustled through her hiking stuff and threw together a pack of sorts. *Where the fuck are those poles I bought?* She found them hidden in a corner of a closet. She wanted to call a friend and vent but looked at the time: 10:30 p.m. She sat on top of her bed, unable to think of anyone who'd want to listen to her rants at this hour. She set her alarm but needn't have bothered. She peeked at her radio clock most of the night.

CHAPTER THIRTY-NINE

Paul SAT IN TEEPEE'S RUSTED Ford F-150 pickup, which he sometimes borrowed, on the hardpan with a view of the chief's office. He waited there for several minutes and watched members of the tribe go in and out. Two of them gave a nod as they saw him sitting silently, and he stared back as if not seeing them—because he hadn't. After the time given for Hendricks to retract his rumor expired, Paul had been summoned. Hendricks had put the tribe's interests in jeopardy and had ignored the demand to fess up. The chief said the biggest problem with Hendricks was that he would always divert water away from the tribe for his Front Range developments. It was an untenable mess, and Butane must kill him. He was running through his mind, again and again, how he would phrase his plea. Every time he did, he either made a false start or became illogical, understanding that he might not get out of this. Daring not to delay any longer, he exited the vehicle and went to the chalet. "There you are, Angry Bear," Teepee said, expecting him. He received him and told him to wait in the vestibule.

He was summoned several minutes later and sat before Running Waters again in his private office. This continued change of venue colored Paul Christo's thinking. Running Waters had always met him in his den by the fireplace, where there were couches, his cats, easy conversation near his bar. Here there was one measly window, the room unheated. Butane glanced at a framed picture that hung on the opposite window wall: Running Waters shaking hands with Frank Sinatra. It was autographed, and he could make out the word "Denver."

Running Waters watched him. After Christo, sitting in a hard maple chair that could have come from a New England kitchen, finished looking at the framed photo, the chief said, "About a week after that picture was taken, I saw you wrestle Ippolito at the arena."

Christo removed his glasses, wiped off an imaginary speck with his thumb, and put them back on. He did this often if backed into a corner. "I lost that one."

"You didn't seem focused and dropped a beat."

Christo accepted the bait. "I'd been thinking about your offer to be your aide all that day. The opportunity consumed me."

"We've set up Ippolito. He is the anti-diversion member we need, and we will not rest until he replaces Hendricks."

Christo looked up.

"We kept you out of it. The water board gang would fight having a biased American Indian replacing Hendricks. The senator has moved on. We can no longer depend on him. We are setting up someone new."

"Will the board accept this?"

"Part of the final deal we made with the senator. Your senator all but refused to dump Hendricks. We got his word that he would push in Ippolito."

"I see. Ippolito accepted the idea of supporting the tribe?"

"To tweak a phrase, we gave him an order he couldn't refuse."

Paul nodded, remembering Ippolito's happiness with a newborn son.

"So why are you here right now?" the chief asked.

Christo went off script and laid out everything as best he could. Indian to Indian. Ute to Ute.

Running Waters said nothing the entire time. But he blinked when Christo told him of his affair and love for Ginger. At the end, Christo threw up his hands. In a voice pushed an octave higher, he managed to squeeze out, "I betrayed you, by his daughter. I'm sorry. I can't do what you ask of me."

"I may have you thrown off Weeminuche," Running Waters said. "No one has betrayed me and gotten away with it."

"I should be thrown off that cliff. You have done everything for me. I accept that, if it's what you want."

"No. That wouldn't be punishment for you. That would be relief for you. It's the coward's way out."

Christo, out of character, stifled sobs for several minutes. He looked down and covered his eyes with his hand as he convulsed.

"Enough!" Running Waters hollered. "Straighten up. Take heed."

Christo pulled himself together, understanding that he had failed. Knowing Running Waters wouldn't speak until Christo looked at him, he looked.

Running Waters said eight measured words: "You will do what I asked of you."

Christo said nothing.

He heard Running Waters's last five words. "Do I make myself clear?"

"Yes."

THE NEXT DAY, HE CALLED GINGER on her private cell. "Got some bad news."

"Let me guess. You've been arrested and all your pornography has been confiscated."

She always liked to play these kinds of games; it was one of the things he loved about her. Today, he was lost, afraid, alone.

She picked up on the bead of silence. "What happened?"

"I can't come over tonight."

"Why?"

"Do you remember the spot where I explained why . . ."

"Of course."

"Listen carefully. Have at least two of your friends pick you up and bring you there, the parking area near the sheltered sign. Do not come alone. Do not use your car. Have your friends wait there."

"What time?"

"Six."

Butane had several hours. He knew he wouldn't be able to sleep tonight after seeing Ginger, so he prepared. He'd maintained all his CDT hiking gear. He'd been able to disappear numerous times for a few days to see Reardon, and thankfully, during those times, he didn't reveal his whereabouts. He'd been able to escape from other matters and gear up for the tunnel mission. He didn't discuss his frequent hikes, figuring the clan would let him hold private his near death in the wilderness. Teepee knew bits and pieces but couldn't draw him out.

Butane needed supplies, but he had enough to get by for now. He knew he might be followed tonight, so he kept his stuff in trash bags as if they would be discarded. The foods he took from his pantry, as well as the refrigerated items, which he wrapped in tinfoil and inserted in baggies, he loaded in his backpack, putting trash bags over opposite ends of the pack. He arranged with an off-reservation friend who owed him a big favor twice over to pick him up again late tonight, after he'd seen Ginger, to drive him to another trailhead he'd selected.

He prepared for the second owed favor by placing a closed atlas on his kitchen table. He hid it partially under a newspaper, which is how Teepee or another aide would report it to their chief. But one page of the atlas was earmarked—New Zealand. On a night table, next to his cot, he scribbled out on a pad a New Zealand phone number given to him by his friend, a native New Zealander. His friend had arranged for his brother, who lived in New Zealand, to wait for a call at the number provided. The New Zealand brother would ask in his native accent, "Paul, is this you? My driver in Christchurch, New Zealand, is waiting."

———————————

BUTANE EXITED HIS FRIEND'S vehicle and met Ginger as she stepped out of a car. Her friends parked away from his friend and kept the engine running.

"I have," Butane said, "an insurmountable problem." He took her elbow and walked her to a bower away from the lot. He sat down on a park bench beside her. She said nothing.

He began again but couldn't continue.

"Oh, for Chrissake, Paul, man up."

"I have to go away for a while."

"Why?"

"I can't tell you."

"It's got to do with my father. Water rights."

"I can't get into details."

"You supposed to kill him?"

"Yes. I refused."

"Which means?"

"It means that I at first refused, but last night, I said yes."

She stared at him.

"I'm going away. Some place where they won't find me."

"And my father?"

"He's in danger. But he can cover himself if he spills everything to the press immediately. This is one reason I wanted to meet you privately. Have him call the number in this envelope. The lady at this number knows it's a scoop and will interview him as soon as he calls." He looked at the envelope. "Inside are details that your father needs to know to protect himself."

"Can't he call the police?"

"Only after he gives a complete interview to this person. Our government may have been breached."

Ginger put it together. "Senator Rodriguez. My father is to call the Admiral's wife."

"Yes."

"How long will you be gone, Paul?"

"Could be a year. Or more."

She shook her head and turned to him. "I guess you'd better hustle your tidy little ass out of here."

That hurt. But Paul knew that's who she was. He wasn't surprised.

"Right. Listen, Ginger—"

"No, I want you to listen to me. Yeah, I love you and all that. But it's over. I do appreciate you telling me in person. I'll give you that."

"Ginger, please."

"I'm not finished," she blurted.

He gave her his handkerchief. She wiped her eyes and threw the cloth back at his face.

"I was your setup. You duped me."

Paul jumped up. "Yes. Of course I did. That's how it started. That's how it was supposed to work. Okay? You've got me cold on my original intentions."

She got up and faced him. "All right. But I can't wait for you. I'm sorry, Paul. It's all changed for us now. Gone for good." She placed a finger on his cheek. "Good luck, Paul." And then she walked away.

CHAPTER FORTY

BUTANE DIDN'T THINK ABOUT sleep after his meeting with Ginger. He had less than five hours before being picked up at midnight here at the trailer. Up next was the one thing that would refocus his mind, the obvious thing left to do.

He hid the Vespa near the cemetery and gathered himself within the Spirit. The doctor of all maladies had been right, listen to the wind, watch, study the signs. That last night at the cemetery, he'd smelled distant campfire smoke from the reservation and sensed it drifting to his nostrils. The wind was slight, and, truthfully, as he'd concentrated, he may have imagined conversations of his mother, Medicine Man, Teepee, and mixed breeds like himself. Unable to sleep in the early morning hours that next day, he'd had sat up from his sleeping bag, which topped his cot, and emerged from his trailer. The occasional spot of light was from Teepee's cigar as he smoked by his teepee. The Ute refused to live in any other domicile. He couldn't stand the metal of trailers or the painted, "desecrated" wood of typical houses. Always the teepee. Butane had turned his collar up, aware that the coolest times of night were before the dawn. The Utes had explained it to him, something to do with the Spirit steeling itself for the day ahead, but he couldn't, or didn't, try to process it. You have an attitude, they'd said.

Now, after Ginger and Chief Running Waters had closed him down, Butane was about to enter the proper cave tunnel entrance and descend. It wouldn't be a setup with demo. He would reconnoiter, get a feel for the true mission. The chill of excitement swept through him. He was made for this. This was payback for all the shit he and his people had been through. There was a half-moon above the coyote howl, and he tried to remember what that meant in Ute lore. As opposed to full-moon howls, the message within could signify a handful of meanings depending on season, alignment of planets, weather, mood. It was as abstruse to Butane as unknown Indian dialect. He hadn't studied or listened, and now he wished he had. Was it all junk? With maturity came wisdom. He knew that signs were everywhere. He used to think that one's mind could create signs on the spot about anything. Now he realized that it was a matter of discarding the faulty, the foolish, the inhumane, and selecting the meaningful, the true. That's why Teepee came out in the mornings with his cigar. While so-called normal white people scan the headlines around coffee and toast in wood and brick mansions, the Utes listen, watch, and read the signs of the day straight from nature, the creator. *My God,* thought Butane, *white people have thrown it all away. They don't have a clue.*

Butane, in the moment, saw as his purpose to send a huge and obvious message. The earth provides water. We don't divert it to the detriment of others, especially those who were here first.

Butane stuck the shaved limb of pine he'd taken from the reservation into cracks and crevices on the other side of the boulder. After a number of tries, the limb went all the way through an opening close to the bottom. Using the limb as a lever, he managed to slide aside stone. After squeezing himself inside, he maneuvered the rock to re-cover the crawl space, pulling his hand away in the nick of time. Thinking ahead, this time he'd left flora rooted outside the cave to hide the entrance.

Butane kneeled inside the cave and put on his headlamp. He had to stoop as he walked, and soon he headed down at what he figured was a thirty-five to forty-degree pitch. This was steep, and he was glad he could restrain forward momentum by reaching to the rock ceiling above him. The climb back up would be arduous, but without the weight of explosives and attendant gear, he'd be fine. The air was stagnant but tolerable. Butane had trained in worse conditions and remembered the coal-mine canary story. He'd been counting steps, and at 236 yard-length steps, he came to the fork. He turned his head right and the headlamp showed a narrowing tunnel. He angled left and advanced into a similar narrowing tunnel. The air quality diminished, which worried him. He barely had room to walk, and with the stoop bothering him, he got on his knees to crawl on all fours.

He kept on measuring arm lengths, shoulder to wrist, as instructed by the medicine man. This was easy to do as the walls crowded him on both sides. Butane kept himself lean at 160 pounds and was glad of it. He'd done that one right. But the air bothered him. He moved slower to conserve oxygen and took shallow breaths to force-acclimate himself. Again, part of his training. But thirty arm lengths wasn't far, and he panicked when he felt he was getting close and the headlamp showed nothing but the same rock all around him. At forty arm lengths, he did panic: the air was depleted. He would die in here if he didn't back out now. How could he have missed it?

It was impossible to turn around, and Butane strained to breathe. He backed up and shone his headlamp on the walls, left and right, no longer relying on arm lengths. The ceiling? That's what he'd missed. He chanced going forward once more to where he'd stopped and shined on the ceiling and saw nothing. With a sick feeling in his stomach, dripping sweat, and unable to breathe properly, he backed up. He was in a bad fix. He had to creep backward, uphill. In his gyrations, he prayed the headlamp would show the rock arrow as he drove himself backward. Nothing. He gasped for breath, and sweat seeped into his eyes. He hyperventilated and tried to remember what they'd taught him in the army. With Olympian effort, he closed his eyes and concentrated on one tiny breath, another, one more. He'd been facing down on the pitched floor, and as he opened his eyes, he viewed a most wonderful sight. Right before him was a squared-off rock scored with a heart and arrow angled at 135 degrees. With shaking fingers, Butane felt around a different stone at the end of the arrow and with both hands got purchase. He lifted the rock up and air, oxygen, flowed up into his face. He could have cried as he sucked in the dank air. *Breathe, breathe,* he told himself. *Stabilize.* Like a diver experiencing the bends, he instructed himself to do nothing, sit for a moment, and he did.

He heard a distant thrumming. The thrumming stayed constant and came from the right, the direction of the arrow. Butane took out his flashlight and shined it straight down into the hole. Railroad track. *Praise be to God,* Butane thought, *this is the Moffat train tunnel.* He took a picture through the hole with his cell phone. Hearing nothing below and seeing nothing on the track, he searched with flashlight and headlamp. The combined light revealed an iron ladder built right into the rock underneath him to his left. Butane pulled out more stones that had been lined around the squared one and realized he was uncovering a perforated manhole cover, which was connected to a short length of manhole-sized pipe. He took more pictures. He confirmed it was a manhole pipe after he lifted the cover, which fit in the tunnel he'd been crawling in. He dropped himself to a hanging position and felt the ladder next to his foot. He maneuvered himself to the ladder and went down a few rungs. It would be an easy drop to the track, four feet, if that. He looked around while on the ladder and saw nothing. He must be right on the Divide, for he couldn't see daylight at either end of track or the other exits or entrances built into the wall, but as he looked back up through the man-sized hole, he saw that the underside of the cover was camouflaged with stone that pieced into the natural ceiling, making it look like everything was sealed permanently.

Butane dropped down near the track and took out his cell again. He took pictures of the hole he'd emerged from, the ladder, the train tracks, and then went to the huge water pipe angled slightly down, which hung overhead. He climbed a planked scaffold, put his hands on the pipe, and felt the thrumming. Flowing water. This time his light revealed other staging and platforms, which went up over the track to the pipe. He took more pictures. He climbed up the other staging, felt the vibrations again, and took extra pictures. His flashlight revealed a dirt-stoned recess farther on, but he still couldn't see daylight at either end of the track. The stone-marked arrow had aligned with where he stood. Butane congratulated himself. He would bring rope and tie it to the inserted ladder rungs of the main hole so they could get back up quickly. As it was, Butane had to reach and scramble his way up. He was nervous, and his sweaty palms made it difficult. He couldn't wait to see Reardon, explain how to enter the cave and tunnel, and show him all the pictures.

CHAPTER FORTY-ONE

BUTANE WENT INSIDE HIS TRAILER to drink hot chocolate and think. He had an hour before his midnight escape. He was torn about writing another letter to Ginger, but he'd already left her one declaring his everlasting love in the envelope he'd given her with the reporter's private number. There wasn't anything he could add to change her mind. He knew her well enough that she wouldn't want him to be weakened any more for her. But it'd gone badly, and despite his success at the cave, he was sick over the breakup. He sat on his cot and tried to figure a last way out but knew it was futile. He needed to disappear. The chief would give him peace for at least another day, maybe two, before having Teepee check on him. That was the Ute way. They would not expect a sudden escape. He'd be gone within twenty-four hours of his last spoken word to Running Waters.

He'd taken another sip of hot chocolate when his phone chirped. The New Zealander would be there in ten minutes. Awol went outside and circled his Vespa for a last look at his pride and joy. He gathered his trash bags and took a final look while listening to an approaching rumble. His friend pulled in, shut the lights but left the engine running as both lifted the Vespa into the pickup.

Butane had little to say on the drive to the trailhead, which puzzled the Maori New Zealander who drove the pickup.

"Don't you worry, Paul. I'm solid on this. It's the least I can do."

"I know you're solid. I was glad to help you before. We're square."

"Should I know this place where I'm taking you?"

"Yes. This is where you will take your other vehicle, the Dodge Ram pickup we talked about, and hide it. I'll show you. As discussed, my Vespa is yours for procuring that other vehicle. Keep everything a secret."

The Maori stuck over his hand and they shook.

After giving him a right, left, and straight, Butane said, "Up at that large oak—see it—there is a path right beyond it to the left. Drop me there. But when you come back, move the other vehicle to the right about fifty yards into the brush."

"And ride my accomplice back on your Vespa," the New Zealander Maori said.

It was Butane who stuck out his hand to the Maori. They shook again.

Butane got out and removed his trash bags. He told his friend to remain in the truck. After a few switches of gear and adding some things to his pack from one of the bags, Butane saddled up. He pulled his belly strap tight and fist-bumped his friend.

"Until we meet again," Butane said.

"Anything else you need me to do?"

"No. You haven't seen a thing. You don't know a thing. Stay cool."

After the Maori left, Butane fastened his headlight around his forehead and advanced. A mile later, he walked by a CDT trail marker.

BUTANE CRAWLED INTO HIS BAG outside the Arapaho National Recreation Area. From the oak tree turn-in to the cabin was a little over fourteen miles, and it took the average hiker eight hours. In daylight, Butane could do it in four. Halfway to the cabin, Butane had set up camp. This night it would drop to the low forties, but he'd packed his down sleeping bag and had taken extra clothes. Seven miles away, Reardon was unable to sleep, which was, for him, unusual.

Butane looked at the tiny section of stars above as he checked off in his mind his packed supplies for the diversion as well as for the tunnel mission. He went through every step he'd have to perform as he looked upon the brightest star and saw a cloud cover it. He couldn't sleep.

Chief Running Waters was also awake at the reservation, looking at the same stars. All three had their reasons for sleeplessness, and they were not unconnected.

Giving up, Butane crawled out of his bag at 10 p.m. Ten minutes later, he poled again toward the cabin.

———————————

THIRTY-SIX HOURS LATER, Teepee found his 1995 Ford F-150 pickup at the airport. Running Waters had kept the New Zealand map, which had been discovered earlier.

"It's a ruse," Running Waters had said. "He's too smart to play us this dumb."

But after his Ford was found, Running Waters called the New Zealand number and got a message. He refused to tell his people what the message was. The previous night, he'd watched a breaking story on Denver's main news station. He'd refused calls from the press all day about his alleged threat to Bruce Hendricks of the water board to not divert more water east of the Divide. Running Waters was beyond fury: one of his own had betrayed him. He'd read the scoop in this morning's paper, and seeing Hendricks on the news incensed him. Hendricks was shown telling the top news reporter that he had information that he couldn't reveal. "Was it a bribe?" she asked. "I have nothing more to say," he responded.

When he readied for bed, he asked Teepee about any leads on Christo.

"None, Chief."

"Mark my word. He'll show again. Not here. But he'll reveal himself."

CHAPTER FORTY-TWO

BUTANE MADE IT TO REARDON'S cabin before 1 a.m. It was hard enough to find the cabin in the daylight, isolated in Indian Peaks Wilderness. But he'd explored the area , once with tribal friends but mostly on his own, and he'd met Reardon out here. With his headlamp, he was able to spot that particular jagged rock, off the CDT, that was marked with charcoal squiggles resembling a large caterpillar. Rain and snow had smudged what was left of the charcoal, but because Butane had once put those squiggles there, he could always find the rock. He followed an obscure path for another mile, stepping through blowdowns that Reardon had placed to deter others, crossing a brook in his moccasins, and making two more zigs and zags before the final two-hundred-yard approach to the cabin. Butane didn't use his sticks the last several yards for fear of waking Don, but as he drew within a few feet of the door, it opened.

"Whoa. Didn't think you'd be up," Butane said.

"My man, Butane. I had a hunch you were coming tonight. Are we on track?"

"More than ever. There is no turning back." Butane had briefed him on his cell but left out the parts about Hendricks and Ginger.

Reardon heaped three split oak logs on the dwindling stove fire.

"Good. I don't have to say goodbye to anyone. Done that years ago."

Butane looked at a spot across from the bed. He pointed a stick to it and looked at Reardon for approval.

"Yours. And I made you some honey and tea."

"I've been hoping that was mine since I smelled it from outside the door."

As Reardon went for a cup, he looked back at Butane. He was spreading out his Ridge Rest pad. He rolled his sleeping bag down on top of it and placed his sticks aside as if he were cowboy camped on the trail. Reardon noted the care he took in setting up his spot and convinced himself that Butane was ready and focused. Reardon felt a rush of delight; the long-planned goal would soon be a reality.

"Got some big news," Butane said.

Reardon smiled.

"The cave leads all the way to the Moffat Tunnel," Butane said. "I know the secret access point, and no one else knows except for Medicine Man, the oldest Indian on the reservation."

"All right!" Reardon said, and they bumped fists. "Hallelujah."

Butane felt proud and on his A game.

"How are you sure?" Reardon asked.

"Because the project was intended to be a train tunnel providing traverse under the Continental Divide. A train still travels through it, usually with skiers. Medicine Man's father and two of his brothers were laborers. The Indians were treated worse than coolies. They had to live in their own wickiups."

"Go on."

"Back in the day, engineers bored a parallel tunnel used by workers to access the main tunnel. That parallel tunnel is now the Moffat water tunnel."

"What about the cave tunnel?"

"From what I understand, it was a natural cave with other tunnels inside. Medicine Man's father and brothers extended it to reach the Moffat system."

"His father and his brothers wanted revenge, and that's why he gave you the information."

"I'm told his father and brothers weren't invited to the 'holing-through' ceremony in 1927 or the actual opening of the Moffat a year later."

"How old is your doctor of all maladies?"

"He was born in 1920. Eighty-eight."

"Now I know what your people mean by many moons."

"From the hidden cave, I made it down to the train tunnel, which is right near the water tunnel. Now, do you really want to send a message?"

"Absolutely."

"We can blow both at the same time. Go big or go home!"

Reardon smiled. "Good work, Butane. What rocks is that I had always wanted the Moffat."

"Any special reason?"

"That's where Denver Water first envisioned bringing water from west to east to the Front Range. The Moffat started it all." Reardon nodded as he spoke. "Denver's first major transmountain water diversion."

"Yep. Steal water from Fraser to South Platte and give it to the Range. That fucked us Utes. Denver upped the diversion, and that fucked us for good."

They looked at each other.

Butane smiled. "I know what you're thinking: the news about expanding the Moffat. Before that has a chance, we're gonna blow what they have to smithereens."

They sat in Reardon's cabin looking at and feeling the warmth of the wood-fed stove. Butane had brought two Coors Light to celebrate, and they drank with satisfaction. Now that their most important hurdle had been removed, a way to get to the actual tunnel without being detected, they earned the right to relax for a moment.

"You ready to roll on this?" Reardon asked.

"I need a few more days to prepare supplies and to run a trial."

"Did you run trials in Afghanistan?"

"No, but . . ." Butane swallowed, "that's how we were trained."

"Do what you need to do. But, Jesus, Butane, you're returning to a future crime scene. Let's not leave any tracks."

"Right. Tell you what. I'm going to treat this like a combat mission. I can do this without a trial."

"How close did you get to the actual water tunnel?"

"I could hear the thrumming through the pipe. I headed right to it and felt the vibrations with my own hands." Butane looked at his hands. "It won't be a problem."

"You sure? I know we want the train tunnel too, but this water tunnel's gotta be the main objective."

"I'm sure. We gotta have the water tunnel. Don't worry. I'm locked and loaded."

For the next hour, they talked about the upcoming mission. Butane was fired up as much as Reardon because he had escaped his chief for good.

Reardon asked, "Doesn't Medicine Man worry you? You know that he knows."

"Yeah, he knows. But you don't understand the Ute. Not in a million years would he, the oldest man on the reservation, have given me his secret if he didn't want this mission to happen."

"He won't tell the chief?"

"Nope. He told me as much with his last words."

Reardon looked at him.

"He said, 'Don't come back to see me anymore.'"

"That a Ute thing?"

"Yes. That is the interpretation he wanted to give me. And he sealed it—his eyes glazed over as I left."

Reardon stared.

"The doctor of all maladies has, in effect, checked out. He'll be dead before or die the day we carry out our mission."

"I believe you. What about Ginger? She's not Indian."

"True. But she knows nothing about our mission. Nada. She does know that her father is in danger, and of course he knows nothing."

"She has other things on her mind than you?"

"That's right," he laughed. "I'm history, and she knows it."

"Will you miss her?"

"Ha! She was a royal pain in the ass. I had a job to do for the chief, and I failed."

Reardon was concerned but dropped it. "You did well, Butane. Let's get some sleep. We detail plans tomorrow. Send copies of all the pictures you took to my cell and educate me on the mechanics. We'll accomplish our mission together."

They high-fived. Reardon was satisfied. Butane was all mission. If Butane had designs on developing a relationship with him, it was clear that he would wait until after the mission was accomplished. Reardon barely felt sorry for him.

Before going to sleep, Butane was satisfied as well. Ginger was gone; that part of his life was over. But Reardon was here and would be after the mission was accomplished. Reardon had saved his life. He would always love him for that alone. And he'd found a way to help his tribe despite his betrayal. They would have their water because the tunnel would no longer be able to divert it. The busted tunnel would force the water conservation board to store runoff west of the Divide. The reservation would have extra water ipso facto. The chief wouldn't have approved the mission Medicine Man had sacrificed for the tribe. But the authorities wouldn't trace the terrorist act to the Utes. The tribe would be investigated, but they were clean. The chief would put it together. *Perhaps after a year or so, I could . . . Well,* he thought, *let's focus on the present.* Butane checked his watch. Reardon had scheduled the blow for one week from today. "Fourteen years to that day in August, I found my father hanging from our garage rafter," he'd said. Butane would see to it that Reardon's timetable held.

CHAPTER FORTY-THREE

Awol WAS TAKING A MUCH-needed zero day near Lake Granby in the northwest section of Indian Peaks Wilderness. He'd hitched back most of the seventy-odd miles, figuring that if the government was paying for modest lodging, he might as well stay in an area he'd been reading about. Unfortunately, he'd slipped on an outcrop of shale yesterday near Granby Dam when a rattlesnake frightened him, and he was feeling the aftereffects. He'd gone down hard on his left elbow. He was lucky twice over: nothing was broken, just a swollen bruise, and the rattler slithered away. Blazer had been ahead and missed the action. Awol hitched to the Granby library, and after sending and answering a few business-related emails, he wandered through the periodicals section and picked up a magazine with an article on the Hoover Dam. He skimmed it and thought about water diversion under the Divide.

A half hour later, Awol was reading a periodical about the Big Thompson Project: ". . . one of the largest and most complex resource developments undertaken by the Bureau of Reclamation. It consists of over 100 structures integrated into a transmountain water diversion system. Specifically, the system stores, regulates, and diverts water from the Colorado River on the western slope of the Continental Divide to the eastern slope of the Rocky Mountains." Awol read on and learned that the project "features dams, reservoirs, power plants, pumping plants, pipelines, tunnels, transmission lines, substations, and other associated structures." He'd had no idea. "The project diverts 260,000 acre-feet of water annually from the Colorado River headwaters on the western slope. Some of this goes through the Alva B. Adams Tunnel under the Divide." Awol noticed that one of the features was the Granby Dam, which controlled Lake Granby. He remembered the waitress back in Pie Town and her story about a drifter and his threat to that dam.

"The Alva B. Adams Tunnel is 13 miles long and almost 10 feet in diameter. It has a capacity of 550 cubic feet per second. The Big Thompson Project consists of 12 reservoirs, 35 miles of tunnels, 95 miles of canals, 6 hydroelectric plants, and 700 miles of transmission lines." *We are sitting ducks for a terrorist attack*, Awol thought. He paged to accounts of other tunnels. The Moffat was the first to "conquer the Divide." Additional water rights had been secured east of the Divide, but a tunnel had to be bored into and through mountains—and they weren't called the Rocky Mountains for nothing. Both a railroad tunnel and a water diversion tunnel were constructed. *Hell, I'm between two tunnels below me.* Completed in 1927, the Moffat Tunnel was enlarged in 1958 and became the property of Denver Water. Before reaching Denver proper, the Front Range enjoyed the benefits.

Awol discovered that as of late, Denver Water was looking to increase transmountain diversions from west to east through the Moffat Tunnel. A shortfall was expected in Denver in 2016, and plans were being made to address it—expanding the Moffat Tunnel was one of those plans. He checked the map and saw the Moffat was back near Berthoud Pass, which he'd hiked. It was near the Ute reservation, he noted. He'd learned that over 70 percent of Colorado water was west of the Divide, and plans called for yet more diversion. He remembered again the conversation with the waitress. Lots of people were angry.

He skimmed a few more articles and came to one on the Roberts Tunnel, which was farther south. This was a twenty-three-mile artifice that diverted to the Front Range. *Twenty-three miles!* The Dillon Reservoir west of the Divide, south of Silverthorne, held the water, and the aqueduct carried the water deep below the Divide to reservoirs in the east.

The chatter pointed to homegrown terrorists, not international. He wondered how things could fall so far off track that people in his own country fought each other tooth and nail for water. He concluded that it was a combination of global warming and misused resources over the years. There were more people, and water availability was dropping. Awol didn't figure in greed and the chance to make millions or revenge and the chance to wield a mighty blow. These things could have been in the recesses of his mind, but he was about to see them unfold right in front of his own eyes. His curiosity and thumbing of other pages informed him that though 80 percent of Colorado's precipitation occurred in western Colorado, over 80 percent of the population resided in the large metropolitan areas of Fort Collins, Boulder, Denver, Colorado Springs, and Pueblo on the eastern side of the Divide. More and more people were moving to northern Colorado east of the Divide, and Denver's Front Range, in particular, demanded more water.

———————————————

WHEN AWOL REENTERED THE Continental Divide Trail, the first time he crossed over from west to east, he had the uncanny feeling he was chasing someone and that he was running out of time. *It would have to be dams. Hard to get underneath the rock here.* He concluded that a terrorist would want to take out a dam as it would visually show the horror in the act, the catastrophe. Terrorists couldn't wallow, and normal citizens wouldn't be struck dumb in something they wouldn't see, like a tunnel. Yet something always made him think back to the tunnels under the Divide. The hideous and secretive act of blowing up a tunnel would create havoc harder to fix and control. And it would also be less top-of-mind for federal agents.

CHAPTER FORTY-FOUR

HENDRICKS WAS MORE PUZZLED than annoyed as his cell buzzed him awake in the night.

"Who is this?"

"I'm hearing that there is a major storm brewing with the banks and investment houses."

Hendricks scratched his head. "Richard, what the fuck time is it?"

"I don't give a shit what time it is, Bruce. I want you to get a handle on the scuttlebutt and call me right away. Clear?"

Hendricks scratched the other side of his head. His fellow classmate was poised, not like this. "Okay, okay. Settle down, Richard. I'll call my inside man in the morning, first thing."

HENDRICKS FELT A TINGE of unease as he watched his over-easy eggs break yolk on his plate. *Sunrise or sunset?* he asked himself. Hendricks always started his day with a proper breakfast, before compulsive eating took over and despite the overeating of a previous day. He pushed away his unease after two cups of *café solo*, not the Americano brew but strong and vigorous like they made it in Spain, his favorite European country. He'd waited until his personal aide had mastered it. He told himself that Richard felt overextended. Well, no shit, he was! Like himself and his six other select clients. Hendricks could now be a billionaire in fourteen to fifteen months. If need be, he could do the unthinkable: rob from some clients to pay—no, that's what happened to Ponzi. Hendricks was too sophisticated for that. Richard had heard false rumors.

Hendricks eyed his watch and called his Wharton contact. He had trouble getting through, but after he was transferred, he had to leave a message. *Not to worry. My Lehman man can run, but he can't hide.* He called Jake's personal cell number and got a message that his mailbox was full.

By noon, EST, after two trips to Moe's bakery, he finally got Jake live. "Yeah, Bruce, sorry."

"What the fuck is happening, Jake?"

"Keep your shirt on. Hold on a minute." Hendricks heard the shuffling of paper and muffled voices.

"Gotta make this quick," Jake said. "Got a meeting."

"Jake!"

"Calm down, Bruce. You're solid. Some inconsistencies with a few ancillary mortgage-backed securities. Don't worry about it. I'll get back later."

"Hey, Jake—" But he'd hung up.

That afternoon: "Mr. Hendricks. It's your senator, in case you've forgotten who I am."

"*El Patrón*, I've talked to my inside man. Everything is fine. No matter what you heard, he says we are solid."

"Listen to me, Bruce. It's not just what I've heard, it's what I'm continuing to hear from top-level people." His voice had escalated, and Hendricks moved the phone away from his ear.

"Now, Richard, don't panic. We are fine. Don't forget, I'm in this a lot more than you are." Even while saying this, Hendricks knew he would regret saying it.

"Mr. Hendricks. I don't give a rat's ass if you are in it a million times more than me. I want all my investment back, wired to my bank by the end of the day. Understood?"

"Your funds, sir, are tied up. I can't just—"

"By four p.m., EST, and not a second later." Click.

So, Bruce Hendricks robbed from Genevieve, a rich and faded widow, and from Benjamin, a sycophantic parvenu, and from James, a near comatose hanger-on better off in a nursing home, to pay his boyhood friend $250,000, half the senator's total investment, by the end of the day. It was so simple. He updated the Front Range Equities company Excel spreadsheet to show a 210 percent profit to all clients that left no trace of his transgressions. He would tell Richard that half was the best he could do in the time given.

That night, on second thought, he called the senator to attempt a delay of further payment, but the senator wasn't available. That's because Rodriguez had taxied into the heavens over Washington, DC, and was on his way to Denver to personally collect the rest of his investment.

At the same time that Rodriguez landed, Hendricks could not believe what he was hearing from Jake.

"I'm all done. Me, my staff, my boss."

"Jake! What in Christ's name are you telling me?"

"I'm all done. You have to call the main office number from now on. Good luck with that," he said with a sneer.

Shock as if from a bolt of lightning shook Hendricks to his core.

"I'm sorry, Bruce."

"Sorry!"

"For me too. I had as much riding on this as you." The phone clicked.

HENDRICKS WATCHED THE BEGINNING of the end on CNN. Like a rat in a rathole, he hid in his private emergency office on the other side of Denver. A year ago, he'd set up this office, thinking it prudent. He didn't expect to use it. It was a triple-size cubicle with a twin bed and wardrobe, sink, shower, toilet, fridge, and freezer, wired for computers and assorted electronics. He was told by a friend, a hacker, that he would not be traced at this location. An hour ago, Hendricks raided a bodega and a Chinese supermarket. That was after he'd raided a bakery and two candy stores. He was set for two weeks. He'd taken a taxi, and only his daughter knew where he was.

Hendricks rolled up his sleeves and put on shorts, a jar of peanut M&M's beside him, as he watched the free fall of his investments on two separate monitors. That got him sick. He tried puking in the sink, but after a dribble of oily looking phlegm, he went back to his monitors and a large Snickers. He rechecked his messages—"Where the fuck are you hiding, Bruce?"—and set to work. He took every remaining cent out of Richard's fund as well as every cent out of all his other clients' funds and transferred the money into his main personal account. He added all protected profits to this fund, profits from his company, his clients, his bank, and everywhere else he could think of. He wired a cash note of $2,230,000 to a bank in the Cayman Islands. He spent the rest of his evening reapportioning all his stocks into safer categories, with some going into long-term futures. It was clear the housing market had toppled. For his own individual FRE fund, he had $410,000 he could call his own.

But they couldn't take his land. It had been inherited and paid for. Land was always the safest investment. Yet Hendricks had one huge problem. Water. The way things were heading, all too clear to Hendricks, whose lifelong business was realty and banking, if he didn't get the water needed for his acres, they would plummet in value, that damned casino-resort would rise to the west, and his development plans would be relegated to the back burner. But if water was diverted for his Front Range developments, Hendricks could and would rise again. *Absurd*, Hendricks thought, *but true*. Water. He opened a large bag of Fritos.

"LOOK, RICHARD, I CAN'T meet you. I've lost everything. You at least got back half your investment. I have nothing."

"Ask me if I give a shit." The senator had given up trying to find him. "You get me my other half, or else."

"Or else what?"

"Not one drop of water."

"Now look here, old friend, we, and I mean you and me, if we don't get that water, you can kiss your other half goodbye."

Silence.

"Think about it, Richard. For Chrissake, think. Lehman is shut down. I've got zero. All my other clients have zero." *Which is true*, Hendricks thought. "We will get out from under only if that Front Range land increases in value, and that happens when we are assured more water for development."

Silence.

"Richard, we are not talking mere houses here; we are talking schools, hospital, assisted living. This is *primar.*"

"If you get your goddamned water. Yeah, yeah, yeah. Well, I'm going to think long and hard about that, Bruce. Meanwhile, you be where the fuck I can reach you. Understand?"

"Yes, Richard."

Hendricks heard the phone click and wiped sweat from his brows and forehead. He felt drops of sweat coursing from his armpits. He needed to shower—he smelled his decadence—but the shower would have to wait. He wanted to finish pigging out. Then he had an important phone call to make to the Caymans and a taxi trip to his backup bank.

CHAPTER FORTY-FIVE

Awol looked at his sunglasses and cringed as he put them on. They reminded him of Moonwalker, his former AT nemesis. *Hope I don't meet him in hell,* Awol thought as he squinted while looking at the enlarged map board screwed to the campground posts. The sun hit the board at an angle and reflected light back into his eyes. He was to meet the FBI undercover operative in less than an hour at site sixteen, and he didn't feel like hunting for it. At least the agent was driving to him. The field office had requested they meet as hikers near a trail, and Awol dug out his map and suggested a campground. He decided high-tech had its uses. He pulled out his digital camera and took a picture of the map board. Under the shade of a pine, he enlarged the photo and moved the cursor, finding the campsite. He reduced the size of the picture and absorbed the layout. He oriented himself and moved smartly, Blazer beside him. To reconnoiter was in his army DNA, and Awol kept scanning right and left at other campsites and tents, some of them big for families. He noted trailers, mostly the pop-up kind, and stopped to watch a larger trailer unhook and pull out.

He reached campsite sixteen and stared at an empty spot of tramped grass and gravel. It had rained hard during the night, and he noted fresh tire marks. He walked around to other sites, found a baseball cap lying on the ground and hung it off a branch of a tree, and twenty minutes later, as he drew back to site sixteen, he watched a hiker about fifty yards away round the path by midsized pines. He didn't look like a hiker the way his sticks flashed new in the sunlight. As he drew near, his pack tilted off his right shoulder, something a serious hiker wouldn't put up with. *It's a woman.* She came closer, and her boots gave her away. Unblemished with a one-knot tie, like one would lace up a pair of dress shoes.

The middle-aged woman looked familiar, sported a Nike cap, lip-smiled at Blazer, and addressed Awol. "I've parked my rental up yonder," she pointed her pole, " 'bout a half mile."

Awol stood stock-still. "You're that bartender's friend."

"Yes, I'm Diana Santos." She held out her hand.

Awol stabbed both poles in the ground in front of him. "Thank you for the extra drink." He didn't shake her hand, and she withdrew it. "I assume you were checking me out back at the bar?"

"Yes, Awol. And this is Blazer?"

Awol hadn't moved. Blazer let the woman pat him. "How did you know?"

"You left him outside the bar. Listen—" She smiled and touched his arm. "I was under instructions to suss you out about the chatter, but you moved ahead to, you know, another subject, which is funny, because you asked me to go camping."

Her touch brought a chain reaction of thoughts to Awol. His ex-wife, Gloria, had touched him at the same spot the last time he saw her before she left him forever—"Good luck, Karl." And a few months ago, Linda, after her touch—"Karl, can't we be civil about it?"

"What's funny about that?" he said to Santos.

"I don't mean it the way it sounds, and I didn't want to leave you at the bar. But I'd been assigned a task that I would mess up and do you a disservice if I . . . you know. It went in the wrong direction."

"I don't understand what you mean."

She poked her poles in front of her, meeting his. "Let's say woman's intuition. Okay?"

"Ouch."

I didn't want to take advantage of you. How would you have felt if I dragged it on and revealed myself later?"

Awol stared at the ground between their poles and shook his head from side to side. The way she'd touched his arm seemed to Awol like a lid shutting on a box of memories and hope.

The rental was a Dodge Grand Caravan Stow 'n Go. Diana keyed the back hatch door open and suggested Awol retire his gear inside. "We can talk seated in the front," she said, and placed her pack and poles next to Awol's.

After a few more attempts at cordiality, Diana stopped talking. She knew her face told a different story. She'd rather use her poles to bash and bloody that prick Avery than hike. She looked in her mirrors and said nothing. Neither did Awol. Both watched Blazer lie down outside the car at a pine angled closer to Awol.

"Okay," Diana said. "What can you tell me?"

Awol took time rubbing his nose. "I don't want to be nasty, but . . ."

"What?"

"I've already told Sacco all that I know. I've got nothing new."

"And I don't want to be difficult. First, I called Sacco after reviewing your file, but I haven't met him. Second, this is standard procedure. And, I might add, in this case, in order, as you have not been briefed by anyone in person. Am I right?"

"Yeah."

"So . . ."

"Before I recount what little I know, you need to understand that I didn't want to get involved. Just wanted to pass it on and keep on hiking. I've been through this kind of thing before."

"I read all that and the commendations. I'm impressed."

"I will keep on trekking. Whatever I see or hear, I'll be glad to pass it on. Okay?"

"Back to square one. Tell me everything, and start at the beginning." Diana angled her head and peeked up. "Okay?"

"We could have done this back at that bar."

"I knew you would say that."

A half hour later, after repeats, which drove Awol nuts, he threw up his hands and excused himself to void. He stepped by Blazer, who opened an eye as Awol stepped behind brush and firs, out of sight from other campsites. If he'd had his pack and poles, he would have kept on going.

"I've told you all I can," Awol said upon his return.

"So you think it's a dam."

"Could be a tunnel. Again, I ask you, what's your opinion based on my story?"

"I try to avoid opinions until I have enough hard facts. Based on all you've told me, everything points to a dam here in Colorado. West of the Divide."

"Then we share the same opinion."

Diana nodded. She went to the rear of her car and threw up the hatch. She came back with a sealed container and removed a packet from inside.

"Call your dog."

Blazer trotted over and after one sniff of the packet gave a passive alert. The animal was as still as a statue.

"Good. Your dog was trained well. He remembers. Here's what I want you to do." She restored the packet to the container and sealed the cover. "This is heroin, bought on the street less than a hundred miles from here. Meet me tonight at Ajax Bar & Grill. Here's the address. Come in sometime between nine-thirty and ten p.m. with Blazer. Stay away from me, but at some point, I will walk over to pat your dog. He will give an alert. You will pull Blazer away, and I will walk out the door. As soon as I leave, pull out your phone and call this number. Sit away from the bar. That's all you have to do. Got it?"

―――――――――――

AND SO IT WAS. Within twenty minutes of Awol calling the number given to him, two police cars drove into the lot, and an official-looking civilian in a sweater and sports jacket was escorted inside by two cops. He showed his badge, pocketed it, and pulled out a photograph. He started with the bartender.

"Have you seen this woman?"

"You a narc?"

"Showed you the badge, didn't I?"

The blonde bartender put two hands on the bar, said nothing.

"Please answer the question."

"She was here and left twenty minutes ago." She looked over to a man sitting by his dog.

"Who's that with the dog?" He pointed to Awol, who sat at a nearby table with Blazer beside him.

"That guy with the dog? He with you? After she patted his dog, it stood up and sat in front of her. She left. He pulled out his cell phone, and now you're here."

The agent showed the picture to the six adults sitting on stools at the bar. "Do any of you know this woman?" They all said they hadn't seen her before tonight.

"Are any of you hikers?"

A guy and the woman next to him perked up. "We are," she said. "We're doing the CDT."

"Thru-hiking?"

Several others, including another woman, gathered around. "That's the plan," her partner said.

"And the rest of you?" the agent asked.

"Just doing sections," another said.

"What's wrong?" a woman asked.

"That woman hiker that was in here is dealing heroin. That's why the dog alerted. And that's why the dog and my friend over there are out checking sections of the CDT. We've had reports of several drug sales on this trail."

"Why did you ask me who the man with the dog was?" the bartender asked.

The agent ignored the question.

"We haven't seen either of them," another said.

The agent passed out his card to the bartender and gave cards to the other hikers. "If you hear of drugs being sold on the trail, please call it in."

CHAPTER FORTY-SIX

Awol took Diana's post-operation call that night and had to admit the plan looked promising. The word on drug enforcers would get out, and terrorists might not expect other motives.

"You're good around bars," Awol said. "How did you set me up back in—?"

"Another time, okay."

"As you wish. However, something is bothering me about tonight."

"Let me guess. We shouldn't be seen together because my picture is being shown as a dealer of heroin. And I connected with a hiker and his alert dog."

"Exactly. We're linked."

"I did that to get off this trail. I don't like it out here."

"Where are you now?"

"Back at the campground."

"We're all done here?"

"I wish it was that simple."

"What's the story, Diana?"

"My fucking boss says I . . ." She hadn't meant to holler.

"Says what?"

"I'm supposed to stay out here. That was the original plan."

"You disobeyed orders."

"Right now, I don't give a shit."

Awol had to smile. Things were working out for him after all. Somebody else had screwed up.

"Well, we can't be seen together. Right?"

"The agent who you saw come into the bar retrieved my rented vehicle. He took it back to the airport."

"Un-huh. We'll be hiking separately."

"I didn't pack my fucking tent!"

AWOL LOOKED AT HIS TENT, which was in place. He'd journaled his notes for the day before he'd cooked and eaten his dinner, a matter of boiling water for chicken with rice. It was delicious after he'd filled the Mountain House bag, stirred, and waited the suggested seven minutes before opening and stirring again and then waiting for another three or four. He closed down his tiny Esbit stove, which had sustained him on the AT, the PCT, and now here. *What was once good for the NATO troops is good enough for me,* he'd thought when purchasing it. It was worn but worked fine.

He wondered what Diana had eaten. Did she bring food? It felt like rain, so he pulled out his cell and called her.

"Look. I'm a few miles away according to my map. Why don't you come up here for a proper meal? If it rains, I'll share my tent."

"Thanks, but . . ."

"What?"

Silence.

"Now, don't get your hopes up about the tent." Awol paused. "Ah, Diana, that's a joke."

"How funny."

"Call it a weak attempt at humor."

"I'll be fine. I have my sleep pad and bag."

"Synthetic or down—as in goose down?"

"I know what you mean," she snapped. "Sorry. It's down."

Awol sighed. "Oops. Okay, I won't say it. Let's hope it doesn't rain."

"I've got pines nearby for cover."

"Did you pack a meal?"

"I don't want to talk about it. We'll go over next steps tomorrow."

NOT MY PROBLEM, Awol thought as he felt the first sprinkles and a temperature drop. But after he'd gone in his tent and rain pelted the rainfly on top, he couldn't sleep. He knew what he had to do, so why waste any more time?

He took down his tent last and, under his headlamp, looked around his campsite for the last time.

"C'mon, Blazer. Help me apply for sainthood."

Despite his hooded shell, rain and moisture had seeped through, and Awol was cold and wet upon reaching the campground an hour later. Under unrelenting rain, he looked at an empty site sixteen. *Where the hell is she?* He took out his cell and called, but it went to voicemail. He spat and left a message. *Shit.* Nearby pines, she'd said. He went to three nearby sites near pines and found nothing. He yelled out her name several times. Feeling stupid as the rain continued unabated, he went back to site sixteen and unpacked.

"C'mon in, Blazer." He wanted to rant but stifled himself, as the dog lay down in his tent and tried to lick Awol's face. Awol was sweaty and soaked to the bone. He shivered and downed the last of his water, telling himself he'd already changed into night clothes back at the other site, and he was damned if he'd do it again. He went to sleep.

"BROUGHT YOU SOME coffee. Awol?"

"What?" Awol turned over, his bag hood snorkeled about his head. He opened an eye and sat up looking at her while she crouched at the entrance of his tent.

"I got your message a few minutes ago. Sorry about that."

Awol hauled himself out of the bag and gimped out of the tent. He was dressed as he was last night, disheveled, with bloodshot eyes.

He put his hand up, halting her offer of coffee. "Could I trouble you for some water?" he asked, pointing to the plastic Nalgene hooked to her pocket. She handed it over, and he uncapped it, took a swallow, got wide-eyed and spat.

"Do you always put lime in your water? Where the hell were you last night?"

She stared at him.

"Tramped all around here, hollering your name, checking under trees." He picked up the mug of coffee, which she'd laid down, and took a sip.

"How's the coffee?"

"Just ducky. You haven't answered my question."

"Yes, I put lime in my water. It gives it that certain *je ne sais quois*."

Awol eyed her over another sip of the brew. "Diana!"

"Now hold it right there. Look, Awol, I didn't ask you to come out here. Okay? And right now, this is the last place I want to be. So—"

"So, scram! And thanks for the coffee."

She walked away.

"I deserve an answer about last night."

"I stayed at the campground office," she hollered in profile. "I was offered bedding and a cot, given a hearty meal of chili with homemade corn bread and a Diet Coke. I turned off my phone when I plugged it in over there to charge and didn't check it until a little while ago." She turned and faced him. "And I'm so goddammed sorry that I messed up your evening, Mr. Awol."

He looked at her. "Just why did you disobey FBI instructions?"

"To get back at my fucking boss." She realized she'd yelled again. She lifted her eyes to a gold-streaked sunrise slipping through the pines. "It's another story for another time."

CHAPTER FORTY-SEVEN

AWOL READ WITH FASCINATION and concern. He had no idea that water rights had always been a source of contention. He was at the library again, this time near Winter Park, about six miles from Diana. The campground manager had told Diana about a new hiker hostel off the south side of Berthoud Pass, near the CDT. Impressed with her credentials, which Diana had told him to keep private, the manager arranged for a friend to take her shopping and to the hostel. Awol didn't know the arrangements she'd made with the hostel, or with the FBI, for that matter, but she told the hostel that she would be meeting with hikers from time to time. Awol had to admit, the hostel was a perfect cover as word was out about her dealing drugs. Her picture had been shown to people, and two hikers had already eyed her suspiciously. Diana hoped hikers in particular would ask about her and make contact. She would feign ignorance about providing a fix but keep their hopes up. Meanwhile, her eyes and ears were open as she planned the next steps.

Awol studied water rights and water shortages from articles on the internet. "First in time, first in right." "Use it or lose it." "Beneficial use." Water scarcity was a problem everywhere—Georgia was trying to redraw its border with Tennessee to gain more water rights. California, Arizona, and Nevada battled to divert greater portions of the Colorado River to meet their needs. The problem and contentions were acute in Colorado. He read again about the growing needs of the Front Range. Although water had been diverted west to east to Denver and the Front Range for decades, more was requested. The biggest transfer of water continued via tunnels through the Continental Divide under Rocky Mountain National Park.

He studied a new article about Lake Mead, the snowmelt-fed Colorado River reservoir, a man-made reservoir that supplies 90 percent of Las Vegas's water. He knew about the problem, but the picture accompanying the article, which showed an abandoned skiff lying on a large swath of cracked mud, unsettled him. In the distance, you could see water. The lake was drying up—and this was from an article written over two years ago. Awol couldn't believe that the original high-water mark, shown in the picture, was one hundred feet up the bedrock wall. The report went on to say that if global warming continued along with the rapid population growth in nearby urban areas like Las Vegas, the lake could be dry by 2021. Awol reread another sentence, "The situation has stressed the rest of the Colorado River basin, which provides water to farmers and cities from Colorado to southern California."

Las Vegas was referred to as "the driest big city in America." He scanned one more article about glaciers. "Rapid melting is underway in all seven states that have significant glaciers. Some are on a fast glide toward extinction." *Can that be right?* It was getting hotter, too fast. Yet the melting of glaciers should be contributing to water. But if they were, and we were already having such significant problems with water availability . . . What would happen when the glaciers were gone?

———————

BEING BACK ON THE TRAIL felt good, and Blazer romped back and forth along the skimpy dirt path. He raced around picking up scents and bounded off where his nose directed him. Awol decided to keep on hiking throughout this magnificent national park. People from all over the country came to Colorado to hike in the Rocky Mountains, and he would use this "wait and see" opportunity to stay in shape and explore. He'd let Diana and her government people do the legwork. Awol would be available. He'd compromised; he stayed local and loyal for the benefit of the bureau but could hike the Rockies and see some of the great vistas of North America on his own. Today, he was taking a different ascent to Berthoud Pass. The Colorado mountains to his left and right never failed to awe

Awol. Compared to the Appalachians in the east—which had contoured, gentler slopes and peaks, covered with pines and oaks, along with some firs—the upper slopes here were acute and spired with buttes. Peaks were exposed granite and rock, serrated, ragged. Below these rugged peaks a preponderance of spruce and evergreens displayed themselves.

Later, Awol chose a well-marked trail and his mind wandered, hardly noticing vermillion-hued granite cut from box canyon walls. He'd come to understand and sympathized with ranchers and farmers and families that depended on water. If Awol had been an American Indian, he would have been brokenhearted by the signs around him. Tiny tinges of smoke came and went with the wind. His sense of smell didn't register them because he figured the fires were small, local. Yet mighty forest fires were getting close; he'd seen it on the news. He was in a drought that showed no sign of relief. He didn't dwell on the high-water marks he could see on the rivers and streams he crossed. He was ignorant about the depth and speed of the flow and assumed it was based on rain. Despite some recent rain, he noted obvious signs revealing the lack of precipitation. Patches of earth were not continuous dirt; the patches were cracked, and feet broke the earth like crumb cake. This was old, forgotten mud that had crusted. Branches and tiny limbs broke apart like pretzels. The sun pushed along its curve and beat down through depleted ozone on baked valley and lea, on dried-up pond and stream. The American Indian would understand that the earth was in pain. That the pain was growing worse. The Ute would be disconsolate and feel that pain internally. Awol admitted that he himself hadn't paid much attention.

Things were terribly wrong. He was reminded of something he had read years ago, could have been in a poem. *The center cannot hold.* He accepted that water rights and associated development issues would become more contentious and would bang head-on with government reclamation projects designed to manage water. He would mind his business about that and plow on. But he would not be wasteful with his water. He had his own issues to contend with and an arduous hiking trail to complete, and he had to pay constant attention lest he become lost. Awol was in one of those few stretches near the CDT that had a marked trail. He could tell it was a snowmobile trail because of the triangular blue blazes nailed to trees. He'd been tramping for over two miles, and it was a joy not having to keep checking his compass—he had a habit of pulling to the right—or to remember specifics on his maps and take bearings, gauge distances, confirm direction, and check off items from the maps. As he walked and thought, he was slow to realize that what appeared to be a root in front of him wasn't that at all. He was startled when it moved and coiled and rattled.

"Christ!" Blazer had come up and stood behind him, barking a fit. Awol backed up to the side and looked on a diamondback rattler the diameter of Linda's Chevy tailpipe. The snake remained coiled, and the rattle sang like a thousand flying bees. He and Blazer emerged back onto the trail, well ahead. Looking back, Awol heard and saw the rattler, coiled, dead center on the path.

That night, he decided not to return to the motel, and he and Blazer camped several miles from Berthoud Pass. While setting up, Awol saw a sun dog to the west. The half-rainbow slanting toward a clear sky was apt. The back of his mind wanted to announce that he was in command out here, in charge of his woodland affairs. He was shaken by the snake and realized how the expressions "he got rattled," "you rattled him," and the like came into usage. What bothered him was that he hadn't been observant. The reptile resembled a root, but he should have noted the uniform size along the entire length and seen a diamond on the snakeskin. He was depending too much on Blazer and had gotten sloppy. He noted this in his journal, and after he had described the day, Awol, ashamed, took a pole and inspected his campsite inch by inch. *Get a grip. Pay attention.*

CHAPTER FORTY-EIGHT

AWOL HAD TO STOP and stifle a laugh. There she was in an oversized, ripped, plaid-checked mackinaw and stocking cap with a pink pom-pom on top, fussin' with something that resembled a tent. *Jesus H. Christ.*

"Diana, how nice of you to invite me for dinner." He gave her a forced smile. "And where did you pick up that tent?"

Awol had arrived at Diana's request. They needed to share every bit of new and old information, and this was the best way. She didn't think anyone would find them, as she'd taken the time to bushwhack to a secluded spot two miles from the hostel and four miles away from the CDT.

"I'm partial to Chianti," she said. "However, I'll overlook that fact if you haven't packed a bottle." She smiled in profile as she finished setting up her tent.

"I've got freeze-dried spaghetti and meatballs. Okay with you?"

"Of course. Wasn't being snarky about the vino."

"Of course."

"Got this mongrel tent at the hostel. For the last three days, I've managed to add something here, cut off something there to make something else work."

Awol walked around it. "No rainfly?"

"Not yet. I can use my shell."

"That might work. Thank God for duct tape," he said as he poked a grommet-repaired hole by a stake.

She sat on a downed limb several feet away from him, and while he boiled water for the freeze-dried meal, she walked their campsite perimeter.

"Where did you serve?" Awol asked. "What bases?"

She admired his observation skills. "Basic and AIT at Fort Jackson, Fort Benning for OCS."

After the shared meal, he boiled more water for instant coffee.

"Ah, the coffee is good. Better than Chianti." She looked up at a darkening sky while holding the stainless steel cup from her thermos in both hands. She blew on the hot liquid and sipped the coffee again.

"Didn't know you were an army officer," Awol said.

"I'm not, and I wasn't. I was pregnant at Benning, though I didn't know it at the time."

"Oh." Awol looked at her. He poured her more coffee and handed the thermos cup to her.

"Thank you," she said.

They sat on the limb, long shorn of leaf, beside each other but about three feet apart.

"Aren't you having any?" she asked.

"I might. It keeps me awake and makes me urinate."

"I appreciate the food and coffee."

"I shouldn't ask, but—"

"I left Benning after I'd gotten an abortion."

Awol nodded. "That must have been rough."

"It was."

"Was he army? The father?"

"No. After basic, before AIT, my boyfriend came down to visit me. That's the only time it could have happened. He arranged the abortion back home in Jersey." She took a sip of coffee. "I thought about going back to a new OCS class. They told me I'd have to start over again, but I didn't go back. Finished up in the reserves."

"Did you marry him?"

"No. He paid for everything and disappeared in the air force."

She looked over to him as Awol stood. Temps were dropping. He put on his shell and attended to Blazer, who had been napping by Awol's tent the entire time. He packed up the dog's bowl, and Blazer, seeming to understand the day was ending, stretched and sat down next to Awol.

"Beautiful dog," she said.

Neither knew why they didn't get down to planning, to the business at hand. It was as if they had to spend a night in peace before they could mesh gears together. Awol journaled in his tent. Diana tucked into hers and did whatever it is women do.

WHEN THE RAIN CAME, it pelted straight down, waking Awol. He came out of his tent with his shell and met her as she draped her own shell over the top. They said nothing as he adjusted both shells. She'd already gotten inside again, but as he tramped back to his own tent he heard, "Thank you."

He tried to go to sleep, but the rain smacked the roof of the tent. He made room for Blazer, and the dog licked his face and twirled around three times before settling into the one available spot to cozy in for the night. The rain stopped, and he could hear her snores. He readjusted his pad, trying not to disturb Blazer. He was thankful he hadn't had coffee. Awol felt like he was in his own mystery novel and wondered what the next days would bring.

THE NEXT MORNING, the two tenters shared everything they knew, which wasn't considerable other than a dam was in the crosshairs.

"Shouldn't we bring in extra security for dams?" Awol said.

"I've discussed that with my people. 'Which dam?' they ask. I tell them that Granby has come up. Which leads to a discussion of all the dams in Colorado—and there are a ton. Not to mention lakes and reservoirs like Dillon, which could also be compromised."

"And tunnels."

"Right. I've sent warnings to beef up security at Granby and other large dams near the Divide in Colorado. Confidential bulletins have been sent."

After they discussed every option, tore each of them apart, reassembled and discussed them again, they had to accept the fact that they had no smoking gun. The challenge was to not only foil the act but to find the terrorists.

"It could be a suicide mission," Awol said. "What's the use of finding dead terrorists after a dam has blown, causing death and environmental chaos?"

"Yes. But if we show our hand, bring in police or federal, the perps will wait it out. They have control."

"Got to find them before anything happens," Awol said.

"Back to square one. We find them on our time. We surprise them and close it down."

Diana would hike back to the hostel and try to get more information. "I've made an arrangement to help there for free lodging."

"I'm going to follow river and stream near the east side of the lake, west of the CDT. I'll stay isolated."

"Be careful. If a chopper was sent for you, where would it land out here?"

"Right. And it would tip the thugs off."

Diana patted Blazer, who sat between them.

Awol looked at her profile. "So," he said.

"If I don't hear from you, I'll call you in the afternoon on your satellite. Every day, including today."

Awol nodded.

"We get something, we call the other ASAP."

Awol nodded again.

Diana could tell he was deep in thought. "What's on your mind, Awol?"

"You." He fluffed Blazer about the ears and smiled while looking at the dog.

"Let's get these bastards," she said. She put on her backpack. The tent tied underneath didn't seem to hinder her.

Awol stood and did the same.

"Yeah, okay. First things first," he said as they parted in opposite directions. Awol felt as if he were in a duel: march twenty paces, turn to face the other, and fire.

CHAPTER FORTY-NINE

AT THIS NADIR, all Rodriguez wanted was the rest of his investment back. If he could get his other $250,000, he could right himself. His wife had moved out—"until you get our goddamn money back"—and took the kids with her. He couldn't get a cent out of Hendricks and wanted to wring his neck. But the bookie business was up, and his shady contacts were all over him to place bets.

He wanted to go to a casino and do it right. Rodriguez didn't miss the irony. Gambling at a casino at the moment was counterproductive to the senator. He had to agree with his old classmate from E-4: the game now was to get water diverted. Fuck any casino-resort. Enhance those eight hundred acres with water and demand payment from Bruce. But with no end to the contaminated housing market in sight, it would take too long for the senator to recoup his losses. And no one expected the water board to consider any changes right now—except the tribe. He knew firsthand how that worked. They'd bribed Hendricks to no avail. Could the senator call the tribe and hint that he would accept a bribe, telling them he would block the diversion of more water? He was reminded of the old saying, "Grab him by the balls, and his heart and mind are sure to follow." But it was Hendricks, the bastard, who had him by the balls, not the tribe. Of course, if he did renege on Hendricks and go with the tribe, he would be in their clutches forever. And the tribe wouldn't pay the bribe until Rodriguez accomplished their request anyway. But Hendricks owed him and would pay if he could wait it out while Hendricks righted his ship. So how the fuck was he supposed to get money right now? Unless . . .

To the senator, it made sense: Arrange a bet for $250,000. All at once. Win and he had $500,000. Back solid again. He didn't think he would lose and, unlike the riffraff, the senator felt he knew when his luck would run out. At the last second, he bet $125,000 on baseball—and won! That tingling feeling for the senator was better than sex. A second later, he chastised himself for not betting the entire two-fifty. *Too late now. But be prudent*, he instructed himself. Before doing anything else, he would go to another meeting of Gamblers Anonymous.

———————

RODRIGUEZ COULDN'T CONCENTRATE. The GA meeting was holding him back. He felt time was being lost and feared he was losing an opportunity. He punched in his driver's cell number as he moved out of his back-row seat, "Scuse, scuse." Then, to his driver, "Pick me up."

This time, forgetting about senatorial paperwork piling up in his office, deciding he would not vote on tomorrow's agenda, canceling other appointments in his mind that he'd phone to his secretary tomorrow, the senator made a private call to his same bookie and placed another bet. "Double—no. I'm sorry, make it one hundred twenty-five thousand."

He won again. But the senator didn't get that same tingle. It was bullshit that he had chickened out again at the last second and changed the two fifty to one twenty-five. He blamed it on the incredible ease of the system, the fact that high-end big-sum bettors could do it this way, a mere phone call. He understood that as a senator, he was fodder for any type of scandal, and for the big-time high-end bookies, that was all the collateral they needed.

The senator didn't attend any more GA meetings. And for the next week, he let senate work pile up. He felt overwhelmed, stifled, and of course he knew why. Twice now, he'd cut himself short. He missed the action. His mind was set on winning a million. That million, the senator convinced himself, would make up the profits he'd lost to Hendricks and probably not see again, plus the 5 percent the prick skimmed for himself. He was almost there and would shut it down for good, get the wife and kids back. One last time, and again he got that tingle. Yes. One more time, and he could kiss the world goodbye if he had to. This was life on the edge, which a true gambler understood, and the senator was a superior gambler. The tingle reached critical mass. He placed another bet—all or nothing—"Five hundred," he said.

And lost.

Was the senator crushed? Yes and no. Would he jump off a roof? Certainly not. He was an experienced gambler. The good news was that he had enough to get by. He was below zero, but he wouldn't be outed. He had a good job. He didn't have to worry about broken legs. The senator was a positive gambler, and he had the rest of his life to gamble the loss back. In the meantime: *Where the fuck is that little prick?*

CHAPTER FIFTY

THE LATE AUGUST SKY dimmed. *Strange*, Awol thought. He didn't sense a storm brewing. Blazer stopped and sniffed the air north of west. Awol thought of smoke but couldn't smell any. The afternoon was a painted sun over a painted forest. Awol looked at oak leaves on trees, willing them to move. They hung still. He looked up to the highest limbs of oaks and pines. They were as motionless as on an artist's canvas. It was bone dry on the west side of the Divide, due west of Denver. Awol poled north, crackling the twigs beneath his boots.

Smoke teased Awol's nostrils. He looked up again and noted that more darkness had developed northwest. In Awol's mind he imagined a huge conflagration in the forests west of the Divide. He stopped and looked all around him. It was too quiet. The trees and understory watched him from every angle, thick and patient.

Awol took out his maps. He was ten miles from the south end of Lake Granby and thought of hitching to the notorious dam he'd been hearing and reading about. The smoke feathering his nostrils tried to tell him this wasn't a good idea. If he had to escape, he couldn't have been in a worse location. He was halfway to the lake and didn't want to backtrack. He'd already checked out of last night's motel in Fraser and was planning to get a new one in the Granby area. The question was whether he could make it to the lake before he hiked into flames. *My imagination is running wild. It's too soon to panic.* Yet he prayed a spark wouldn't fall near him. He'd learned from junior-high science about spontaneous combustion. Don't keep oily or gas-soaked rags piled together in a hot garage or attic, his teacher had said. Awol felt vulnerable and was glad he wasn't a smoker. He reminded himself not to heat up his stove for evening meals until these forest fires had burned themselves out. He wouldn't chance it and felt better from this one decision.

He moved deeper into the wilderness and camped that night, until the smell of smoke began to trouble his sleep. Within a dream—he told himself over and over it was a dream—the smell was real. He woke in sweat, with smoke-filled air lodged in his throat. The heat of the night was unlike anything Awol had experienced. It was worse than Desert Storm, but in the Middle East, he'd smelled tinges of oil. Here he smelled smoke and felt a heat that was beyond oppressive. Awol shoved open his tent flaps and saw Blazer, crouched to the west, eyes open, nose sniffing. Awol checked his watch—3:10 a.m.—and broke camp.

At 4:30 a.m., Awol accepted that he could go no farther without risk. He had to cover over five miles to the nearest egress; he wouldn't make it as the smoke had thickened, so he reversed. He backtracked all the way to the campsite and took out his maps again. He didn't want to backtrack the other six miles to the nearest jeep path he remembered from yesterday, which would take him too far away. He noted on the map a blue line—water, not a river perhaps, but for sure a stream—east-southeast, in the Arapaho National Recreation Area, where he was. He would bushwhack the mile to the stream and follow it east. He waited until after-dawn light fought a darkened sky and advanced.

It was rough going, but using his ax where needed, he made it to the stream less than an hour later. The stream should have been fifteen to twenty feet wide, according to the viewable water marks, but the drought narrowed the water channel to six or seven feet. The good news was that the sere conditions had converted the western side to floodplain, which made bushwhacking easier. Awol was taken off track but still on alert. Since signage along the Continental Divide Trail was poor and often confusing, bushwhacking away from it offered relief. He kept his bearings and relied on his map and, for the time being, didn't have to fuss to find the next CDT marker or waypoint.

The floodplain lasted less than a mile and narrowed into gumbo. Soon, both sides of the rock-choked shallow stream thickened into larger rocks that required balance and focus. Awol moved upslope into shrub

and thickets. He sat down on the flat but slanted portion of a protruding rock wondering if that was the tip of a buried "iceberg," a sedimen-
tary boulder. He looked at the further-darkening sky and was happy he'd
moved east. After break, he would cross the stream and hike the eastern
side, yet he knew that sparks, if it came to that, would jump this water
path in a heartbeat and cause new conflagrations. Blazer cocked his head
for a pat and looked refreshed after walking in the stream the entire time.
Awol rubbed his ears. "You feeling good, Blazer? Atta boy."

Awol hadn't had a decent breakfast other than a handful or two of
gorp. He took out a baggie of crackers and hard Vermont Cabot cheese
wrapped in tinfoil. After eating that, he spooned sludges of chunky peanut butter from the plastic jar. Blazer hopped up and barked at a brace
of grouse that had settled on a rock in the stream, but they flapped off
as Blazer approached. The dog waded into the stream and sniffed the
rock. Awol hadn't gotten enough sleep. He peeked at the sky and settled
back with his pack underneath his neck for a quick nap. Fifteen minutes
later, he woke and saw Blazer curled in front of him sleeping soundly. He
didn't want to disturb Blazer and shifted his eyes and head about him as
he always did after waking from a wilderness break. The force of habit
revealed nothing downwind. With practiced eye, he scanned upwind to
more of the same and settled on a spot that looked like the background
but in some way was peculiar. Then it moved.

Awol watched a camouflaged man emerge from a stand of scrub pine
and thickets and advance toward him. Awol wondered why he gave no
voice, gave no nod or wave. "Camo" came within twenty yards, stopped,
and unshouldered his bow. He wore a canvas haversack on the other
shoulder. Awol saw several arrows attached to the bow and realized it
was a high-end compound for the serious bowman. Awol waved and
stood. The man looked at him and eyed Blazer, who stood by Awol and,
strangely, didn't bark. One could scratch the silence.

"Smart looking bow," Awol said. He also noted what looked like
army field glasses hanging about his neck.

Camo moved forward another ten yards, saying nothing until he
stopped.

"I hunt."

"Deer?"

"What are you doing here?"

The bowman's tone was ominous.

Awol pointed to sky. "Was doing the CDT. Didn't like the looks of things."

"That's a Malinois with what?" He motioned with his bow to Blazer.

"A pinch of shepherd."

Camo nodded and looked at the sky. "That won't come here."

"No? What makes you think that?"

Camo looked at him, eyed the dog a second, and leaned on his bow. "Head downstream. There's a limb-strewn bridge 'bout a mile. Take that and go due east until you hit the access road."

Awol didn't like the tone but was in no mood to test Camo. At least he would be heading toward the CDT. He packed up.

"Thanks for the advice. Can I shake your hand?"

Camo looked straight at him. He was a living statue.

"Later," Awol said.

Awol looked back not five seconds later. Camo had disappeared.

CHAPTER FIFTY-ONE

HENDRICKS WAS IN A SNIT. Denver Water would postpone water diversion issues until the recent forest fire was handled. "For God's sake, Hendricks, this is the biggest forest fire we've seen in ten years," Anderson said.

The last time Hendricks felt like smashing his TV was after the Broncos lost in overtime. This time he watched the TV as helicopters dropped water into orange and yellow flames west of the Divide. Every time he watched the chopper approach the flames and release water, his stomach revolted. He heard the announcer say that the water came from Lake Dillon, one of the biggest sources from which Hendricks needed more water to be diverted from. He pushed the remote to off and contemplated about getting his fix. Hendricks needed to concentrate, and he convinced himself he could do it better while looking at plates of food. His spirits rose right away, and he went for his keys. *Pasta*, his brain said. *Pasta*.

THAT EVENING, HENDRICKS called Rodriguez's private cell. Both of them needed each other. Hendricks would support and campaign to get the senator reelected. The senator had reluctantly agreed to work with Hendricks to get out of their mutual mess.

"I'm warning you, Bruce. If I don't get my—"

"Please, *El Patrón*, let's not go there."

The senator bit his lip as he gripped his cell in a sweaty palm.

"Have you seen the big story down here?" Hendricks asked.

"Yeah, I've been following it."

"You gotta do something."

"Have you lost your mind? What shall I do, a Ute rain dance on the senate floor?"

"I've heard mention of an iceberg that could be floated down the Pacific."

"You're in Denver, for Chrissake. You have lost your mind."

Hendricks picked his words carefully. "What state will emerge as having the biggest water problem?"

Silence.

"I'll give you a big hint. It starts with a C."

"Okay, California."

"That's right. And we all know that our mighty Colorado River has to allot water to them. We can't keep doing that and have a future that you and I call home."

"The future being your particular Front Range development."

"And that's your future too. Right?"

"Continue . . ."

"Get an iceberg for California. Position it over there, and give the Colorado waterways some relief."

"There's not enough science behind it. It's premature."

"Richard—*El Patrón*—not for nothing are you a senator."

Silence.

"There's a lot riding on this for both of us. Do it right, and you can be a hero."

"Other senators will be suspicious of motive."

"*El Patrón*. Water is a problem everywhere. Position yourself as having Colorado's best interests in mind. Your constituents need relief. Help California with an iceberg and—"

"Hendricks! I get it. Okay? I get it. I'll get some wheels rolling."

"Godspeed."

The senator considered the fix he was in. If there was any way he could get his money back and thwart Hendricks, he'd relish that opportunity. With that in mind, he calculated ahead and considered possible linkages to . . . *One never knows.* He wanted to be involved in the chatter he'd been hearing about ecoterrorists. Time to call Avery.

———————————

HENDRICKS—WITH A nut-covered hot-fudge sundae with butter-pecan ice cream and whipped cream sitting a hand's reach from his laptop—Googled and skimmed all the science and articles he could find on icebergs as a water supply source. Each time he scrolled to something suitable, he copied and pasted the URL to Rodriguez, while shoveling ice cream into his mouth. His stomach hurt. Accepting that he had no choice, feeling like a damned woman, like those deceptive women who contrived with their bulimia to fool the public, but not Hendricks, into believing they were gods of discipline when it came to food and nutrition, Hendricks lurched to his bathroom. He dared not peek into the mirror as he loomed over the toilet bowl and stuck two fingers down his throat.

CHAPTER FIFTY-TWO

As AWOL HIKED AWAY from a troubling encounter with a puzzling dude, he felt his emotions shift. He had no idea why at this particular moment thoughts of Linda, Kenny, Gregory, even his ex, Gloria, tumbled inside him. He wanted to get a handle on the chatter, but other than a malaise of discontent and confusion, he couldn't put his finger on anything tangible. He started with what he knew. Water scarcity was an ever-growing problem. The frequent droughts increased forest fires, and in his mind, frequent forest fires contributed to more droughts. It was a vicious cycle.

His other encounters along the CDT had, in some way, been related to water. His lack of and need for it, strangers fistfighting over the availability of it, threats people had made about dams, the self-evident truth of global warming.

But added to this, he was rattled sick over his son's suicide. That had broken Awol's hard-earned sobriety and was one of the reasons he'd come out here in the first place—to become sober again. The thing of it was, the ironic if not downright cruel thing, was that he had reached out to Gregory a year ago. Awol shook his head from side to side as he almost wished he hadn't seen him. He had failed to connect with his troubled son. Awol still took it personally and held himself responsible. The fact that he'd tried and reached out to him held no muster. He'd failed. Gregory ended his life on Awol's watch.

Linda. He tried to see a way back from the separation. He wondered if she was seeing someone. His stomach tightened at the thought. He was trying to think how all these different things connected to his life and what his next steps should be when Blazer yipped and barked. Awol looked up to see Butane smiling at him. For Awol, this new jolt—

"Where is the rain when you need it?" Butane said.

"Huh? Yeah, right." Awol reached down to pat Blazer. He avoided looking at Butane, annoyed that he'd lost focus.

"Trying to escape the fire?" Butane asked.

"Yes." Awol looked up and squeezed his poles harder. "You see a guy in camo come through here?"

Butane smiled. "Why do you ask?"

Awol swung a pole at some weeds behind him. "Wasn't very friendly."

"I wouldn't worry about it."

Awol looked into Butane's eyes. "You know who I mean? Looked like he had army field glasses."

"He hunts all the time around here."

"Look, I'm getting off the trail for a while." Awol pointed his pole in the direction Camo had given him. "Your friend says go down to the bridge and cross over."

"That's right. The path after that is the best way out. Might get a hitch from a camper."

As Awol paid attention to Butane's eyes, he had the feeling both of them were being watched. Awol shifted his eyes, but without persistent focus, he wouldn't be able to find Camo. He kept Blazer beside him and noted that the dog sniffed in the direction past Butane's right shoulder. He wondered if Camo was there.

"Adios," Awol said.

Awol poled off and told himself not to look back. But he couldn't help it. He glanced in the direction where he figured Camo was but saw Butane, who gave him a wave. Awol raised a pole as a final acknowledgement and moved on. His eyes and ears were on high alert. Something wasn't right. All the way to the bridge Awol asked himself why he should continue the Continental Divide Trail under these conditions and uncertainties. He wanted to be a triple crowner, but . . . He revisited his previous thoughts of Linda, Gregory, and Kenny. Kenny was a success story, and Awol tried to drink up the proud father satisfaction he'd had on finishing the PCT. But it troubled Awol that he didn't have access to Kenny other than on the phone, and it always felt to Awol that he was interrupting his son. Awol missed Kenny, and at the bridge he sat down a moment while Blazer romped in the water. He wished Kenny were here to help him understand his thoughts.

Awol, unsure of his next steps, lingered on the bridge. What should he do? How long would he have to wait for his government to shut down this terrorist thing? He was on the cusp of something he couldn't put his finger on. He wasn't sure how to get back to the lake from here. He didn't want to renege on the verbal commitment he'd made to Diana, but he didn't want to go back and run into Camo either. He was about to take out the radio to try and reach Diana, but he wasn't sure what he'd say. It bothered Awol that he had such thoughts after agreeing to stay in Colorado. He might hitchhike to Wyoming after being released by the bureau and do this section later, after the forest fire burned out. Hikers referred to this as a flip-flop. Acceptable in the thru-hiking community, so long as you completed every foot of the hike some way within the season. But this stint for the government could take a while. It would still be considered a thru-hike, except for a minority of "purists," if you completed it in one year. Awol thought about that. At odds with himself, he toyed with the idea of going home to check on the business, give Linda the dog, and thereby see her, but what if it was more of the same: a detached relationship that had gone south? Only to come back to the CDT having lost thru-hike time.

When Awol got to the access road, he hadn't made up his mind about what he should do and was in as much of a muddle as he could remember. The one thing he knew for sure was that he'd been waylaid by a new appreciation for water as a natural resource. Now there was chatter about wrecking a water system. He'd seen a future problem of humanity, at least right here, and people were squandering this resource if they had to use it to fight forest fires. And fires were amplified by droughts. Awol slowed and stopped and watched Blazer, who accepted the stop as an invitation to romp for new scents. Awol watched his animal and thought about how the life of a loved and cared-for animal was better than the life of any king or queen. He wondered if he should put himself into the hands of God. This opened up a new canvas that served to weigh him down as he considered it. He piqued at the idea that if things got too rough, he would consider becoming more Christian, more faithful.

Would he go to church regularly, as he did in his youth? At one time in his teens, Awol had been president of Luther League at his church. He shuddered at the recollections. He'd taken huge chances but was lucky. His first sex was with a girl from Luther League, but he'd told himself at the time that because she was from a different church, it wouldn't matter. Here in the wild, he wrestled with reaching out to God and becoming a churchgoer again. But he knew he wouldn't. He'd right himself and disappear from the church, like he'd always done.

He headed down the access road with Blazer. The feeling that kept nagging him was that he was in a cauldron of imminent trouble. Every step he took, every thought he had was somehow hooked to this section of Colorado. He'd hiked into a center of controversy he didn't understand. *Why not Wyoming? Just get up there and hike on.* He'd think about that. *Yes. First things first. Get back in town, freshen up, think it through.*

Blazer turned as Awol heard a rumble. A vehicle was coming up behind them. He watched it stop.

"Would you like a lift?" Butane asked.

AWOL OPENED THE PASSENGER door of the pickup after closing the tailgate where Blazer sat in the bed. Awol noticed Butane clear a binder from the front seat and stuff it under the driver seat. Awol smelled gunpowder once inside the vehicle and, looking to his left, spotted the end of an army pistol belt sticking out from under Butane's seat. Butane read his thoughts.

"My gun is on the floor beneath me."

"Expecting trouble?"

Butane looked over to him. "Always a possibility."

Awol said nothing as the vehicle swerved to avoid rocks strewn on the path. He felt safe enough—they were army veterans, after all—but being in the vehicle with this acquaintance contributed to Awol's overall mental malaise. He reached back for his water bottle and noticed Butane stiffen.

"What was your mission in Desert Storm, Awol?"

Awol took a gulp and capped the bottle before answering. "Main mission was to rout the insurgents and secure an airfield."

"That all?"

"Now, what the hell do you think, Butane?" Awol had no idea where that came from, but he couldn't stop himself. "That's the easy answer. You served in Afghanistan; what the hell did you do?"

Butane smiled. "I'm beginning to like you."

"Doesn't answer the question."

"I blew up things."

"That all?" Awol mimicked, then looked out the passenger window.

Butane stopped the vehicle and cut the engine. He said nothing.

Awol took his time turning from the window and took a big chance as he faced Butane. "This country has gone to fucking hell, Butane."

Butane said nothing and stared at him.

"I've been told I have PTSD," Awol said. "Bullshit! We need to kick some ass, right here. The government doesn't have a fucking clue."

"About what?"

Awol gave him a startled look from head to foot and back up. In a composed and restrained effort, he said, "For starters, we kicked your people off lands that were yours. Now we are contaminating and destroying these same lands. Our country, your country, doesn't give a shit about its natural resources."

Butane said nothing as he restarted the vehicle and inched forward.

"Ah, what the fuck do you care," Awol added. He looked out the window again.

After a mile, Awol uncapped his water bottle, took a swig, and offered it to Butane.

Butane shook his head. Awol took one more swallow but held the bottle in both hands as he stared straight ahead.

"So, what should we do about the mess?" Butane asked.

"Whatever we do, we have to draw on all our training and experience and keep it under wraps."

"But what can one do?"

"Look, I'm not from around here. You gotta decide that. From what I'm seeing, this area is in a world of hurt."

"So, we have a forest fire. That our fault?"

"You miss the point. Back in Separ, New Mexico, I witnessed a fistfight between two ranchers over water rights. One rancher had more cattle but less water, so he diverted some belonging to the other rancher. They wanted to kill each other. You tell me if that isn't compounded in local, state, and federal government."

Awol heard Butane take a deep breath and knew he'd hit home. He capped the water bottle, returned it to his pack, and turned his palms up as he faced Butane. "I can't tell you if the forest fire is our fault or not. But global warming?"

Butane said nothing as he glanced at Awol.

"Now that *is* our fault," Awol said.

Butane rubbed his nose, and Awol, knowing that Butane's tell could signify contention, wondered if he was overdoing it.

"All I'm saying is, collectively, we've fucked up. Our government doesn't give a shit about global warming. Those dicks are in it for the short term. Greed. Money. Am I right?" He looked into Butane's eyes.

Butane smiled as the access road came to a trailhead. "Where you staying?"

"Going into town for a while. I can hitch from here."

"No. I'll bring you to a place. It's cheap. Just a few miles away," Butane said.

Awol bristled. He couldn't tell Butane that he'd been staying up in Grand Lake. If Butane was part of the chatter, that would make him suspicious.

Twenty minutes later, Butane dropped off Awol at Harley's Cabins. It had a rundown, rustic look and had seen better days.

"This place has internet. Good breakfast in the restaurant."

"It'll do. Thanks, Butane."

"Listen." Butane opened the glove compartment in front of Awol. Tangles of wire, wire cutters, and electrical tape were stuffed inside. As soon as Butane pulled out a sticky notepad, he slammed the cover shut. "Give me your cell number so we can stay in touch."

Awol wrote down the number. "What about yours?" he asked.

"I'll be in touch." Butane held out his hand, and Awol shook it.

THAT AFTERNOON, AT REARDON'S cabin, Butane told Reardon everything.

"I don't trust him," Reardon said.

"This guy's an army vet like me. I can tell he's legit."

"How?"

"Okay, it's hard to explain. We've both served in or near the Middle East. Both of us have been in combat."

"So?"

"He told me he has PTSD. That's what they told him."

"Who's they?"

"He didn't say. I can tell, by the way he talks, his animation, his look. He's legit."

"Don't buy it. He's pulling you in."

"Well, he says you aren't friendly. Guess he's right on that." Butane smiled.

"What do we want with him?"

"If you don't know, I sure as hell don't know. I'm saying, he shouldn't be in your crosshairs."

Reardon looked over to the one cabin window and sipped from his mug of coffee.

"We don't need to do anything with him," Butane said. "I'm saying don't worry about him."

"Why did you get his cell number and tell him you'd be in touch?"

Butane threw up his shoulders. "Don't know, other than I figured he could be a resource for us."

"You've made him suspicious. I don't trust him."

"Wait. I said little. I let him talk. How does that make him suspicious?"

"You picked him up. You hauled him to the trailhead. You took him to lodging of your own choosing and got his cell. And right now, the dude is wondering why you did all that."

"Because we're fellow army. The guy's got baggage. Can't I help a fellow vet out?"

Reardon set his mug down and stared at dwindling light from his small window.

"Listen," Reardon said. "Here's an opportunity to find out if he could be a resource. We'll give him the name of a dam. See what he does."

Butane turned and looked at him.

"You have the army thing going with this guy. You've met him a few times. Let's role-play for when you go back to see him tonight. What you will say. Ready? I'm Awol."

CHAPTER FIFTY-FOUR

Awol SAT IN AN ADIRONDACK chair atop a hill facing a setting sun smothered by smoke. As he watched, he entertained the notion that the forest-fire smoke was interfering not only with nature and the doings of planet earth but also disrespecting the greater system—the solar system. Awol watched and concluded that the sun was finding it difficult to call it a day. Like a child who is too tired and cranky and fights going to bed, the sun didn't want to give up that fight. Then it disappeared beneath a blackened, smoke-filled horizon.

The temperature had dropped, and Awol put on his fleece, which he'd taken from his pack back in his cabin. As he zipped it and adjusted his long-sleeve shirt underneath at the wrists, he heard a familiar voice say, "May I join you?"

Awol admonished himself. He hadn't heard him coming. He admired the moccasins, perfect for stealth, and looked up at Butane.

"Of course." Awol pointed to another chair. There was a third, also vacant. "Help yourself." Butane, in an army baseball cap that he hadn't worn in his truck, took the more distant chair after placing a paper coffee cup on the near arm of the empty chair between them.

"You get that coffee inside?"

"I did," Butane said. "I know the owner here."

"And bring him business from time to time," Awol said.

Butane took a sip and nodded.

They both watched a darkening sky, and Awol turned his fleece collar up.

"What do you do out here?" Awol asked.

"Mostly, I try to forget."

Awol crossed his legs. And waited.

"The drought and fires are screwing up the reservoirs," Butane said.

"I'm sure they take water from them to fight fires," Awol said.

"Yeah. Water restrictions on the Front Range are in effect."

"The Front Range. I've heard of that. What kinds of restrictions?"

"People can't use underground sprinkler systems. Hand watering every other day. That type of thing."

"Well, serves 'em right. Don't you agree?"

"Yeah." Butane took another sip. "Something else should be done."

"Your friend in camo?"

"All I know is, it's going to get worse," Butane said.

"What is? The water problem?"

Butane tapped his fingers on the arms of his chair. Treble clef was active, bass clef silent.

"You hear anything about a dam?" Butane asked.

"As a matter of fact, . . . Why do you ask?"

"It's scuttlebutt, but I think it's true."

Awol pulled his zipper up. The smell of smoke was prevalent.

"I met a veterinarian back in Cuba, New Mexico. Blazer here got some type of beetle bug in his ear. Had to flush it out. Anyway, he says a dam's gonna blow."

"I should contact the authorities about that," Butane said.

"Should I go with you?"

"What do you know?"

Awol looked at him and crossed his other leg. "Look, I don't know squat. I want to get through here as quick as I can. But I believe he said the Grandy Dam?"

"The Grandy? Close enough. But I think you heard Granby."

Awol shrugged. "Guess that's what it was. What have you heard?"

Butane finished his coffee and stood. "The same as you," Butane said.

"Gotta be it."

Butane sat back down.

"The officials, state, local, and federal, have gotten us into this water mess," Awol said.

"Awol." Butane looked over to him. "Why am I not convinced you give a shit?"

"Hey, Butane. For Chrissake, I almost died out there. Twice! Because of no friggin' water. Okay? Where are all the trail angels with water for the hikers? Huh? My guess is, Butane, that they can't even manage water for themselves. Okay? Butane?"

Butane said nothing as he rubbed his chin.

"Right," he said later. "You had some water problems. You get north of here up in Montana, you'll forget all about us down here."

"From what I've read, Butane, from all that I've heard from people like yourself, water problems are everywhere. It might be more serious down here, I'll give you that, but don't delude yourself, Butane. The science points to a planetwide problem."

"Awol. Here's my question: Why in hell do we, I mean some people, want to blow up a dam if we have a serious water problem? I'm sorry, but that doesn't compute."

"Here's my answer: It's the rich and power-hungry greedy people who don't have the problem and don't give a shit. Not me or you."

"And?"

"We need to send a message. Gotta take a stand. Where it hurts."

"You think it could be a dam?" Butane asked.

Awol took some seconds to consider this. "Truthfully, Butane, I have no idea. What about a tunnel?"

"Tunnel?"

"Well, yeah. Don't tunnels transfer water under the Divide?"

"Awol. It ain't gonna be a tunnel."

"Do you know for sure?"

"It's gonna be a dam."

"The Granby?"

Butane looked at him and said nothing. Awol didn't say another word as Butane stood for the second time.

Butane reached down to shake his hand.

"You want a ride to town tomorrow or farther on to another trailhead?"

Awol thought about it.

"Sleep on it. I'll be here tomorrow morning at eight."

"Mighty good of you, Butane."

"We're army."

"OKAY, I'M ON TO SOMETHING." Awol had Diana on his cell.

"I'm all ears."

"The Granby Dam."

"How sure are you?"

"I can't remember the conversation word for word, but this is the second time Granby Dam has come up."

Awol went through other details about Butane and his apparent connection to the camo man.

"Okay. Don't do a thing until I get back to you. Let me shake up the powers that be."

"How long do I have to wait here?"

"I don't know. I'm hoping to get you out of there and on your way. Butane and his friend sound ominous. I believe they are vetting you."

"I thought you had implied our government would take it from here."

"Let me get back to you. Hang tight."

CHAPTER FIFTY-FIVE

THAT NIGHT AWOL COULDN'T SLEEP. No matter what, he twisted and turned so much that Blazer got annoyed and yipped at the door of the cabin room. Awol let him out and stood outside. He felt it right away under a three-quarter moon—if he left here, something bad would happen. The scary dude in camo who'd questioned him, the follow-up by Butane, the fact that Butane put him here and came back tonight. As clear as ABC to Awol: they were in cahoots. Butane was playing dumb. Okay, he would be ready for Butane tomorrow and wouldn't leave until he was certain that these were the guys for the FBI to take down.

"I VETTED HIM," Butane said. "Like I told you, he's legit."

"Okay. Don't pick him up in the morning. You've convinced me. Now walk away from him."

Butane nodded. "All right, boss. If that's what you want. But that's a helluva way to treat a fellow Middle East army vet, don't you think?"

"You were Afghanistan."

"Close enough."

"Can't take a chance with what's coming up. You, if anyone, should know that. Walk."

Butane nodded.

AWOL, FEELING RESOLVED, let Blazer back into the room, and they both went to sleep. Next morning, Awol was ready at 7:30 a.m. and waited outside the owner's office with a cup of coffee.

At 8:30 a.m., Awol knew Butane wouldn't be coming. A fellow army vet would either be on time or would have called his cell or the cabin's office by now. At 9 a.m., Awol walked out to the road, and rather than attempt a hitch beyond the town and back to the CDT from there to avoid the fires, he decided to take the one-lane blacktop and hoof it himself direct to town. At 10:30 a.m., Butane pulled over to the shoulder in his Ram pickup and braked. He pointed to the back for Blazer and opened the passenger door for Awol.

"So," Awol said as everyone got settled.

"Owe you an apology," Butane said.

"What happened?"

"Sorry. I'll drop you in town."

They rode in silence, and Awol was determined to say nothing and wait him out. Butane rubbed a knee and checked his rear mirrors.

"What again did you do in Desert Storm?" Butane asked.

"We secured airfields."

"Shoot anyone?"

"Blow anything up?"

Butane regripped the wheel and looked over to Awol. Awol stared right at him.

"Awol. I'll give you some advice, this one time."

Awol nodded.

"Get as far as you can away from here. The sooner the better."

"Is the guy in camo a terrorist?"

Butane started to say something, pulled to a stop at the side of the road, and smacked the wheel. He looked straight ahead, turned to Awol and stared. Awol knew. He was about to stake his life on it.

Butane put the vehicle in gear and dropped him off near the post office without another word.

Awol held up his hand before closing the passenger door. He stared at Butane's profile.

"You got my cell number, right?"

Butane said nothing and drove away.

IT WAS BEFORE MIDNIGHT, and Butane was deep in thought about how much he hated his assignment. He wasn't a man who relished diversion and deceit. His interest was to complete the main mission, once and for all. But Reardon had saved his life and confided in him. And, he had to admit, the one diversion planned here, away from transmountain tunnels, would keep eyes off the Moffat. In the time the feds would take to secure other area dams, the Moffat would be history. He would plant the evidence for the diversion and get out.

He arrived at Granby Dam at 2 a.m. Right away, Butane sensed more than he bargained for. He moved the Ram behind a stand of trees, then hoisted on his backpack and waited. He'd yanked up weeds and left other clues, like an empty Snickers candy wrapper and deliberate tracks from his moccasins. He looked again with Reardon's night vision binoculars and saw what looked like security patrolling the top of the dam. Why hadn't he seen that before?

He watched the dam and timed the guard as he walked from the near end to the other. The guard moved slowly as he looked from side to side—sixteen minutes. Butane figured he had a good twenty minutes before the person would notice or hear anything as he approached the far end and started to come back. Butane waited three minutes after he had turned and started to walk away from him. He hiked in behind a storage shed and then past a maintenance shed. He grabbed onto the iron ladder bolted to cement that he'd seen last time and climbed it to about ten feet. He unrolled explosive wire, snipped a section off, and tangled it about the ladder in plain sight. Reardon had said he wanted it on the news and covered in the papers. Butane had told him how he would make that happen.

Butane heard something while reaching into a pack pocket for the detonator but attributed it to a wild animal and nerves. But seconds later, he shined his small flashlight toward the sound and, for a brief second, noted small, wild eyes looking at him. It looked like a bobcat and jumped away. He'd be glad to finish by leaving the detonator wired in an obvious area, low to the dam. He smiled at how the recovery team would high five each other after they told everyone they compromised the charge. Who knows, maybe they'd make a mess of it and blow the dam up anyway. Butane knew how to stage it to make it look like the real thing. "Why not make it the real thing?" Butane had asked. Reardon told him that was reaching for too much. "The Moffat is symbolic and is at the core of the message. The dam is ancillary but a perfect diversion. The people will panic, breathe a sigh of relief. And *boom*!" He remembered how they had hollered "boom" together.

Butane finished the diversion and retraced his steps. He'd accomplished his objective before security turned at the far end. Butane got back to the pickup and climbed in. When he could see the sentry at the near end of the dam, to leave a last clue, he refired the ignition and sped away. Before Butane neared his CDT turnoff to re-hide the Ram, and long before he'd made it back to Reardon's cabin, he'd stopped the truck at the side of the road and pulled out his phone to call the Channel 4 tip hotline.

CHAPTER FIFTY-SIX

THE NEXT AFTERNOON, Awol set the wash cycle for his laundry at the town's laundromat and restocked his food at a nearby grocery, where he saw the headline in the local newspaper. He returned to the laundromat and while waiting for his laundry read about the compromised sabotage effort on Granby Dam. *Butane?*

He called Diana, who was at the hostel. She said she'd have to call him back after a conference call with her field office.

"It doesn't make sense," Awol said when she called back. "Granby Dam was either aborted somehow or you got to it in time. The US Army corporal goes by the name Butane."

"You said he's also known as Angry Bear," Diana said.

"On the reservation, I guess. Not off it."

"We'd already sent our undercover to Granby. The dam was patrolled."

"Didn't do a very good job patrolling."

"Because of your feedback, we asked yesterday for police presence. They had set it up for noon."

"That hurts. Late by hours."

"Stay there and try to monitor this Butane."

Awol knew that was coming as he watched Blazer chase a cat who'd wandered into his area. The cat dove under the steps to the laundromat as Blazer yipped.

"Why?"

"I'm betting Granby was a diversion. My people say the terrorist made it too obvious. Blatant footprints, a fresh candy wrapper, for Chrissake."

"Look, he told me to get away from here ASAP. If it's a diversion, we give our hand if I stay here in town and Butane, or someone he knows, sees me."

"Understood."

Awol waited as he heard muffled words to someone.

"Something else has come up. Let me get back to you," she said.

That next evening, Awol watched CNN from a small motel room, miles away from his former cabin. A full story about a failed terrorist act had made national news. As background to the story, a news clip of Joan Denley, reporting live on CBS Denver, mentioned how she had received an anonymous tip from a caller telling her he'd seen a person wearing a pack wandering around Granby Dam. She'd notified the local police and went herself to the scene, which is where she was reporting from. Awol wondered about Butane. What did he know? And where was Camo?

CHAPTER FIFTY-SEVEN

REARDON WARMED AS HE listened to the news with Butane from his emergency radio. He was lucky that at 2,300 feet, with the added wire antenna, he could gain reception from Denver's main stations. His little emergency radio was the type used by the Red Cross and could be hand-cranked to recharge the batteries. Reardon used the radio to listen to an hour of news once a day. It was Butane who had added the antenna for him. Within twelve hours of the incident, Joan Denley gave her scoop, and it was carried on all the main stations, including CNN and other national networks. "Stay alert, be careful," government officials said.

Reardon was ready. D-Day was two days away. He'd been an apt student of Butane and had learned his lessons thoroughly. Butane had explained and showed him how to set a charge. Reardon could do it blindfolded but insisted Butane instruct him one more time.

"I've got duplicates of everything you have, including tools and tape," Reardon said.

"But why? I'll handle the charges."

"Because we are in this together. What happens if you're caught?"

"That won't happen."

"You didn't answer my question."

"Okay. You got me."

Reardon took both Butane's hands and looked him in the eyes. "We *are* in this together, right?"

"Absolutely."

"I've got your mission pictures on my cell and a copy of the map you drew. Watch me and make sure I do everything right, as your backup, to carry out *our* mission." Reardon squeezed Butane's hands. "I'm your student."

Butane watched, and Reardon, like before, was more than up to the task. Butane felt good that, one way or another, the mission would be accomplished.

Reardon felt more than good. "Ya see, Butane, diversion was one thing. I didn't need to get involved with that. But this," he nodded at the detonator, wires, tools, "this is the mission, and now I can back you up if . . ." He looked into Butane's eyes. "God forbid."

ANY REMORSE FROM REARDON about Butane and the way he'd used him was nonexistent. He'd told Butane not to trust Awol, and it turned out Reardon was right. Why else had new security already been stationed in the area? And the news revealed that the local police had been called. Butane was quiet about Awol. But they both knew. Reardon left it alone. Butane was becoming an albatross around his throat.

CHAPTER FIFTY-EIGHT

"**K**ENNY, WHAT DO YOU KNOW about explosives?"

"Dad?"

"Yeah. Listen, can you put your scientific mind on a project for me?"

"What are you up to, Dad?"

"We don't have much time. A dam is going to blow. Put some things together for me and email me the attachments. I'll get to a computer this afternoon."

"What kinds of things?"

"You know, where would charges be placed? How do you negate the blow if a timer is used? How does a layperson foil the operation? That sort of thing."

Silence.

Awol was at a trailhead. He had a headache and knew he was yakking foolishly. But he had to initiate something. He'd remembered to call the motel at Grand Lake, telling them he wouldn't be back in case Butane or his friend traced him.

"Let me call Sacco," Kenny said.

"No. Out of the question. Do that and he'll telegraph what I know to these thugs. American Indians are involved. They are uncanny and will pick up the vibes, compromising—"

"Isn't that what you want, Dad? To compromise the operation?"

"Yes and no. Must be done on our terms or they will wait us out and blow a dam a month from now, or six months, on their timetable."

"I want you to get off the trail, Dad. Promise me. You need to get off right now so we can talk through this more."

"Kenny, listen to me. I need *you* to get me this information"—Awol stabbed his finger in the air—"and I need it now. If you ignore this request and I try to get the info, I'll raise suspicion. The FBI, Homeland Security, will both stir up the hornet's nest here in Colorado, and that could move up the terrorist's date. You're in California, and as a grad student in chemical engineering, you can get it for me without hassle."

"Dad! You are loco. Get off the trail. Do I have to come out there?"

"Son, I'm going to tell you one last time. I'm not leaving the CDT until I see this through. I'll be at a computer and printer this afternoon. I need that information. *Comprendes?*"

Awol shut down the phone. His son was sane—he was not, and he knew it. This was how it always was. If pressed, Awol would reveal his next steps, which surprised him as well as anyone else. He wanted to leave this part of the CDT, take a bus up to Wyoming. Yet as soon as he spoke with Kenny, he knew what he would say. Awol wasn't looking for recognition, so what *was* he looking for? He blotted it out of his mind. He took fifty-fifty odds that Kenny would send the info. If he didn't, Awol would get what he could himself from a library computer and take his chances.

That afternoon, after collapsing his poles and attaching them to his pack, Awol got a hitch to Fraser and walked into the Fraser Valley library. He signed in for one of three computers, got a password, and booted up. There was an email from Kenny without an attachment. *Dad, I'm working on it, but you worry me. Be careful.* Awol was comforted. He made sure his cell was on and retreated to the reference section. He picked up two encyclopedias, and seeing nothing to help him, he decided he could get away with Googling detonators, explosives, charges, TNT. He read all he could, and nearing the end, his eyes sore, his cell emitted the tone for an incoming email: Kenny. This time there were eleven attachments. He got change, as the library charged to print, and without anyone looking over his shoulder, he printed out all the attachments as the printer ran out of paper.

IN TOWN, AWOL BOUGHT hook-up wire, a wire stripper, extra duct tape, and needle-nose pliers with built-in wire cutter. That evening, back at his campsite several miles from Diana's hostel, using an oak stump for a table, he was Travis Bickle in *Taxi Driver* as he played around with the wire and perfected—at least in his mind—a bypass unit which could be used to compromise a set charge. From what he'd learned from Kenny's attachments, he would have to have a surgeon's unshaking hand when applying the bypass, and he was uncertain about how to find the correct connecting points. Added to this confusion, there was a particular sequence to connecting and disconnecting that had to be followed in attaching the bypass. But he had something, and with further study, he had a chance to abort their mission. He would give the feds clues and the best chance for follow-up and arrest. Awol shushed the notion that the bureau and Homeland might pursue him. Kenny would back him up. Awol made the mental note to "call it in" as soon as he was ready to foil the act.

But two nagging questions persisted. Which dam? And when?

Awol looked at the wrinkled and sweat-moistened papers, highlighted in yellow and underlined in ink, with arrows pointing to notes in the margins. It had been a long evening under his headlamp, and Awol wondered if he'd overlooked the forest for the trees. He remembered how President Carter, during the hostage crisis, doggedly studied maps and detailed information—and later, the attempted Middle East rescue was a disaster. Awol looked at what he'd done and picked up the bypass with its wire-stripped ends. He couldn't yank wires on a detonator—that guaranteed an explosion. The person setting up the blow could also booby-trap the unit and leave it to unsuspecting hands. From what he'd learned, an amateur who knew nothing of explosives would have to enact a bypass.

He learned he was to meet Diana tomorrow afternoon. He shook his head, wondering if he could make things better and save those in the flood zone. People would drown; homesteads would be lost in towns along the Continental Divide. He was so enervated that he could hardly maneuver himself into his sleeping bag.

CHAPTER FIFTY-NINE

DIANA AND AWOL had gone over every detail—except for his study of demolition and the bypass, which he held private. He felt foolish, well aware that a little knowledge is a dangerous thing, and didn't want her to overrule. It was late afternoon, but the sky looked clearer than usual. *At least there won't be rain,* Awol thought, *but it'll be a cold night.* Awol scanned about him, and Diana read his thoughts. "You want to tent over there?" she pointed. "I'll tent here?"

Awol bit his lip and complied. As he set up, he eyed her. She was attractive, even with her back to him, which spoke volumes. His loins charged. Tonight would be his last chance.

"Give me a freeze-dried. I'll cook," she said.

"Would stroganoff be suitable, being it's our last night together?"

"Oh, indeed."

"Won't you be surprised when I open my secret stash of instant sangria packets."

She looked at him and smiled.

At least she smiled, Awol thought. And he had sangria.

Their dinner that evening in front of a hidden sunset, which flamed up from distant forest, was quiet and uneventful, except for one exchange.

"You want me, don't you?" she said out of the silence.

Awol shuffled his feet and thought while he chewed. They sat side by side on rocks a bit closer than the last time.

He looked at her. "Yes. I do."

She looked to the pine grove in front of them and crossed her arms. Awol couldn't figure out if she was deep in thought or getting cold. He took up his fleece, which lay beside him, and sat closer to her. She said nothing as he put the fleece over her shoulders. He looked skyward and sensed the moon behind them.

"I would like to make you happy," he said as he patted her back, letting his hand linger there.

"Awol."

"Yes."

"I'm sorry."

"Sorry for what?"

"I can make *you* happy. Don't worry about me."

Awol took his time. He put his arm farther around her and gave her shoulder a squeeze.

"Diana, what I want you to understand is that you will make me happy when I make you happy. I don't want it one-sided."

"Let me think about it, Awol."

Blazer cared nothing about their struggle with words and had already gone to sleep. Awol disappeared into the bush with his tiny toiletry kit. He cleansed himself using Mountain Suds, voided for the last time, and went back to his camp spot. And there she was. Her hair was down, shoulder length. He smelled deodorant as he drew nearer. Her smile was slight, but her eyes told volumes.

As he took her in his arms, she closed her eyes, and he realized she was naked beneath his fleece. She planted a kiss on his cheek. "I've been rude. I'm not unappreciative. Let me make it up to you."

"You already have," Awol said. "Keep in mind I'll be happy if—"

"Shhh." She kissed him on the lips as he steered her to his tent. He remembered Blazer rolling over to his other side.

"Juice me—it's been a while. Then do me," were her words as he maneuvered on top.

CHAPTER SIXTY

THE NEXT MORNING, Diana and Awol were cordial but not relaxed as they realized their tough assignment ahead.

"The down and dirty. I got ten minutes," Avery barked.

"You did ask me to call."

"The down and dirty, I said. You got ten minutes."

Fifteen minutes later, she stared at her phone.

"The bastard hung up," she said to Awol. "As soon as I said, 'It could be a tunnel,' the bastard hung up on me."

FORTY MINUTES LATER, Awol got a hitch back to the trailhead. As soon as he watched the driver disappear around a bend, Awol turned around and headed south, right back where he'd hiked from. He could tell from the smoke that forest fires blazed, but he wouldn't be going that far back. He was determined to get to the bottom of things and had argued about it with Diana.

"Diana, I know you are having a bad day, but don't boss me."

"Okay! Go off half-cocked and keep screwing up."

He had looked at her. "Can't we—Last night was terrific, by the way."

She'd stared at him and rolled her eyes. "Jesus Christ, Awol. Go away," she said as she flicked up a hand and double-tied her boot. So he had. Back to hunt for Camo.

This ignored Butane's advice as well. Awol didn't care. He had to do something. "Right, Blazer?" The dog yipped, and Awol, content that somebody was in his corner, snapped up an oxeye daisy and sniffed. For an instant, it muted the smell of smoke.

When he got to the spot where Butane had picked him up, Awol took a compass heading. He knew if he bushwhacked east-northeast from here, he would intersect the CDT about a mile past a stream. He looked at his map through the plastic baggie and thumbed a spot. But Awol wasn't planning to do that. He wanted to search the area where he'd met camo man. Awol's hiking skills, his memory, his sense of déjà vu, told him straight east was a dead-on target to that place. He reran the conversation he'd had with Diana.

"Why the fuck didn't you call me about Butane? You knew he was coming to pick you up."

"There's this strange guy, camouflaged, compound bow, who appears to live off the grid. I need to find him."

"Goddammit, Awol. Answer me."

"I wasn't sure, Diana."

"Wasn't sure? You told me what he had in his glove box."

"That was the next morning. I couldn't call you then."

"You could have detained him. Did he threaten you?"

Awol put up his hand. "Look. If I fucked it up, and it looks like I did, he didn't give me a thing other than what I told you. He's army, a fellow combat vet."

"I'm army too!"

Awol stood with arms akimbo in front of her. "Shit!"

"Avery should have come out here to work with you. You don't work well with women."

"Now, what's that supposed to mean?"

"You had the demo guy. You let him go."

"I'll make it up to you. I'm gonna find camo man."

"And if you do?"

"I'll call you?"

"What if he's not the guy?"

"I'll call in any case."

"But you'll be isolated. Avery refuses to give me a backup plan. Said I'm toast if I mess with orders again like I did coming out here. It's screwed up. You can't kill Camo unless it's self-defense, which gives us nothing. Butane can do the act we're trying to prevent."

"Do you always see a problem with a new opportunity?"

"I can't back you up out here. If Camo is some recluse with an attitude, you could be the one killed."

"That'll take care of the working-with-women problem."

THREE HOURS LATER, Blazer picked up the scent of human. Awol could tell this because whenever Blazer traced a human scent, the dog became rigid and took longer to sniff. It could be the scent of a different person than camo man, perhaps Butane, but when Blazer sniffed nearby tracks that were of common sole and not moccasin, which Awol had noticed Butane wore, his confidence grew.

Two hours of careful and quiet tracking brought Awol and Blazer to a small patch of gravel near a clearing. Awol looked down at a line of palm-sized rocks forming an arrow. Below the tip, under another rock, was a handwritten piece of cardboard in a Ziploc that said CDT. The arrow puzzled Awol. He'd come off the CDT a few days ago to avoid fire, and his memory and maps told him the true course was north of this arrow. He rechecked his map and took a compass bearing. The proper direction was twenty degrees east of north, and this arrow pointed southeast. True, it would reach the CDT eventually, but this arrow was placed wrong. Awol now performed a service any hiker would appreciate and do for another. He corrected the mistake by redirecting the arrow and adjusting all the rocks and the bagged sign. Hikers looked out for each other, and Awol was glad to help. As a habit, Awol also kicked aside any wobbly or pointed stones that were in the hiker footpath.

After a drink for he and Blazer and after gorp for himself, Awol followed Blazer in the direction of the corrected arrow along a barely discernable path. No wonder he was surprised by camo man the other day. He slowed his pace and paid attention as he followed what looked like a less-used trail, not even a footpath.

THAT AFTERNOON, after Reardon had taken his practice shots, he went to check his patch that showed direction by the rocks he carefully placed. Before he got to it, he sensed something different in the air. Attuned to the woods, Reardon wasn't sure if new or different birds alighted in the trees near him or if the smell of fire smoke had new tinges of animal, but he knew something was different. He studied the change in his redirect. In the seven years he'd checked his patch, only twice did a repositioning of his rock-arrow occur. Once, three years ago, a ranger left his card and a note saying that he'd gotten himself off track but corrected the arrow according to his compass. Of course, Reardon had put the rock arrow back the way it was. Nothing happened. Another time, the rocks were all jumbled and animal tracks covered everything. But this here was different. Reardon concluded it was Awol. Who else could it be? He was in the area several days ago and, according to Butane, was a serious hiker, army trained. Reardon thought about changing the arrow back but knew that would be an instant giveaway. Reardon stiffened as he nocked an arrow to bow string and thought of the possibility Awol could be watching him now.

THAT EVENING IN HIS CABIN, with fishline tucked around his perimeter at ankle level, Reardon thought it through. He didn't think Butane was involved, but he'd done something to alert Awol. For that alone, he could no longer trust Butane. And if Awol was tracking Reardon, that meant Butane had seen Awol again after he'd told Butane to walk away from him. If Butane had disobeyed him, Reardon had a reason to off him. If Butane was caught after the mission, he could implicate Reardon. Reardon decided to eliminate Butane before the mission. And Awol would be child's play for Reardon.

CHAPTER SIXTY-ONE

THAT AFTERNOON AWOL camped in thick brush near a granite cliff, which eliminated any approach from the west. He assumed that Camo had prepared the rock arrow—incorrectly for what purpose?—which meant he traveled this area. Awol understood that he had to keep Camo alive. He could be working with others besides Butane. What about this WINJA thing? Camo knew when, where, and probably how. Awol had to admit it: Diana had a right to be upset by the way he let Butane off the hook. The thing that surprised Awol was that he didn't feel more compunction about it. He didn't because any delay with Butane would tip off camo man. Camo was the initiator, Awol was sure. He couldn't pin that title on Butane. So why couldn't he articulate this to Diana in their verbal fray? He'd have to let that one hang.

Awol was forced to think about the here and now. He figured Butane would do the dirty work for Camo. And Camo thought they were in the clear. Awol shivered at the possibility of Camo doing it himself. Impossible. Butane's the explosives expert. Could he have beaten the info out of Butane? Should he . . . could . . . ? He wanted to slap himself. *Focus.*

Things had evolved to where any action might give better odds than doing nothing. Awol had to do something—but what? He looked at Blazer, remembering how his animal helped save the day on the PCT. Awol couldn't think of a scheme and tried to focus on what Butane had told him of the Ute way. He studied for signs. Nothing. He tried making connections to his senses. How did trace skunk smells moving into his nostrils connect to the cloud-covered moon? He felt a breeze and saw agitation of limbs and heard creaks, but try as he might, nothing presented itself as a course of action. As evening closed in, he drifted into sleep. Awol dreamed of bobcats and was sick with fear and confusion, jerking himself awake.

Awol went out to void after patting his buck knife, which he always kept on him, always within reach. Unable to sleep, he stepped into his Crocs and walked to the cliff, leaving Blazer at the campsite. Within two minutes, he heard Blazer howl louder than a Baskerville hound. The howls got louder as Awol rushed to his camp.

A fury of tails and paws swished outside the tent. The bobcat had Blazer by the neck and was trying to make a kill while Blazer, with the fury of a cornered wild animal, tried to force him off. The cat was joined by another smaller bobcat as Awol grabbed one of his poles. He couldn't swing, for he might hit Blazer, but he warded the second one away from the frenzy. The first cat dragged Blazer, and Awol chanced a swing, the pole hitting the male tom on the head. The cat released his bite, but the other cat charged Blazer. Awol stabbed the female with his pole, and she ran off. As the bigger cat readied for another try, Awol sliced it with his knife. Awol made the kill through the cat's neck, hustled back to the cliff, and dumped him over so other cats wouldn't trace the smell to the tent. Awol remembered blood oozing above the eye of the she-cat who'd run away.

"Oh, boy. Look what happened to you."

Blazer continued to yelp like a pissed-off infant. Awol used his bandana to wipe blood off Blazer's belly and was thankful that the dog suffered no bite there. The claw wounds from the cat were superficial. The bite in Blazer's neck was another story. He could feel Blazer's neck throb as blood coursed. Again, the animal was lucky. Blazer could breathe, but the bite had ripped open skin on a fold in his neck. He carried Blazer into the tent and washed the wounds. He stemmed blood flow by tying his bandana around the upper belly and shoulder. He prayed the dog would recover properly. The incessant yips intensified in volume and frequency as Awol patched and taped the neck with gauze from his first aid kit.

For the next half hour, Awol held Blazer. The dog quivered, and Awol thought for a minute that he might die in his arms. More blood seeped around the bandana. Blazer needed to rest on his left side, but as

Awol positioned him, Blazer fought it. Awol talked to him and was able to turn the dog on his side.

"That's it, boy. That's it."

The animal whimpered, yelped, whimpered.

"I'm with you, Blazer. Trust me, boy."

Whether out of last hope or deciding to obey, Blazer rested on his side and began to stabilize. Awol hoped he had done right and felt relief as Blazer's whimpers became less frequent and more muted.

Now the worst fear obsessed Awol: The commotion had revealed his whereabouts. Wild animals and humans knew where he was. While the moon rose, Awol listened, waited.

A short while later, while watering Blazer, Awol rethought all his options. His situation with Camo was bleak at best. The quasi–mountain man had lived in these woods for years. Awol was no match, but drawing on a lifetime of survival skills and gut instinct, he had to find some advantage. He crept back to the cliff and looked down. Even under the full moon, he could couldn't see but sensed the dead bobcat at the bottom. Again, he considered every possible option, and a preposterous one presented itself.

With a heavy heart, Awol whispered into Blazer's ear, "I will be back, boy. Trust me, Blazer. I'll come back." He rubbed the animal's ears. He couldn't get a response from Blazer, whose dead-looking eyes stared beyond Awol. Awol tried again to get a response, but Blazer stayed silent except for a tiny grunt deep and low from his clawed gut.

Awol packed what he needed and left Blazer water and food. Awol turned the dog's head again and held up his water pan so he could drink. Blazer yipped and growled between laps.

"Okay, Blazer. I hear you, boy."

Awol zipped up the tent but left room by the flap for Blazer to get out, though he didn't expect Blazer to emerge any time soon. Awol crouched and plastered himself with what dirt and slime he could find and, his senses keen under a full moon, commenced an odyssey to get camo man and save as many lives as possible.

Awol was disgusted with the idea of using Blazer for deception, but it was the chance to elude Camo and gain the upper hand. If Awol was willing to sacrifice himself, he tried to convince himself that Blazer would too. Blazer was torn up, but the animal would recover if left alone. Awol locked that thought down without thinking further. Two hours later, Awol was at the bottom of the cliff while Blazer remained at the top, nursing wounds, sleeping, doing whatever animals do to survive. Awol strew items from his pack along the jagged rocks: his CDT baseball cap, pack strapping he'd cut off with his knife, which he placed near a chasm, where from the top of the cliff, it would look like the pack had disappeared. He crushed a water bottle, watching the water wash down a boulder, and left it. He took out his knife again and cut pieces of his hair, taking chunks as close to his scalp as possible and placed these on and around the rocks, so they would be seen. He needed blood. After gut-draining and smearing blood from the dead bobcat on a few rocks, Awol could have smiled. The savage tom had nearly killed Blazer before Awol slit its throat and threw it off the cliff, but now the cat would give Awol time to relaunch. And the other wounded she-cat would also leave blood.

He couldn't capture Camo if he wasn't one hundred percent certain he was the villain. If Camo was working with Butane, by the time anyone got here to help, the blow could be set. He fretted about not contacting Diana but convinced himself she would interfere with action. Awol was so taken with his plan that he planted his feet and looked at his hands to confirm he was of sound mind and body. What stunned him was that of all things possible, his next best move involved going *to* the bobcat. Awol needed to send a strong message to Camo, spook him, take him off his game. *Yes.* He'd seen a similar idea in a movie somewhere. It was a strong move, but first Camo would have to come to him.

Awol fought the emotion of giving up Blazer. He'd learned in the army that the accomplishment of the mission took priority. The next priority was the welfare of his men, and he put Blazer in that category. The thought of poor Blazer made Awol sick, but Awol would stick to his training and his decision. *Blazer, forgive me.*

CHAPTER SIXTY-TWO

AWOL LAY HIDDEN, supine, almost like Blazer. But Awol was at the bottom of the cliff, under scrub and windblown debris. It was a way fate had given him to show penance to his animal. He lay there with a view straight up to the top of the cliff but angled away, out of arrow range. He could see from peepholes amid leaves, but from the overhang far above, he was out of sight. He waited and napped because he was sure Blazer would warn him.

Several hours later, he heard yips and barks that he recognized immediately. He waited another hour after the yelps had subsided. Complete silence. Awol prayed Blazer was alive. Awol kept his senses keen but couldn't hear or smell or see anything unusual in the predawn darkness. The full moon was straight above him, and Awol worried that Camo would hunt down to him. He was startled by rustling, which he hoped was caused by field mice. Awol dared not move, remembering that Camo's field glasses looked like army night vision, maybe Butane's.

Awol concentrated on his surroundings. Moonlight poked through a stunted pine, a pine that looked forgotten. He wondered how roots dug in to force the trunk to rise straight up at an acute angle from the rocky surface. A childhood friend, a Mennonite from Lancaster, Pennsylvania, said all trees and flora grew heavenward to reach for God, claiming a tree wouldn't develop sideways. Awol counted three birds that soared across the moon. *How in the fuck did I end up here?* He concluded he owed himself to humanity. To make up for a twisted past and a horrific mistake.

He looked around by shifting his eyes and accepted he was as helpless a soul as he felt.

More yips and barks. Predawn, the beginnings of light. Awol saw him. The person had a bow and arrow in one hand and held what looked like field glasses in the other. Camo. He was looking down to the bottom of the cliff. Awol sensed Camo making corrective adjustments to his field glasses with his fingers. He could sense the binoculars moving in ghost-like fashion above him, but Camo would not see Awol who remained silent as a log. Awol knew what Camo would do next. He watched him let the binoculars hang from his neck. Camo drew up the bow, and without hearing any twang, Awol heard a *pffft* and saw an arrow stick out of scrub not ten feet in front of him. If his head had been the opposite way, Awol could have reached behind him and touched the arrow's feathers. Awol didn't move and continued his watch after the man disappeared. Awol imagined hearing scuffles, and he heard renewed yips and now howls from Blazer.

Awol's blood turned cold. Camo stood at the top of the overhang and held a yelping, clawing, howling Blazer out over it. Awol wanted to scream as Camo looked ready to drop him. The poor animal was beside himself and shrieked an octave higher than he'd ever done before. Awol had to close his eyes and fight off tears. He gulped phlegm and willed his heart to slow, but Awol did not move, and upon reopening his eyes, Camo and the dog were gone. Awol would have heard the noise if Blazer was dropped, but he was frightened that Blazer was quiet. *If only this could be a dream.*

Awol did not move for another hour or more, until light brightened around him. He stayed right where he was and kept shifting his eyes. He listened and waited. He hadn't heard any human sounds, but it bothered him that his dog was silent. *Unless* . . . Awol abolished the thought. *If true, Camo will pay dearly.* He heard something fall and crash through debris and scrub near him. *Blazer? Blazer, you poor boy.* Awol felt a black rage build and surge through him unlike any other. Linda would never understand the loss of Blazer. He'd promised her and he'd promised Blazer. He could not do anything for Blazer, who was in all likelihood dead. Killed, or thrown over and killed. But Awol did not move. He heard no animal sounds. What's more, he did not sense Blazer.

An aroma of wildflowers brought on a gloomy thought of the cemetery where his son Gregory was buried. He said a prayer. Ninety minutes later, by Awol's inner clock, he rolled himself over. He flattened himself like a lizard and slithered to shadows. He low-crawled toward the bottom of the near-vertical cliff, brushed off, and sat up. After sensing nothing, he crawled to the spot where he could see something had been dropped.

He toed something hard amid the scrub and reached down to feel a moss-covered rock, which he felt certain was dropped from the top to try and flush him out. Awol squinted and moved to his left a few more yards. He felt the arrow by his leg, amid brambles, and yanked it up. He felt the three-pointed, triangular tip, the arrowhead that hooks. Camo for sure.

Awol thought back to his original plan now that Camo had come to him. If he could hunt and kill him, this game would be over in a matter of hours. Alas, it could not be. Camo was too valuable. Awol discarded all options except one. He crept to the dead bobcat and slipped out his knife.

CHAPTER SIXTY-THREE

"**T**HAT'S THE WAY IT IS, Diana. I want you back here."

Diana was at the hostel talking to Avery. "What's changed?"

"We're pursuing other angles, which I can't get into right now. You were upset about going in; now I'm taking you out."

"Just because—"

"Save it."

Avery closed down his cell. He didn't understand it either, but Senator Rodriguez had a part in future events. He'd told Avery that he would be his personal point man on the chatter and intimated that, at the right moment, Rodriguez would lift him to director of Denver's field office. That wouldn't be hard, as everyone in Washington knew the current director was useless and had shown signs of ever-worsening age-related memory loss. Rodriguez would get the wheels in motion, he'd said, and corral his cronies to push him out and promote Avery.

REARDON COULD NOT BE 100 percent certain that Awol was dead without going down to check himself. If the blood and what looked like scalp tufts he'd seen with his binoculars was a ruse, it was an good one, and this man deserved close attention. Reardon had done all he could to flush him out. He wouldn't have dropped the dog. Reardon loved animals and had nothing against Awol's dog. And why make it certain to Awol that his dog was dead? Not knowing would make him come back for his animal if he cared, and the way he'd patched up his dog showed that he cared. But if Awol came back, that presented a problem; the dog would warn Awol as well as Reardon, and the two could be forced into a Mexican standoff. Awol wouldn't walk into a trap, and with advance warning, Awol would reason Reardon would be waiting for him. So Reardon came up with another idea.

FINISHED, REARDON WAS exhausted. If he didn't get a few hours of sleep, it would be costly. One thing he accepted: Awol was no backwoods amateur. Reardon crept back to Awol's tent and listened. Convincing himself that no one was nearby to ambush him, Reardon laid a perimeter of narrow-gauge fishing line by snagging it around roots and scrub. He'd be able to hear anyone approaching Awol's tent, which Reardon commandeered to wait for him. Satisfied, Reardon stayed dressed and had his bow ready, arrow slotted to string, beside him. Inside of two seconds, Reardon could let the arrow fly. Sleep came at once. Reardon had conditioned himself to fall asleep any time, any place.

THAT EVENING, at the last instant, Awol sensed trip wire. He knew Camo expected him to come back, at least for the dog. He dared not wear his headlamp, and the moon wasn't enough to see by. But he sensed it. He jumped into Camo's mind and asked where he would place trip wire. He took no chance and went prone. He low-crawled like an alligator for twenty yards before he made out what felt like fishing line strung at ankle level around a juniper. The fact that Blazer hadn't barked bothered Awol. But if he was recovering, Blazer could be sleeping soundly. He listened, eyes closed, not to rounded snores but to a person breathing. And now he heard truncated breaths. Someone was asleep inside his tent. Awol slipped out his knife and cut the thread-thin line. He felt both ends sag. Camo was here, right where Awol wanted him to be.

Working with stealth around Camo's truncated breathing, Awol did his work. Ten minutes later, he'd back-crawled the twenty-plus yards before kneeling. Awol had raw hatred for this man who had killed his dog, but he couldn't ruin the advantage he'd soon gain. He'd love to hogtie and threaten him, but at best, Camo would lie to him, and by the time Awol realized the information was wrong, a dam or tunnel would blow. It was out of the question to try to take him as a hostage. That would waste more time and tip off an accomplice, like Butane, to accelerate the time and do the deed. He had to deliver a message and take Camo off his game, watch his next move and make him blunder. In time, he'd do in Camo.

REARDON ROLLED OVER to prone, eyes closed, ears alert. His inner clock told him it was between 3 and 4 a.m. He didn't want to risk morning light but instructed himself to grab a little more surface sleep. After a minute, he rolled back supine, eyes squinted shut. He smelled animal. Good, another human had not invaded this animal's territory. He reasoned he could take more sleep; he was alone with some other animal.

Dawn came soon enough. He hadn't realized how exhausted he'd been. Reardon opened his eyes and saw two wild eyes staring right at him. "Whoa!" In a second his arrow took flight, splitting and pinning a head to the flap of his tent. A short stick fell toward him, and Reardon rolled and mounted another arrow. The bobcat head, pierced with an arrow through a nostril, continued to stare at him.

Jesus!

For the first time he could remember, Reardon felt sick as he examined the severed head. His heart thumped like a jackrabbit's as he pulled the flap and peeked behind it. He widened the flap and shifted his eyes. He concluded no one was outside, but he wondered if Awol—*Who the fuck else would it be?*—was hidden. Reardon couldn't understand how this all happened and was jittery and confused. Finally, realizing that he could have as easily been killed, he grabbed his bow and unzipped the screen. He pushed out of the tent, expecting to see Awol. But there was no one. He fingered the cut fishing line and walked around but didn't want to appear concerned if he was being observed. Reardon did his best to look unconcerned. He sat down after regaining his arrow and heaving the bobcat head like a shotput off the cliff and prepared breakfast. He banged Awol's stove on a rock while setting up and made other noises trying to look confident. But he continued to feel tremors. To his horror, this man, Awol, had mounted a bobcat head on a stick, slit the tent screen, and positioned the head so that the arrow secured it right to the flap. And Reardon hadn't heard a thing. Reardon understood his knowledge was too valuable for Awol to kill him, but he was not calm, and his hands trembled.

Awol saw it all. He was fifty feet in the air hidden behind the trunk of an aspen, angled sixty yards away from the front of his tent. He had his binoculars trained on Camo and felt, for the moment, in command. *Definitely off his game*, Awol thought. What would Camo do now? And when would he blunder?

CHAPTER SIXTY-FOUR

From his perch in the aspen, Awol had seen what looked like a footpath to the northwest. As Camo left the campsite, he was surprised to see him avoid the path but move parallel to it. Awol worked his way back down and looked back to the granite cliff and tent site where he'd left poor Blazer to die. *I fucked it up. Oh, how I miss you, Blazer.*

He went right to the tent. No sign of Blazer. Awol sickened as he looked to the cliff. If Camo was to pay, if Camo was to be shut down, he had to get a move on. No time to pack a tent. He picked up a light backpack and looked inside. Beacon, GPS, satellite phone, food—all gone. *Bastard!* And where were the nippers and electrical tape he'd bought? *He leaves me the ice ax?* Under a fold hidden in the top, and under what served as a daypack, he'd flattened the bypass and stuck it there next to his emergency water bottle. He fingered both of them with a sigh and, realizing he couldn't take time to disassemble his tent, removed a daypack from his main pack, grabbing a few things to stick into the smaller one, and armed into that. It was about the same size as what Camo shouldered.

Awol rechecked his blood-streaked map and headed northwest like Camo had, following vestiges of a path. He thought it through. Although Awol hadn't worn a holster during their first meeting, Camo expected that Awol was armed. Camo had to wonder why Awol didn't kill him or take him hostage. Camo figured Awol was a fed, which meant he had backup and was in contact with other feds. But if Camo figured all this, why wouldn't Camo ambush him now? Wasn't he suspicious of wire cutters and electrical tape? Awol expected it and remained keen as he neared every tree, every bolder, every thicket. But he sensed no one. *Why?*

It pressed on Awol that Camo *was* harmless and not a terrorist. Camo had tried to flush him out with the dog and had staked a perimeter around his tent because these were his environs. He was in charge out here, and Awol didn't get that obvious message. A loose-wired recluse who—*No,* Awol thought, and now he was of the notion that Camo wanted Awol to follow him. With uncertainties mounting, Awol realized that without his satellite phone, he couldn't call Diana. He was on his own.

The other questions remained: Which dam or tunnel or whatever? More than one? What was the first and most obvious choice? And when? Awol took out the tiny box of raisins from his pants pocket and dumped the contents down his throat in one go. *Think,* he told himself. *What would I do?* Again, he told himself he would begin the terrorist act with a diversion, which had been the Granby, already seen on the news. For one person, it was too dicey to enact a diversion and rush somewhere else to bomb another dam or a tunnel without encountering a snag of some sort. From all he could put together, two people were involved, and only one of them was a demo expert. These two rebels needed time between the diversion and the final act. It was not lost on Awol that he kept thinking of tunnels. Back to square one: Which tunnel?

Awol couldn't process what he was hearing. He heard dog sounds, muffled. He didn't think it through as he crept to the shaking weeds below the tree. He smelled dog. He knew it was Blazer before he parted the wild weeds and grasses. Blazer, muzzled about the mouth, shook trying to nose up to Awol. He was straitjacketed somehow around the throat and mouth and couldn't bark. Awol didn't notice the torn paper coaster, Coors Light, tacked to the tree. *That bastard left him here to die,* Awol thought, and with emotions clouding his thinking, Awol reached down to his animal and, dropping to a crouch, steadied himself at the tree. The arrow went straight through Awol's left palm and crucified it to the aspen. He heard footsteps behind him.

"Awol! My man. I've been expecting you."

CHAPTER SIXTY-FIVE

R<small>EARDON ADMIRED HIS WORK</small> but didn't want to overdo it. Awol was in shock, and Reardon wanted information but couldn't wait, as Butane was about to arrive. Before aiming this one-point arrow, the kind he used to practice shots, he'd decided to test Butane one last time. Reluctantly, he broke his arrow so he could slip it out of Awol's palm without further damage. In the process, Awol passed out. Reardon tied him to the tree and left.

A<small>WOL HAD LOST TRACK OF TIME</small>. He was in shock, and—*What did he say his name was? Reardon?*—Awol remembered him twisting the arrow out, but he didn't remember being tied at all. His left hand throbbed, and he wobbled his head to try and clear up dizzy double vision. Blazer, strait-jacketed, lay on his back and looked up at him. It was noon, judging by the sun, and the temperature had risen. He needed water. He was tied at the ankles and the arms around the tree. He couldn't help Blazer. He tried to move his arms and fingers, but his damaged palm hurt too much.

Later, as the sun tipped west, Awol heard footsteps behind him. He dared not try to turn his head. He ached all over and felt deranged.

"Did Reardon do this?" Butane asked.

"Water."

Butane got out his water bottle and gave him sips. "What happened?"

"Shot an arrow through my palm, which stuck me to this tree. Get Blazer loose."

Butane cut Awol's wrist bindings with a knife similar to the one Reardon had confiscated from Awol. Butane gave Awol the water bottle and the knife—saying "Here, use this"—and shifted to unbind the dog. Awol managed to cut his own ankle rope and drank from Butane's water bottle. Butane got Blazer unpacked, and suddenly, an arrow thudded through Butane's back and out his chest.

"Jesus!" Awol said. Awol forgot his pain as he looked at the arrow and up to Butane's face. His countenance conveyed—? Butane hadn't even grunted. Butane's eyes conveyed understanding. As soon as he'd brought the extra demolition materials to the cabin, given Reardon the keys to the hidden Ram, and reexplained everything, he'd been, for Reardon, expendable. He gasped for his last breaths.

"Go," Butane managed to choke out.

"Is Reardon going to blow—?" Awol took the paper that Butane managed to hand him.

"Yes."

"What dam?" Awol reached into Butane's pant pocket where he'd seen him keep his cell, realizing Butane was about to fold away forever.

"Not a . . . da . . . a tun—"

Butane gasped a final breath. Awol capped the water bottle, and both he and Blazer hobbled away.

———————————

REARDON HAD NAILED BUTANE from sixty yards. After Butane had answered final questions and given him the keys, Reardon told Butane to go to the practice tree to check on Awol and the dog. Butane went to the tree where he'd once watched Reardon fine-tune his shots. Reardon stepped out soon after with his Quest Storm compound and watched. Through his field glasses he watched him untie Awol, give him his water, and pull the ties off the dog, and that's all he needed to see. At least he wouldn't have to reject Butane's sexual advances later. Knowing he'd nailed Butane, he didn't feel like facing him right now—dead or alive. It was time to accomplish the mission, which fell on his shoulders alone. Reardon ratio-nalized that he'd saved Butane's life already; he would have died for sure at the ravine. His last glance at the tree told him Awol was there, wounded, a dehydrated mess. He decided to go for both of them later. He spent his next moments packing up. Was Reardon getting sloppy? Not in his mind. If Awol managed to hobble away, he wouldn't get far without food, supplies, cell, and GPS—plus the beacon and government satellite phone—all of which Reardon had taken. Reardon would enjoy tracking him after the mission. He felt a rise within him as he remembered one of his favorite short stories, "The Most Dangerous Game." He'd find himself a hound of his own. For now, back to the mission.

AWOL EXPECTED ANY SECOND to hear steps behind him, but he heard nothing as the sun leaned farther west. He took another swallow of water, which shook him alive, and hobbled ahead into thickets, one of his legs half asleep. He wanted to get to a stream so Blazer could drink but felt so bad for his animal that he took the cap off the bottle and held it out for him to lap. Blazer lapped furiously, and Awol promised him more. They hobbled together as a broken team into dense forest. He noted his surroundings and remembered terrain relative to the dimming sun and what he could see of the horizon. Awol had trouble concentrating; he was sore to the bone and tired and thought of food. He and Blazer slowed to a crawl. They came to a hidden patch of moss-covered roots and rocks. Awol pushed ahead to where it was grassier and dryer. And then Awol, in the fetal position, slept with Blazer, back to back.

CHAPTER SIXTY-SIX

Awol STILL HAD HIS WRISTWATCH. His cell had been swiped, but he'd taken Butane's. Under the full moon, he pressed a button, 4:30 a.m. No bars, no signal. Blazer grunted but didn't stir. So why did Reardon let him escape? If, as he remembered reading, one thinks better on an empty stomach, Awol had clarity: Reardon was on a mission. That mission was paramount. Reardon had killed what Awol assumed was his partner. Why? That was a loss in some way. But Awol and Blazer were afterthoughts who couldn't jeopardize his mission in their current condition, so it was reasonable to assume Reardon had rushed off to blow up something.

Awol searched his pockets and felt a tinge of hope as he pulled out his backup emergency headlamp. But what about maps? He searched his backpack. All gone. But wait, he went to another pant pocket. The wallet had been taken, but in front of that pocket on his cargo pants was another fold, and he pulled out a sandwich baggie containing two maps, each facing opposing sides of the bag.

"Up, boy. C'mon, Blazer."

The animal stood, but when he tried to stretch, he shrieked and shuddered. All the while, Awol fixed his location in his mind. He and Blazer retreated their steps and came to the clearing. The near-full moon beamed upon them as Awol reached into his pant pocket for a crushed nut bar he remembered stashing there. His other hand was swollen and useless, but his teeth worked in getting the wrapper open. The nuts tasted good, but they made him hungrier. He looked at the moon, which clouded over, and angled the headlamp to the paper Butane had given him. As he opened it, he remembered Butane's final word, "tun." The five-by-eight-inch sheet was a map, and right at the top, it said "M.T." It had to be the Moffat Tunnel. Sure enough, down at the bottom in small handwriting, it read "Train" and "Water" and was marked with arrows.

With the survival instinct of one who has made these decisions before, Awol took another compass heading from his chronometer. *Yes.* He walked fifty yards and took another heading and then a final one to the east in the emerging light of dawn—the tent on the cliff was that way, three miles tops. The tent was on the way out, which was the sure way back to the trailhead and access road, as Awol remembered it. If Reardon was bent on his mission, Awol didn't think he would go back to his tent, and Awol needed that tent out here as well as his sleeping bag and pad.

Blazer insisted on bearing right at one mile. Awol was wise to follow and was rewarded with a flowing stream. *Hallelujah!* He was out of food, but the water couldn't have come at a better time. Awol clung onto hope. His mind shifted a gear as Blazer drank and sat down in the stream. Reardon jumped into Awol's mind. This was it: he had to get Diana. Every hundred yards, he'd try for a signal on Butane's phone but remembered that only at the trailhead did he see bars on the screen.

They climbed with faded hopes. Both wounded, both hungry and tired. Another drink from the bottle revived Awol for a few minutes, but he slowed again and was afraid he'd pass out and tumble down the mountain. He hung onto an aspen branch to break his fall, but it didn't help much.

They found the tent. It was sliced front to back, side to side, no doubt with his own buck knife. It flapped at the bottoms where Awol noticed all the stakes had been removed. He didn't see them and assumed they were thrown off the cliff. He threw up the tent shambles and looked at a sliced-up sleeping bag that lacked a hood and bottom, with slashes everywhere and a busted zipper. All the synthetic filling had been pulled out and strewn about. Blazer sniffed at the remnants of Awol's former sleeping pad. Awol looked at the cut straps of his mainframe backpack. Every strap cut in half, including the belly strap. Awol wanted to cry as Blazer lay down on torn remnants.

Awol stood beside his animal and collected himself. He opened the ruined pack and took his ax, which he managed to zip into his daypack.

He remembered Reardon swiping his food for breakfast after he'd set the bobcat scare. He'd used his stove that Awol now picked up at the firepit. With field glasses, he'd seen him eat and had smelled tinges of oatmeal in the wind as he watched hidden in the aspen. How he wished he had that oatmeal now. Food would be a problem, but two other things Awol had hoped for were the emergency beacon and the satellite radio. It occurred to him that a password was necessary for the satellite, and Reardon didn't have it. Awol pulled out Butane's cell and tried to reach Diana but failed again.

REARDON WAS ON HIS WAY to the Moffat Tunnel. The forecast called for rain later in the day, but nothing could slow him now. He was pissed at himself. He'd forgotten about Butane's cell, and after he'd gone back, he didn't find it on him. The cell had tunnel pictures, and if Awol had that phone . . . Figuring Awol had hobbled back to his tent, Reardon decided to find him on the way and kill him, which is what he should have done while he had the chance. Reardon smacked the steering wheel of the battered Ram. He hadn't seen Awol and had gotten enraged arriving at the tent, but if Awol was on the way to it, he would be in for a surprise. He kept running ideas through his mind on how he might use the emergency beacon and the satellite he'd swiped from Awol's pack.

Reardon pulled to the side of the road and got out the satellite phone. He shook a fist, realizing a password was needed. Something else occurred to him. Could the feds use this phone as a tracking device? He smacked the phone on the dashboard. He realized he was screwing up and that, yes, he missed the practical wisdom of Butane. He tried to calm himself and remembered how Butane told him to breathe slow and easy in the tunnel. He needed to do that here. He was scared about driving a vehicle again and was worked up about not handling Awol. *Think. There must be a way to use the beacon to foil*—And the idea came to him. He would take a detour, which would cost a good hour, but it would be worth it to ensure the mission. What was the big rush? The vehicle had been where Butane said it would be. He had the keys. If he ended up setting charges a few hours later than what he'd planned, that was okay. He had a way that would allow him to take extra time. He heaved the satellite phone out the widow, out of sight, and pulled back onto the road.

BY THE TIME AWOL MADE it to the access road, he and Blazer couldn't walk straight. The dog had a limp, and the neck wound hadn't had a chance to heal. Awol was sure Blazer couldn't trot. He hoped a vehicle would approach as they tramped to the trailhead, where there would be somebody. As he neared the trailhead, he was dismayed to see Butane's cell needed a charge. Worse, he counted one bar and couldn't get a proper signal. The battery read 7 percent and was in the red zone. He should have turned the phone off. But then he thought, *Maybe Butane had pictures.* He went to his photo album and scrolled without seeing anything useful, but before turning the phone off, he found a bunch of mysterious pictures. Some looked like they were in a cave. He took out Butane's hand-drawn map and spread it on the gravel road. He scrolled farther and saw photos of a tunnel hole, which on the map showed another tunnel hole going straight down off that. A few more pictures convinced Awol he was looking at the Moffat Tunnel. He rechecked the map and identified staging in the photos. He tried one last time to get a signal and couldn't. The phone was losing charge fast. He shut it down completely, thinking he would have one last chance to look at the pictures and where the cave tunnel led to the train and water tunnel. *But where exactly is that X?* He couldn't focus. He needed food.

REARDON HAD GOTTEN TO the junction leading to Granby Dam. He knew he was getting close and pulled to the shoulder a mile before. Using binoculars, he observed two cars with lights on parked near a hill a half mile up the access road to the dam. He hadn't expected security in the area now that the "planned" demolition had been prevented. No matter. He drove to the opposite shoulder and crept along beyond the junction. He stopped and exited Butane's pickup with his backpack. Behind a large oak, sure that no one was watching him, he took out the beacon and placed it below a burl near the bottom of the trunk. He covered it with leaves and pressed the button.

―――――――――――

AWOL HOLLERED "HELLO. HELP!" at the trailhead. Damn his luck. Three vehicles parked, two cars and one pickup, but no one around. The pickup's window revealed two closed pizza boxes, smudged and bent. Awol noted that the pickup's back cab window was cracked open. He hauled himself up into the bed and slid open the window. With pains shooting out his good arm and wrist, he managed to grab one of the boxes as the other slid to the floor. He was furious with himself because he heard movement in the box that toppled off the seat. Try as he might, he couldn't reach the door locks from the little sliding window, but he had the other box and sat on the tailgate chewing days-old pizza crusts and swallowing water. Blazer sniffed one of the crusts and took it like a bone. Awol chewed, his options dwindling and time running out. Then it started to rain.

CHAPTER SIXTY-SEVEN

Famished, beat, standing in the rain, Awol had to lean against a tree. Blazer had drifted away under an oak. Awol headed that way, as it offered better cover. His mind and body worked in slow motion. He sat and leaned back, arms huddled around him. His palm throbbed intolerably. He held his hand to Blazer and let him lick the wound. He fingered through a pocket in his pack and retrieved antibacterial ointment and some Band-Aids. Awol did his best to apply the unguent and Band-Aids. Moving like liquid mercury, he found his other bandana and wrapped his hand.

Awol went back to the truck. Sticking his good hand into the rear sliding window again, he was able to push the driver seat up and found a tarp. *Praise be to God.* He broke the window dragging the tarp back through, but no glass shattered. He returned to the tree and unfolded the tarp to cover him like a poncho, like he'd done in army bivouac. He stuck his nose near grommets so he could breathe and let Blazer come in by his feet. Man and dog slept for three hours, until the rain came full on, the wind picked up, and the temperature dropped. *Now what?* Awol thought.

Back to the same truck. Awol pulled the snapped glass pane out and was able to remove the other sliding pane of the rear window. With his good hand, and with a final one-two-three push and yell, he was able to yank the driver door handle up. Awol climbed in behind the steering wheel, pushed the passenger seat all the way to the rear, and helped Blazer onto the truck floor. Awol wrapped the tarp around himself and stuffed some of it into the broken window to retard the cold. He took out the other pizza crusts that had fallen earlier, and he and Blazer chomped long and hard, savoring every bite. They slept for another two hours.

When Awol awoke, he felt as if he'd woken from a coma. It was predawn according to his watch. Something—he couldn't place it—had pulled him from his sleep. He felt within a spirit, the Great Spirit? He interpreted that he was within a grand intelligence. He didn't know why, and he couldn't make anything out if it, but he felt that a Rubicon had been crossed.

Thirteen miles away, Medicine Man was also awake and was sitting on a horse blanket atop hay in his teepee. He looked with glazed eyes onto a three-quarter moon. He read his last signs and nodded. He was disappointed but accepted the Great Spirit's decision. He lay back down and closed his eyes, forever.

It was at that point that Awol became uncertain again. He was missing something. He closed his eyes and listened with every fiber, with every sense of his being. He was within a great intelligence. In the next few minutes, Awol understood that he was being warned. They'd been fooled. Catastrophe was imminent.

Awol climbed out of the truck. The rain had stopped. Finally, he had three bars and called Diana.

"There you are! We are on the way. Stay there."

"What? Wait. I'm at a trailhead. You're coming here?"

"The beacon reads . . ." She listed coordinates, and Awol realized what had happened.

"That's not where I am. It's the Moffat. Go to the Moffat Tunnel."

"Can't hear you. Go muff it? Procedure dictates we confirm the beacon first."

Awol watched the battery about to expire. Pictures! He needed to see those pictures.

"Moffat Tunnel!" he hollered. He clicked off the phone call and navigated to the pictures. There they were. With an intensity and focus one could only summon if his life depended on it, Awol studied each photo. He absorbed the smoking gun trio: a picture of a detonator, because it resembled the pictures Kenny had sent him, a close-up of a seam right under a huge pipe near the top of a staging, and the following close-up of connecting wires. But wait, the connecting wires were on a table in what looked like a cabin with a stove. The tunnel seam looked real. Awol couldn't process that, but he continued to scroll back and forth through the pictures, scoring them into his mind. He looked again at a cave entrance and studied the boulder and surroundings. The phone screen turned black.

"Blazer. C'mon, boy. Time to saddle up."

Blazer's wounds were worse than Awol's. The animal whimpered and lurched on three stable legs. Awol needed time he didn't have so that the dog could heal.

Awol's mind worked as if he was on speed. He stared at the truck and two vehicles. He needed to get into town and go to the police. Lee Child's Jack Reacher came to mind as Awol wondered what that character would do. Awol didn't know how to hot-wire a vehicle. But he knew what "M.T." meant, and the word "train" confirmed it. If he waited anywhere near here, it could be hours before he got a hitch to the police, where yet more time would be wasted. But he couldn't stay here if Reardon was on his way to the Moffat. Not being Reacher or Hercule Poirot, he dug out his maps. Hope gained a foothold as he focused. The path leading from this trailhead in front of him took him in the direction of the Moffat— not all the way to the cave, but he figured he could bushwhack what he estimated was no more than two miles. He refused to look closer at the bushwhack—he had a marked path right here. The time was now.

"Okay, Blazer. You ready?"

The dog wobbled over and Awol patted him. At least Blazer no longer had the weight of his own belly pack and supplies. "I'll make it up to you, Blazer. I promise I will."

Awol walked to the pickup. He opened the glove compartment and pulled out a bunch of loose mints. He rifled through the compartment but found nothing else to eat or use. He pulled on a side seat handle and tipped up the seat. He opened a toolbox and removed a small flashlight. Using the flashlight, he grabbed pliers and a wire stripper. Thinking ahead, he grabbed the roll of electrical tape. At the last minute, he remembered to take the flashlight and stuffed everything into his cargo pants pockets. A hundred yards up the trail, Awol ate mints. He tried giving one to Blazer, but after sniffing the miniature green hockey puck, the dog turned away as if offended.

CHAPTER SIXTY-EIGHT

Reardon listened to old news on the truck radio: ". . . a suspicious character and probable suspect had been seen in the area . . . authorities are trying to determine if he is American Indian and served in the military . . ." A rehash of events of the past—but still on the mind of Coloradans.

The broadcast went on to say that there was an area-wide hunt for the suspect. "Meanwhile," the news reported, "the FBI and local police are staking out Granby, other dams in the area, and are patrolling Dillon Reservoir." Reardon lip-smiled as the report ended without one mention of any tunnel.

Two miles later, after redirecting himself toward the west Moffat entrance, the pickup that Butane had provided acted up. It bucked twice, and to Reardon's horror, the gas gauge read empty. The pickup stopped, and Reardon rolled off the berm onto the shoulder. He was out of his element and wanted the comfort of his bow, which hung behind him in the cab like a shotgun would. His palms were sweaty as he sat there not knowing his next step. He couldn't imagine that Butane would do this to him after he'd saved his life. Though Reardon had used extra gas to reposition the beacon, he wanted to kill Butane all over again as he smacked his fist on the inside roof. He was Ray Liotta in *Something Wild*.

His heart leaped when he heard a siren and saw a police car, lights flashing, in his rearview mirror. The police car went on by, but Reardon didn't feel any better. He remembered seeing a gas station about a mile back, and it infuriated him that he'd have to backtrack, on foot, away from the Moffat. But what was he to do? He couldn't remember if there was a gas station ahead of him. He could walk for miles and not find one if he went ahead. Feeling exposed in full camo, he got out and started back. The entire time, his stomach growled and cramped. It was the same way he had felt when that bastard Awol pulled his bobcat trick. He felt vulnerable without his compound. He kept patting his pant pocket, ensuring that the truck keys were there and worrying that he hadn't locked the truck, even though he thought he had.

He arrived at the station, and a young attendant with glasses was inside at the register. A mechanic with soiled face and wrench toiled under a lift.

"I need some gas," Reardon said.

The young man blinked his eyes. "Excuse me?"

"Right. I'm sorry, my truck's out of gas down the road about a mile." Reardon pointed in the direction.

"Oh. Got a gas can?"

Reardon blinked and couldn't stop himself. "Excuse me?"

"You need a gas can."

Reardon shrugged. "I don't have one. My truck's out of gas, down that way."

The young man peeked around to the mechanic. He rubbed his chin and stood there in the doorway looking at the mechanic at the lift.

Reardon wanted to strangle him. He walked up behind him.

"Matt?" the clerk hollered.

The mechanic pulled on a rusted tail pipe, gave up, and pulled out the wrench again.

"Hey, Matt?"

"What!"

"This man needs some gas. His truck's out of gas."

"He got a gas can?"

"No."

The mechanic said nothing.

"You want me to . . ."

"No. I need you here."

Reardon stepped in front of the clerk.

"Mister, I gotta get gas. It's important."

The mechanic put his weight on the wrench and lost his grip. The wrench clanged to the floor, and the mechanic held his knuckles.

He looked up at Reardon and took a breath. "Chill, man. This right here's important, see. He'll get your gas and take you back after I finish installing this muffler." He picked up the wrench.

Reardon opened Butane's wallet and pulled out a ten-dollar bill. "Look, here's ten bucks. Give me a can of gas, okay?"

"The last time I did that," the mechanic said, "I lost my gas can. Got another ten, I'll do it."

"This is all I've got. Can't you give me a break?" Reardon didn't realize he had hollered.

The mechanic threw down his wrench. "Hey, asshole. Either you wait till I'm finished or get the fuck outta here!" His face was red.

Reardon wanted his bow. How had he ever lived as a civilian? He looked at the clerk, who'd gone back to the office. Reardon saw the mechanic grunt with the wrench. He went back to the clerk.

"Can you loan me ten dollars?" Reardon asked.

"I'm sorry. I can't."

Reardon leaned into him. "Why the fuck not?"

"I don't have it."

Reardon pointed to the register. "What's in there?"

"Not my money. I can't."

Reardon flushed and his fingers trembled. A bell squeaked, caused by a customer whose tires rolled over the customer alert hose, and the clerk was happy to beat it out to the pump.

Reardon stood there looking at the cash register. He peered to his right and saw the mechanic, rag in hand, looking at him. The mechanic ambled away. Reardon walked out to the car near the pump. "Can't miss it," the clerk said. "It'll be on the right."

"Thanks," the driver said.

The clerk went back to the office as Reardon looked across the street to a grocery. He crossed the street and entered the store. He smelled cigar smoke and saw the attendant behind a counter, lit cigar in mouth, hand a bag to a customer. Reardon was desperate but didn't know what to do, until he realized that he wasn't on a deadline. He'd been so focused on his mission that he'd forgotten another hour, or two or three, meant no difference. But he wanted to act now. He stared at the headline in the local paper sitting in a rack. dam attack investigation continues. Unsettled but realizing he had no choice but to wait, he went back across the street to the station. The mechanic glared at him, and Reardon turned his back and waited outside where the garage intersected with the office.

Ten minutes later, Reardon heard him come up behind him.

"Gonna take me longer," the mechanic said.

Reardon turned to face him. "Most jobs take longer than you plan for."

The mechanic nodded. "Benny, come 'ere. Take this gentleman's ten bucks and give him a can of gas."

"Hey, thanks."

"Sorry for the words," he said as he went back to work. "I know you'll bring back my can."

Reardon wanted to say to Matt that if Benny drove him to his truck, he'd be sure to get his can back. He stifled himself and said nothing to Benny as he filled the can. Benny capped the can while another customer pulled in. Reardon hoofed back toward the truck with the can of gas.

On the way to the pickup, Reardon was disconnected. The continual noise and horns and occasional flying stones from the berm made him think he was on another planet. The mixed smells of oil, gas from the can, roadside animal shit, and fast food made him stop. He could puke right here. What in the fuck were these people doing? As he tramped by small homes, each one was a cage for an intelligent but unwise animal. Some cages were adorned with flowers or a fence or a tiny patio with plastic chairs; nevertheless they were cages in Reardon's mind. Man wasn't free in this so-called society—he was caged. Reardon wanted out of here. He remembered actor Steve McQueen's comment, "I'd rather wake up in the middle of nowhere than in any city on earth."

Back at the pickup, he twisted off the gas cap and poured in the fuel. He hopped inside the vehicle and turned the key. The engine whirred but didn't start. He tried again and pumped the pedal. The ignition caught and stalled. Ready to blow a fuse, Reardon tried again, pumping the pedal harder than anyone pumped on any old-time pump organ. *Fuck!* Aware of "flooding," Reardon wouldn't allow himself to think about it as he reddened and kept pumping. While the engine kept whirring, he stopped, thinking the mechanic had somehow compromised his gas. The idea enraged him as his mind returned to the look on the mechanic's face when Reardon turned to him by the register. Reardon put his face in his hands and covered his ears as a horn blew and the Doppler effect tore through his brain. *Mission. Mission. Mission.*

He tried again and the engine caught. As he veered into the road, the pickup stalled. The scream of horns unraveled Reardon, and he pumped the pedal again. The engine caught but stalled after he made it into the road. Fearing for his life, as vehicles swerved around him, horns blaring, voices hollering, fingers and fists flying from windows, Reardon kept trying as he screamed. The engine caught, and the truck lurched forward again. Reardon thought he might cry if the truck stalled another time and told himself he would split the mechanic's head with arrows if it did. But the truck engine held and began to smooth. Reardon, gasping, was semicoherent as he stayed in lane and followed the flow of traffic. He wanted to bash the gas can over the mechanic's head but kept going.

From here on, it was all mission. He would drive to the trailhead leading to the arête. Butane had taken Reardon before and showed him where to hide the vehicle. Butane had taken him to the cave entrance and pointed out details on Reardon's copy of the map. Reardon had studied it every day and remembered every detail and Butane's descriptions. After he'd murdered Butane and gone back to retrieve his phone, Reardon left him there like roadkill. He'd searched all his pockets without finding it. Reardon knew who had it. He gripped the wheel and accelerated.

CHAPTER SIXTY-NINE

TWO HOURS LATER, as dawn breached the eastern sky, Awol and Blazer had slowed so much that either could have slept on their feet. Awol had ample water but no food, just a lingering mint taste in his mouth. Blazer nibbled wildflowers. As Awol trudged, mental images of food consumed him. He looked for berries as he walked, but nothing presented itself. He knew his mushrooms, and as he dragged his poles through dark places with rich humus from the detritus of dead leaves, he spotted one here and there. He was certain that many of them were not poisonous, but he also knew that you could be tricked. Many a hiker got ill, and some may have even died, and that quashed any desire he had to try some. He had heard of mushroom deaths elsewhere but not along the trail. Violent illness far from medical help was not something he could chance.

A few minutes later, he heard voices coming his way. Two men, one in a cowboy hat, the other in a railroad engineer cap, approached as Awol stopped by his dog.

"Gentlemen," Awol said.

"Howdy." the cowboy said. He looked down at the mutt and back up at Awol. "You guys look a bit under the weather."

"Haven't had food in four days," Awol said. "The dog's better off than me as far as the food goes. I'm hurting."

"Where ya headed?" the engineer asked.

"Long story. Headed up . . . towards." Awol pointed the stick. "Got anything to eat, guys?"

Cowboy pulled off his pack. "Well, let's see, you may be in luck. We're headed back to the trailhead."

"I'll pay you."

Engineer pulled off his pack and looked at the cowboy. "Now I know he's hungry."

"Here," Cowboy said, "some cheese and crackers. That's all I got."

"I thank you kindly," Awol said. Blazer lay down and once again covered his head with his paw.

"Don't have much," Engineer said, "but this should help." He handed Awol a baggie of grapes, rummaged some more in his pack, and held up a crushed banana, hesitating as he looked at it.

"I'll take it. Please," said Awol.

"Three nights ago, we had pizza," Cowboy said. "I'm sure you could use one now."

Awol rubbed his nose and nodded. "The trailhead doesn't have pizza."

The engineer looked at Awol.

"That's where we ate them," Cowboy said. He grinned.

"Thank you, guys. Listen . . ."

"Oh, don't worry about it. Do you need a few bucks to buy some food?"

"No, and I thank you for the offer."

The engineer said nothing and closed up his pack.

"Wish I had more," Cowboy said.

"This saves my ass. You own the van back there with the New Mexico plate?" Awol hoped so.

"I own the pickup. Colorado." He extended his hand. "Name's Hank. This here is Jack."

Awol shook both hands. "Karl. Trail name's Awol."

Cowboy reshouldered his pack. "I like that." He grinned.

"Be seeing ya," the engineer said, starting off.

"Mighty good of both of you. Stay well," Awol said. "C'mon, Blazer. Up, boy."

A mile later, Awol snuck a look behind him and took a break. He chalked up his misstep—*all for a few pizza crusts and a tarp.* He patted his pack and hoped they hadn't noticed the piece of tarp sticking out. He ate everything, including the banana peel. The more he promised himself to save the cheese, the quicker he chomped it down. The food revived him.

Two hours later, an elderly hiker approached and stopped. Awol tried to look desperate and mimicked putting food into his mouth and chewing.

"I've been in the same situation," the man said. "I'm heading back to the trailhead, so I'll help you out."

Awol's eyes moistened as he was given two wrapped sandwiches and a baggie of gorp.

"Don't have anything for the hound. But you got tuna and chicken salad on rye under the tinfoil."

"I want to pay you," Awol said.

"Get out. I won't take a cent. In fact," he rummaged more, "here's my scraps—pack in, pack out—for the hound."

After the man had gone, Awol took Blazer into a clearing off-trail and watched him devour scraps of bread, what looked like sausage skins, some moldy cheese, and olives with pimentos. Later, at a stream, Blazer drank while Awol replenished his bottles. Once finished, Awol patted Blazer. "Okay, boy. Take a nap. You deserve it." The animal understood and turned over to sleep. This time, his paws stayed by his head, and Awol took that as Blazer's sign of thanks.

Awol took his time eating scrumptious chicken salad on rye. He'd stashed the other sandwich in his pack—out of sight, out of mind—but dug into the gorp after he finished the sandwich, as a fat man would dig into dip and chips. He drank plenty of water, and after checking his map, he saw that another stream was ahead. *Thank you, God.* All the while, as he chewed, as he drank, as he dug into the gorp, Awol thought. He might have gotten a long hitch or, more likely, a series of hitches up the twelve miles to get to the ridge above the cave, but like a wormhole leading to an alternate universe, if he scaled this mountain, he would drop down to the area on the map showing the cave tunnel. He closed his eyes several times to remember the picture of the cave entrance, rechecked Butane's map, and cross-referenced that with his own. That mountain—counting map rings and checking scale—he estimated at a height of six thousand feet. He could not move it any more than he could take the time to bushwhack around it. There appeared to be swamp and marshland on both sides, which was dicey on any hike and out of the question if he had any chance of beating Reardon. But he noticed a trail that led up the mountain, and the descent put him on an arête he estimated at a little over a mile from the cave entrance. The fact that he had a marked trail up and down solidified his confidence. He would climb and descend that mountain to the cave.

CHAPTER SEVENTY

"**T**HE LONGER WE WAIT, Senator, the worse it will get."

"Look, ya little shit. You sucked me into your mess. My life is in shambles because of you."

"Wait a minute. Stop. My life, too, but we can get out of the mess if you send more water here. I got no support from the banks. These eight hundred acres are a development sinkhole without the extra water."

"The water is needed elsewhere, and I don't mean for the tribe. More water is needed everywhere."

"What about that iceberg?"

"Get real! That's years away. The droughts and fires have me blocked—all water reclamation is at a standstill. Go ask the Colorado Water Conservation Board."

Hendricks was at the end of his rope. Yesterday, Ginger offered her resignation to spare him the indignity of letting her go.

"How is the reelection campaign going?"

"Why do you ask?"

"I'm sure you don't want any scandal to break."

"The fuck you talking about?"

"I know all about it, Richard. You gambled the tribe's money and lost. They were ready to out you, but you agreed to a deal. They own you."

"You are a scumbag. I didn't think you'd shoot this low."

"Hey, I gave you back half. That's a half more than anyone else got. Rumor has it that now you've gambled all that money away. I'm not all the reason for your mess, Senator."

Rodriguez closed down his private cell. Up till now his life couldn't get much worse. But if a scandal broke exposing his past and the link to the tribe, he wouldn't be reelected. Rodriguez was a spider caught in his own web. If he managed to steer more water to Hendricks, the tribe would expose him. The tribe wanted to keep the past behind them, but if they were not going to get water, they wouldn't care about bad press. And he wanted to crush Hendricks, who might not give him back another dollar. Now Hendricks threatened him with scandal. Either way, he'd lose the election.

That night Rodriguez watched CNN. The usual bombings and terrorist mayhem danced across his screen. He compartmentalized those images in his mind and reviewed the account of a terrorist attack at a dam in Colorado that had been foiled a week ago. He'd already discussed the details with his inside contact, Avery, at the bureau. The situation looked ominous, and they were trying to get more information, Avery had said. The bureau's Denver field office director was as weak as wet toast. He was losing it, and the senator talked up Assistant Director Avery.

Rodriguez calculated like he always did, like any superior gambler. That's why he'd positioned Avery as his inside contact in the first place. Everything had a reason. It occurred to Rodriguez as he watched CNN that an atrocious act of terror could give him an out. *If*, as he repeated to himself, *if* a terrorist were to blow up a dam, the tribe would not see extra water diverted east—the tribe would be satisfied, therefore no more pressure on him. No scandal. And Hendricks would not get his needed water, all because of a terrorist act. Hendricks, greedy as he was, wouldn't initiate a scandal over that, and if he did, the senator would expose the deceit and money grabbing of Hendricks. Further, the tribe would now continue with all development plans and stand beside the senator. Game over for Hendricks.

Ten minutes later, on a hunch, Rodriguez called Avery.

"Keep this private," Rodriguez said.

"You got it. It stays in the vault."

"What's the chatter I'm hearing about another terrorist attack on a different dam in Colorado?"

"Senator, how the hell did you know?"

"Well . . . in this business . . ."

"You know about this Butane's supposed partner?"

"Some. What can *you* tell me?"

"There's another guy out there, off the grid. We know this because an undercover has met him."

"And?"

"Senator, this must stay private."

"You gave me your word. I give you mine."

"Our undercover claims Granby Dam was a diversion. Another attack is planned."

"So, the real target could be another dam."

"Or a tunnel that diverts water under the Divide. That's another possibility."

Even better. "Hmm. I see. Sounds like you have your hands full. Listen, I can't reveal my source, but I may be able to help you."

"That's great, Senator. We need all the help we can get."

"From here on, we discuss this privately. Understood?"

"Yes."

"I have a sensitive issue with my source; he'll walk if this doesn't stay private. You and me only."

"Understood, Senator. I'll not include my field director in any of this."

That's what Rodriguez was waiting to hear. "Send me the latest updates. Keep me in the loop."

"Intra-security inviolate?"

"Intra-security inviolate."

This entire hunch had been a long shot, but now Rodriguez saw a way out of his dilemma. It would require finesse. He'd have to add his own vigorish.

CHAPTER SEVENTY-ONE

AWOL PALMED THE ICE AX, felt its weight, and simulated a slam into ice. He remembered where he bought it, Eastern Mountain Sports, about twelve years ago in North Conway, New Hampshire. At the time, he envisioned doing ice climbs in New Hampshire's White Mountains, and he had, twice. Both times the ax wasn't needed, but he'd dug into ice at Mount Osceola and another time at Mount Moosilauke. He wanted to say, been there, done that.

He hefted the ax again and looked at the ragged surface of iced gneiss facing him. He'd climbed two-thirds of the way to the top of this mountain and hadn't expected this sheet of ice, which hadn't revealed itself at ground level. He wished that he'd tried the traverse around the mountain, but if he was to intercept Reardon, this was the fastest way. It had to be Reardon who'd set the beacon, and whose coordinates Diana had mentioned during their aborted conversation.

His watch thermometer read thirty degrees, and the temperature was falling. He looked for a way to go left or right of the ice sheet, but it was continuous. Fate was cruel; he couldn't go back down. He wouldn't get to Reardon in time.

He approached the ragged edges of ice and packed snow and replaced fear with hunger. He had half the gorp left and bread crusts he'd saved from the sandwiches, but food would have to wait. Awol had done a smart thing. He'd learned to hike in freezing conditions with his water bottles upside down. Water froze to ice on top first, so if they were right-side up, one had problems getting to the liquid. He'd seen frustrated hikers banging their water bottle on trees to try and shake loose hard ice. Awol had put both his emergency bottle and the other one upside down in his pack side pockets. He removed one, which was frozen on the bottom, and turned it right-side up, uncapped it, and drank freely.

He took but six steps and started to slip and slide. He gripped the ax and thought through his situation one last time. One, he knew where Reardon was headed. Two, the only way to beat him to the tunnel, or ambush him there, was to conquer this ice sheet and get down the other side. He'd told Blazer, as best he could, to go around and hoped his dog would figure it out. The poor animal wouldn't have made it up and over this ice patch.

Awol, right-handed, as though the first stroke had to show confidence and determination, struck a mighty first blow, something he could not have done if the arrow had torn through that hand. In a crouch, he maneuvered to the spot near where the ax held and jabbed his right foot, outfitted with spiked crampon, into ice. He swung the ax again for his left foot spikes. Awol tacked right and left and worked his way up the patch of ice. He refused to look down behind him, but the icy patch became steeper, and he could no longer see the top. He peeked behind. Brokenhearted, sweating profusely, he'd gone a mere fifty yards. His hands were cold and stiff, and he lacked the might of earlier swings. Yet he inched up.

At a hundred yards, he had trouble gripping his good hand around the ax. He was soaked in sweat and dehydrated. He stopped to drink and, with trembling hands, tipped the bottle to his mouth. *Oh, that is good.* He complimented himself in that all his water bottles had attached caps that hung on a small chain. As he swung again, he felt in charge, knowing that he'd taken the time to attach garbage bag ties to all his zippers on every piece of outside clothing. That meant he could unzip without removing his precious Gore-Tex gloves. He remembered that time in the Adirondacks during a winter hike with his new polar shell. He had his thickest gloves on, and he'd struggled to unzip to void, finally taking off the gloves and holding them with his mouth, but he'd dropped one and remembered how he'd cursed. That would not happen here. But, already, his hands and toes were cramped and numb. This served to flood his mind with other problems. Diana was stuck on procedure, *Regulations require us to clear the beacon first.* Catastrophe loomed. *My FBI, Homeland.* He had the feeling that the government had left him hanging, the irony, as he hung to his ax sixty yards from the summit. The notion festered in his mind. He'd laid his life on the line in Desert Storm and had been beat up since, *and now my government ignores me?*

Awol slowed. He had about forty yards to go on steep sheer ice, treacherous ice frozen on rock, without snow. He needed the teamwork of companions, pylons, rope. He had the crushing realization that he would not be able to cut off Reardon in time. It was all he could do to survive the climb to this summit. His mind didn't process going down the other side. His thoughts became confused. For an instant, Awol thought that Kenny had notified the FBI and that they would be ready. But Awol had failed using the responder, hadn't he? Or had he? Awol began to get scared. His thoughts were muddled to the extent that he now thought he was over the peak and had to descend backward from here. It was getting dark, the westering sun slinking behind the mountain, and it took him awhile to remember that he had his headlamp.

What was happening to Awol was the same thing that happens to all hikers and climbers in extreme weather: dehydration and the inability to think clearly. He needed water and a change of glove liners. Awol pulled out his water bottle and puzzled at the lack of a cap to open it. He realized the water was frozen as he stared at the bottom of his bottle. He turned the bottle right-side up to get at the cap, and it slipped out of his shaky hands. He heard it fall and slide behind him, followed by a faraway thump. Awol felt sorry for the bottle. Frantically, he reached around his waist and pulled out his one other bottle and crouched as he held it in front of him so it could not slide if dropped. Awol managed to uncap the bottle and drink. He got it back into the side pocket and was revived enough to reach for his gorp. With tired and cramped fingers, he teeth-opened the baggie and tipped it to his mouth. He was careful to make sure the nuts, Craisins, and chocolate chips all fell into his mouth. He chewed and felt tinges of awareness.

He pushed Reardon to the back of his mind. He fumbled for his headlamp and managed to get it on his head and working. Awol decided he couldn't do anything about his sweaty glove liners, which were causing his fingers to cramp. He had other liners, but the effort it would take to get them from his pack overwhelmed him. He closed his eyes to gather himself and stitch his thoughts. He grabbed the ax, swung, and started upward again.

It was almost dark an hour later, except for his headlamp, and in addition to disappearing and reappearing thoughts, Awol began to experience vertigo. He was certain he was falling backward, so he threw his head down in front of him and banged it on the shaft of the ax. He was terrified but forced his mind to one thought, as if the bang had knocked sense into him—*drink! And change out the glove liners, if possible.* He drank, and after more gorp, went to work. Lying on a sheet of ice so steep that he felt closer to vertical than before, he hooked a knee behind the ax. He shuffled off his pack and, in a Herculean effort, managed to find his other liners. Ten minutes later, he had switched them out without losing anything. He treated himself to more gorp and took two more swallows of water.

Forty minutes later, Awol could see a sprinkle of stars in front of him, and the moon rising north of west, giving him some light. He felt a gush of hope but had sweated more and could no longer feel his feet. He banged his toe box against the ice and felt a throb, which served to sting, tickle, and scare him all the more. He was losing energy and mind at a faster rate and avoided another drink, as the problem of how to remove his water bottle and uncap it puzzled him. *How do you do that?*

Water! He struggled but figured out how to remove the bottle and uncap it. He swallowed. He swallowed again. He swallowed a third time, and though his lips had a stinging numbness, he felt the liquid slide down his throat. Gut instinct told him to concentrate on one word. Every time he swung his ax, he yelped: "Up—up—up."

He sensed less vertical terrain. *Up. Up. Up.*

He approached level and hollered again the same word as he, ax in hand, crawled to level. He'd made it to the top. He treated himself to another mouthful of gorp, feeling much less of it in the bag. But the hardest part was accomplished. He figured it would be tricky getting down this other side, but . . . He drank again and noticed that most of the bottle had frozen. His last sips of unfrozen water put a new fear into him. Would God be so cruel as to have him fail here? Awol, his faculties not at full strength, thought back to the map. The west-southwest route down was less steep, and he stood up to head that way. It felt better to walk, but his feet were numb, and that worried him. He tramped with crampons as though marching in place. He pictured the map as he walked to the other side of the summit and believed he could see the less steep route. This time, he was on the money. God was good, though Awol didn't realize it.

He descended, facing the mountain, and swung the ax, but the backward descent brought him a new problem. Going up, he could spike his crampons into previously chopped ax-holes and wait to swing the ax in front of him again. Descending backward, he had to swing beside and behind him and feel for the hole, lest he put himself in an unstoppable slide. Awol knew how to do a self-arrest with an ice ax, but if he started to slide here and built up momentum, it would be as bad as sliding down the entire sheet of ice and scraping over solid rock, tumbling to boulders or trees.

The things saving him were less thick ice on a less steep descent. He worked himself down as best he could, but his muscles rebelled. He was using a different set of muscles in his legs and was convinced that it was so difficult ascending the other side that those other muscles had borrowed from his quadriceps, leaving him nothing for a descent. He felt himself losing his footing and slid about ten feet until he could swing his ax above him and arrest the slide. Flat on the mountain surface, he peeked left, and with the aid of the lamp, he could see outlines of another's former footholds. He would try to slip over to those spots.

Fifteen minutes later, Awol didn't think he could go any farther. He'd shifted to the proper spot but was taking too long to refocus. Winded and dehydrated again, he slid down to an ax hole left by another. He whacked on top to secure his ax and, one by one, he slid to the next and the next, knowing that these holes left by an unknown soul saved his life. *Thank you, my friend.* But twenty minutes later, his entire body was cramped, and he was afraid to pull out his ax to descend to the next hole. He pictured himself sliding and tumbling to the bottom. He managed to reach a few more holes, and sensing the end of the ice sheet, he lost concentration and slid. He couldn't flatten himself over his ax to self-arrest and gathered momentum. To save his nose and face and drawing on what he knew, he turned himself over and held the ax up in the air in front of him. He glissaded on his rump and bumped faster and faster to the bottom of the ice. He tried not to yell, fearing he might alert Reardon, wherever he was, but couldn't stifle himself as his speed increased. He prayed that he would miss boulders.

At the last second, his lamp revealed snow and grit but no more ice. Awol hit those ragged patches, and as one steps off a moving escalator onto firm walkway, he misjudged his entry to rocky terrain and tumbled over himself. Awol was jerked sideways as his left leg banged into immovable rock. He passed out for over a minute, and when he came to, glad to be alive, he felt more than beat up; he was down for the count. Two screwed-up legs, and he couldn't put full weight on either.

CHAPTER SEVENTY-TWO

"**S**ENATOR, I'VE GOT THE NEWEST." Rodriguez took the call from Denver FBI Assistant Chief Avery on his intra-security inviolate cell. "Our undercover says it's the Moffat Tunnel."

The senator had been waiting for a location, and now he knew what to do. "The Moffat? I was about to call you. My source says it's the Roberts."

"We are losing time, Senator. The beacon was found at Granby Dam, but our undercover is missing. We've sent forces to secure that dam. And we plan to helicopter troops to the Moffat."

"You said earlier that the beacon was stolen."

"Right. Procedure calls for us to confirm and clear a beacon first."

"The terrorist planted a ruse. You've walked into it."

"Possible, but—"

"Where do you think your undercover is?"

"We've lost contact, Senator."

"Before you do anything further, give me three minutes to reconfirm with my source."

Rodriguez closed down his phone, poured himself a double Scotch, and stared out his office window until his watch said three minutes and seven seconds.

"Okay," Rodriguez said. "I've reconfirmed. Like you, I pray that his information is correct. Nevertheless, I can't be held accountable."

"Understood, Senator."

"He claims the Moffat is a ruse, like Granby was. It's Roberts Tunnel. Get your people to the Roberts."

"I'll do my best, Senator."

"Plead the fifth. Godspeed."

Rodriguez had already packed luggage if his plan backfired and he was held accountable. He rechecked his private one-way to Hispaniola and conversed in Spanish with Jorge, the pilot on call, another poor schlep who owed the senator a favor.

He proofed his scheme again. If the Moffat blew, he'd say to Avery that his source was missing, but he'd turn up and, until that time, the senator was sworn to secrecy. Further, he'd tell Avery he appreciated his support and that he'd be the next director of the FBI's Denver field office—as soon as he was reelected senator.

And, the senator thought, *if the Moffat blows, Hendricks is screwed for good*. More water wouldn't be coming his way for a long while. If Hendricks hinted at a scandal involving Rodriguez, the senator would tell everyone Hendricks had already known the terrorist and plans because it was confirmed that Butane had dated his secretary, Hendricks's daughter. If Hendricks played tough, he'd figure out a way to implicate him as the secret source. Everyone knew he'd all but got on his knees and begged for more water for his real estate empire. He'd drag Hendricks through the mud from information he'd already gleaned from the tribe. Rodriguez would drive home the point that Hendricks last met Butane at a private meeting in his real estate office and would have to have been involved. Rodriguez felt stronger and poured himself another Scotch. He couldn't wait to destroy Hendricks.

CHAPTER SEVENTY-THREE

"DIANA, ARE YOUR PEOPLE PLACED?" Avery asked. Reluctantly, he'd sent her back to where the action was but accepted that she was the most versed. As de facto director, he needed to remain in charge and couldn't keep his top reliever out of the game. Avery was at the helm of his first crisis in FBI Denver. He would prevail.

"Not quite. Indications I've received point to the Moffat, not the Roberts."

"Stop! Don't you say another word about the Moffat." Although he was on the phone, he pointed an accusing finger at a person over a thousand miles away. "Not—another—word. Get your people to the Roberts Tunnel. Understood?"

He heard a click and noticed that he had his cell in a rigor mortis grip.

"BASTARD," SHE HISSED.

This was *the* moment for Diana. Her entire government career came down to this moment. First, she took several deep breaths. Second, she told herself that she would neither do something for personal revenge nor because of her admiration for Awol, who was pushing himself beyond what she'd asked of him. Third, she would do what she felt was the right thing for those in peril. But who was right—Awol or Avery? She felt in her gut, from all discussions with Awol, that the Roberts would be a diversion, like the dam was. Avery was a thousand miles away, and if her hunch was right, he was being fed wrong information. She reminded herself that that was not his fault. Though he was a . . . *No. Let it go.*

"Chief of Police Adkins?"

"Yes."

"Listen closely. I'm agent Diana Santos, FBI. We need some of your best men to go to the Moffat Tunnel immediately. There isn't much time."

"How do I know you are who you say you are, Ms. Santos?"

She knew that was coming. "If you feel you must, you can call my field director."

"Please give me a direct number, Ms. Santos."

After giving Adkins Rachael's direct line, Diana pulled away from the curb. She made one last futile try to reach Awol and sped off to the Moffat. Her Scout Maps program said she'd be there in thirty-six minutes.

AVERY SPAT INTO HIS CELL PHONE after she'd hung up on him. He would file for agent Diana Santos's expulsion from the FBI as soon as all this was over. He'd drilled down to her top man, who said he was positioning at the Roberts, awaiting instruction.

"You're the bomb expert, right?" Avery hollered.

Before the man could answer, Avery yelled, "Get in there and do your job!"

"I'M DIANA SANTOS. I need to get in this tunnel."

"Sorry. Got a call from police. Tunnel is locked down."

"Good." *Thank you, Rachael.* "Glad they followed my advice." She showed security her badge. "I called Chief Adkins."

AVERY NOTICED THE WOMAN standing in his doorway. "Can't you see I'm busy, Rachael?"

"The Moffat is being locked down. Security there called it in."

"On whose orders?"

"I don't know, sir."

"Get out and shut my door."

Avery covered his ass. He called his field director. "I'm locking down the Moffat too."

He couldn't believe the nonchalance of his boss. "It's in your hands, Avery."

How in the hell could that bitch pull this off? He called in reinforcements to the Roberts. "It's done, Senator. I've seen to it."

He left a voicemail for Agent Santos. "You have countered my orders. You are a disgusting disgrace to the bureau and your country."

He hoped in his heart that the Roberts would blow. Sooner rather than later. He prayed the Moffat stayed free. After locking his door, he sat and steepled his hands to his forehead. He would power nap for ten minutes.

CHAPTER SEVENTY-FOUR

Awol REACHED BOTTOM, first using his poles like canes, then using brush limbs he'd found as hasty crutches. It became warmer as he neared the bottom of the mountain, and remembering how his father told him at a young age not to baby aches and pains, he sideways-crabbed his way downward. He'd removed his crampons, which revived his feet and toes, and shoved his ax through a loop on his belt.

He became lightheaded at the bottom of the mountain. He yearned for food and sleep, in that order. He removed his pack and saw a rip in one of the straps from the ice slide. He unhooked two bungies he always carried underneath the daypack in case a strap failed. The pack repair finished, he rested on it and did everything he could to regroup, hoping Blazer would find him. After several swallows of water, less than a half bottle remained. He rethought his objective. He checked his watch and accepted that Reardon was not on the way. He was in the cave and could have already set the charges. But Reardon would delay the blow to allow time to escape clear of the cave, clear of the area that would burst open like Butane told him it would. Awol ate the last of his gorp standing up, tramping in place, trying to unfreeze his toes. He un-Velcroed his pocket and took out the map and drawings so he could review them one more time. He committed the details to memory, rechecked his pockets for the wire stripper, cutters, and electrical tape. One last time, he fingered the outline of the bypass, which lay under the zipper in his daypack.

Awol moved down the moonlit arête, forcing his legs to function. What he would have given for a hot bath . . . He arrived at ridge level and, checking Butane's map, looked to his right and noticed the clear patch indicating a cemetery. He poled over to it and worked his way to what looked like the cave, if his map was correct.

Five minutes later, he was anguished as he struggled to find the opening. He felt sick knowing that every minute wasted helped nobody and hurt everybody. He slumped to the ground thinking about Linda, Blazer, Kenny, and . . . *Gregory, oh Gregory.* He remembered a passage from one of Emerson's essays he'd read in high school: *If I have lost confidence in myself, I have the universe against me.*

Thoughts of his tragedy in the Middle East while in the army waved over him. His ex, Gloria, drifted through his mind, but for an unknown reason, his thoughts settled on something that had happened to him many years ago when he was eight years old. At a church outing, he stood at the top of the ladder of a high diving board. He was supposed to wait until an adult signaled to him that it was okay to plunge off the end. Young Karl Bergman had seen his friend run down the length of the board and leap off. It looked like fun, and without waiting, eight-year-old Karl ran down the board right after his friend had plunged. Awol felt nauseous as he remembered that in the middle of his own plunge, he saw his friend right below him and thought to himself, at the time, that he had done something wrong. Karl cannonballed himself and landed on top of the boy's head. Awol placed his hand on his forehead as though in prayer . . . and remembered. A man was throttling him. He heard screaming. He glimpsed his father pulling the man off him. No one spoke to him for days, not even his mother, and young Karl wished he was dead. After release from the hospital, the boy went to a different church and school. But Awol heard later that the boy had medical issues. He wasn't right. Awol's father had been sued for not keeping Karl in control, which the prosecutor said would have obviated the tragedy. The boy's parents and Awol's father settled the case, and the friend, whom Awol never saw again, moved with his mother and father to a different state. Awol's father and mother would not speak of the incident. They started sitting in a different pew at the back of their church, and Karl felt miserable.

Trying to shake the memory, Awol stood. He would find the opening and enter this cave.

Just at that moment, Blazer gimped up in predawn darkness.

"There you are, boy! Oh, Blazer . . . there you are." The two muzzled cheeks, and Blazer nibbled Awol's ear while making dog sounds. "Blazer, help me find the opening. Where is it, Blazer?"

He pointed the dog's nose to the half round structure of dirt and rock. Blazer started sniffing, and within a minute, the animal stopped. The entrance was lower than Awol had anticipated, which was why he hadn't seen it at first. Awol remembered what Butane had written about a drop inside and the struggle to get through—no place for Blazer, who would also use up precious air.

"Stay here, Blazer." Awol shook off his pack, pulled out the bypass, and removed his water bottle. He wished he still had that bottle he'd dropped and felt sorry for it all alone out there on the other side of the mountain. He slapped his ax to make sure he still had it. "Stay, Blazer. Guard the pack, okay, boy? Guard the pack." He didn't like leaving Blazer again but had no choice. At the last minute, he opened the pack and pulled out the tarp, figuring Blazer could lie down and sleep on it.

When Awol crouched down, he noted a partially open hole. *Could Reardon . . . ? If he came out, he would cover the opening completely*, Awol thought. He pushed the heavy rock aside and low-crawled.

I'm in. Awol had decided his fate. Blazer stayed outside. Kenny was safe at school. Linda was stable. Awol, torn by dreams and ghosts he didn't understand, had had enough. If he failed in saving the tunnel, at least he wouldn't have to live with himself and his failure. He wouldn't know. *God help me.*

The heat smacked him right away. If he didn't hurry and get through this cave tunnel, he would meet Reardon as he emerged from where Awol was headed. That thought quickened Awol, who was already crouched as he scurried down the ever-deepening passageway. The extra effort required to hurry caused him to pant. He knew he should have drank more water, and he should drink now, but first he had to get out of this cave before Reardon got back in. The heat layered onto him. He was in a steam bath, except clothed and pocketed with tools. He'd memorized the directions from Butane's map, drawn to scale on graph paper, each square marking ten feet. He gasped and thirsted, but the descending channel was too narrow to start fussing with his water bottle. He reckoned he'd advanced less than 30 percent of the way as he noted the right fork. He panicked as he remembered Butane being wiry, and Awol worried that the channel would become too tight for him.

REARDON WAS FINISHED. He followed Butane's instructions exactly, but he was about to go the extra mile. He'd set one charge with Butane's unused materials. He then positioned another charge nearby with his own back-ups to blow five minutes after the first, in case Awol aborted this one or the first malfunctioned. Devastation would be complete if either went off. *Ironic*, Reardon thought, *Butane ended up not being needed, like this extra charge won't be needed.* Ten minutes later, he finished setting the second charge. He had thirty-five minutes to get out of the cave and escape. Twenty-five minutes would have been enough, but Reardon gave himself an extra ten.

After Reardon did a last check on the second charge, he headed for the exit ladder.

GASPING AT LIMITED AIR and continual heat, after Awol turned at the fork, he felt tinges of musky air and stale oxygen feather his nostrils. *Of course, the exit hole is open.* A renewal of hope and energy transferred to his muscles as he low-crawled to the hole and peered down. No one, but as he was about to maneuver into the hole, he heard footsteps. Trained not to overthink if at risk, Awol reacted. He picked up the covering stone and waited. The footsteps grew louder, and then discernable speech—"Fuck you, Hendricks." *Reardon!* Awol raised the stone, saw Reardon's hand grab the outer rim, and waited for his head. When Reardon's eyes made it above the plane of the hole, he looked up at Awol. The stone came down skewed, grazing his head but crushing his hand. The stone wasn't positioned right to cover the hole, and before Awol could do any more damage, the hand disappeared as he heard Reardon scream and thump down the ladder.

Awol went through the opening as quick as he could, but by the time he got down, Reardon was gone. After Reardon's initial yell of pain, Awol heard the thrumming of water through the Moffat Tunnel. He unclipped his ice ax and absorbed his surroundings. Everywhere rock and wall. He moved to the tunnel, which was right where the cell picture showed it to be. He approached a platform with built-in steps and noticed wire rising from the back side of the platform up to a huge V-shaped brace supporting iron rigging that held this section of the tunnel. No sign of him, and knowing one of Reardon's hands was as good as useless, Awol stuck his ax back through the belt loop and clambered up the steps. He sight-traced the wire to the V and saw a black box. He looked up from that and saw the wire disappear behind strapping. That's where he needed to be. He climbed up to the iron V and put his ear to the box. It ticked like a clock. Based on Kenny's information, Awol knew the cover wouldn't be wired, and he opened it. The timer said twenty-two minutes. Plenty of time. He looked farther up and climbed.

There it was. The detonator, trailing from the charge. He would have to—

The rock missed Awol's head by inches, and then a second potato-sized rock whacked his shoulder, causing him to nearly drop his bypass, which he'd pulled from a side pocket. *Reardon!*

"I'm a southpaw, Awol. You got the wrong hand."

Awol figured he had fifteen minutes at the outside. What should he do? Deal with Reardon and finish him off? He didn't think Reardon would try to climb up to him with one working hand. Reardon made the decision for him.

"Thanks for leaving the hole open for me, asshole. I'll be sure to cover it tight. You try to race me up, I'll crease your head as well as your hands."

Awol clenched the bypass between his teeth and climbed as he heard Reardon trail away. He got himself into position and yelped as his rock-bruised shoulder banged a strut beneath the detonator. *Careful. Breathe. Breathe in, breathe out. Slow it down. No sudden moves.* He pulled the bypass from his teeth and remembered from the pictures he'd studied that a tiny section of the other connecting wire had to be stripped. He pulled out the special tool to do this and dropped it right after he heard Reardon holler, "Listen to this, Awol." *Thunk!* He figured Reardon had gotten up the exit ladder and slammed the rock into the hole. Awol noted the sweat dripping from himself as he hustled back down for the stripper. He retrieved it, and as he went back up noticed another wire twenty feet farther in, also stretching up to the base section of the Moffat. *So what the fuck is that? First things first,* he told himself, and with trembling hands, he managed to splice an end of his homemade bypass to the connecting wire. Eight and a half minutes. He became dizzy as he tried not to think of the other wire lurking to his right. He got the other end connected, and eyes blurred with sweat, he closed one and read five minutes and some change on the clock, which had stopped. No tick, no movement. He'd done it right and felt a surge of hope.

He reached bottom, and his legs shook uncontrollably. Under him, the Moffat train was approaching. The oncoming train vibrations worsened his tired and twisted legs. Awol was dehydrated. *Ironic,* he thought as he heard water hum through the tunnel. It was all he could do to uncap his water bottle with unsteady fingers as the crescendo climbed. He gulped water and thought of running to the exit hole and pushing off the stone. *Escape!* The flimsy tunnel lights hanging by metal rods from the rock-topped ceiling shook, and the lights flickered and dimmed as the sound of the approaching train became overwhelming.

Awol thought he might pass out but found himself lurching to the next stanchion where he'd seen that other wire. The lights shook more and hadn't stopped flickering. Awol wiped the sweat that continued to fall into his eyes and climbed the V. Something tucked into the back of his mind agitated him as he climbed and stopped, climbed and stopped. He'd made just one bypass for one bomb. He got to the familiar-looking box and opened it. *Fifty-one minutes. Wait. Minutes? Now it says forty-nine, forty-eight seconds!* The noise underneath him was unbearable as the stanchion he was hanging onto trembled. Awol, in the climb of his life, reached the bottom of the Moffat, which threatened to burst upon him. He'd been counting seconds since he left the timer. *Thirty at the outside. What did the attachment say about detonators? No, think! How did the picture Kenny sent look?* He felt a hand grip his right ankle. Before he could react, the hand squeezed and pulled his leg off the V. He went down on top of Reardon, and they both fell to the stanchion. He crushed Reardon, but Reardon shook himself and got to a crouch. Awol whisked out his ice ax. Reardon charged and ducked beneath Awol's first swing, but Awol back-swung the ax in time, catching the back of Reardon's head. Awol was amazed that Reardon grinned and charged again. This time, Awol caught him square in the forehead, and Reardon went down forever.

Awol, adrenaline charged, double stepped up the ladder and hauled himself back up to the V. His mind reached a dead end as he fingered wires from two connections. *You can pull but one wire.* He figured he had mere seconds and couldn't focus. *This connection took one end of the bypass, but you can't pull that wire—or can you? I can't see the picture, I can't* . . . Awol closed his eyes, and with the Moffat train thundering below him, threw his fingers to the wire at the other connection and yanked.

CHAPTER SEVENTY-FIVE

AWOL HUNG OVER A STRUT BRACE, the yanked wire gripped in his hand. He didn't understand that he'd blacked out until he realized the Moffat train had passed. All he heard was the thrum of water, and the lights had become bright and steady. He looked at his hand holding the wire. With effort, he opened his fingers and let the wire drop. He drank Reardon's half-full bottle of water and searched Reardon's pockets but found nothing of use. Awol figured that if Reardon was caught, he didn't want his phone confiscated.

Before hobbling down on a re-sprained and twisted leg, he looked at the second clock timer—stopped at two seconds. *Jesus.*

A tsunami of delayed pain washed over him. He could not move his other leg and knew it was broken. He eyed the stone hanging over the exit hole, but the notion of somehow hobbling there and trying to scramble up made him dizzy. He looked in the direction the train had passed and thought he might try to find an egress leading to somewhere. But he had no idea where to begin the search. He looked back to the exit hole. He wouldn't be able to climb that ladder.

He wished he hadn't drunk all of Reardon's water. He had a mouthful left in his own bottle. He was as soaked as if he'd walked through a car wash, and the heat was like an unending steam. He told himself to think. He didn't have much time. He must have banged his head during the fall with Reardon. His right eye was closing up, and aches in his jaw and head worsened. He couldn't open his mouth. He couldn't holler. He couldn't chew. *Think.* His ax lay ten feet away on the stanchion, and he crawled to it. He remembered the universal distress code he first learned from his father and later in Scouts. Awol gripped the handle of the ax with two hands and positioned himself in front of the iron railing which, from what he could see, extended from stanchion to stanchion. He banged the rail three times one half second apart, then banged the rail three times a full second apart, and finished with three bangs like the first time, one half second apart. S-O-S. He did it again, waiting about five seconds before beginning a new series of bangs. He banged the series over and over. The last thing he remembered was repeating in his mind, $S \ldots O \ldots S$.

DIANA HEARD A PITTER-patter behind her. "Blazer? What are you doing all the way over here?" She bent down to examine the patched-up mutt dragging a beat-up daypack. "Yikes! You've been through hell." She took the pack from the dog's mouth and went to her car for her bottled water. The security woman managed to scrounge up a plastic bowl. Diana took up the daypack again while Blazer lapped at the bowl, his tongue pushing it in a circle. The top of the pack was open and empty, but she recognized it. "Where's Awol?"

Blazer whinnied and tried to yip, his head twisted askew like he was in pain. He sniffed the train track and walked to the train tunnel entrance.

Diana had no idea what to do as she neared the tunnel with the security woman. She tried one last time to reach Awol on her cell and her satellite phone. Nada. She followed Blazer, who led her along one side of the train tracks. The woman said there were some doors that led to scaffolding, but only contractors and inspectors went in there.

"Is that where the water tunnel is?"

"Never seen it up close," she said. "I'm a sub here, but three others that know this place are en route."

With Blazer yipping and whinnying like a sick horse, Diana's gut told her to get going and follow the dog. *God it's hot in here.* She reached down and touched a warm rail that carried a distant thrum.

It grew dark ahead of her, save for a light farther on. She kept walking and discerned a light fixture that hung over a door. She tried to open the door but could see it was bolted. It was warm, and she held an ear to it but couldn't hear anything.

Blazer yipped but kept pattering ahead. They went by two more locked doors, one of which had a skewed light fixture and busted bulb above it. This door was also warm like the others. She closed her eyes as she eared the door. Nothing. Blazer yipped and yammered, and she followed again.

She heard a siren behind her. She'd told security to have the police call her cell as soon as the bomb squad came. Her cell beeped.

"Agent Santos here."

"We've entered the tunnel. Identify your location."

"I just passed a third bolted door."

"We've got two engineers who know the water tunnel. We will open the first door here at the west exit to have one of them check it. We have the other engineer at the tunnel exit—east—to check that first door. After that, each will work their way to meet the other."

"And the bomb squad?"

"A bomb expert is in the squad cars with each engineer as they travel the tunnel."

Diana tried to hurry as Blazer picked up the pace. She had a horrible feeling within herself as the tunnel grew darker. She was sure she had gone a mile but had seen no further lights or a door. Could she have missed a door? She was about to call the policeman again when she heard Blazer yip. He'd stopped, but not in front of a door. He sniffed the sides of the rock tunnel wall and trotted back and forth in front of the same spot.

"What is it, Blazer? Whatcha got?"

The animal kept yipping and pawed at the rock.

Diana placed an ear and her hands on the wall. She heard something, but it stopped. She placed her other ear on the wall and closed her eyes. There it was again, some type of ping.

"Quiet, Blazer. Listen."

The animal couldn't stay quiet and yipped. Diana refocused, moving more to the left and standing on her tiptoes. "Quiet, Blazer."

She heard faint pings and picked up a pattern. Quicker pings, slower pings, quicker pings. Then they stopped again. As soon as they repeated, she knew.

"Agent Santos here. I'm hearing a distress call behind this wall."

"Where are you?"

"About two miles in, but there is no entrance door or light where I am."

"Hold on."

"Engineer Carter here. Do you see a scorched rock above you?"

Diana shined her cell phone light above her. "No. Hold on . . ." She walked closer to Blazer. "Okay! I see—I've got it! A round slab above me with a blackened line on it."

"Stay right there. I'm on the way."

CHAPTER SEVENTY-SIX

CDT—Colorado
Ten months later, June 2009

AWOL WAS BACK ON THE Continental Divide Trail. He opted to hike through Creede in Colorado to avoid snow in the San Juans. At Wolf Creek Pass, he hiked straight north through Creede to San Luis Pass and from there swung east to Monarch Pass. These decisions comprised one of two legitimate routes to hike the CDT, and because he'd had to skip sections in Colorado the previous year, he completed them now. He loved hiking in Wyoming, in particular the Wind River Range area, which bordered a tundra of purpled lupine. Montana and Glacier National Park tested him, but the rugged country and weather there made him feel alive and whole once again.

He wouldn't qualify as a legitimate thru-hiker. He wouldn't complete the rest of the CDT in the required time, which would have been by May 13, the day before he'd started his thru-hike over a year ago. It was a disappointment but not a deal breaker for Awol. He drove himself up and through Wyoming and Montana with the determination of an ox and the patience of a jackrabbit. All his wisdom told him to slow down, to make a complete and final recovery, but he could not do it. He remembered his father telling him, "Son, your health is your wealth." Yet he refused to take it slow and easy. He needed to nail this lopsided and faulty triple-crown hike in his own way. He knew himself too well. If he missed the opportunity to complete the Continental Divide Trail, this king of trails, he would regret it for the rest of his life. Thus, he drove on, and a miracle ensued. His final recovery in body and mind was proportional to his progress. The harder he hiked, the better he felt. He didn't rush—he pushed.

Awol listened to his body and observed all that nature offered. He remembered the teaching of his philosophy professor at the small Lutheran college he'd attended years ago. The professor insisted on a grounding in Greek culture, and he taught about the attention classical Greeks gave to the body as well as to the mind. Awol hiker-hobbled on his previously mangled and busted legs, and he tired easily, but he rested on arêtes close to mountain peaks with Blazer. He unpacked his thoughts as to what was important, his next goals, his future with Linda. He concluded his best course was to make no big changes. He would stay where he had been staying, give Blazer to Linda for a month or so, enabling him to drop by and visit or at least see Blazer. He wouldn't force anything. *No, that hadn't worked.*

The government had treated him properly. Diana Santos, the new director of Denver's FBI field office, had asked that he keep private most of what he knew. The bureau and the Department of Homeland Security had their reasons, he was told. One was the messy replacement of former Assistant Director Avery, who had been forced out of the bureau. Diana got all of Awol's medical bills covered and reimbursed him for lodging and meals for the time he'd agreed to stay in Colorado. She also secured an additional stipend for the time it would take now for Awol to complete the CDT. That was much appreciated, and Awol had thanked her. He planned to visit Diana after he finished, but he never did. He wasn't sure why.

Thinking about his future, Awol thought he might take a course in Spanish. That would open new neural pathways and keep his mind sharp. He could have used the language on the Pacific Crest Trail, and Spanish was the second language of his country.

Awol put all the chaos and bad memories behind him. He reached out to the few he met on the CDT, but he remained alone with Blazer and, for the moment, preferred it that way. The nights became cold and the dawns colder. Blazer appeared content but was still suffering from the aftereffects of the wounds he'd sustained. He rested often and licked where his wounds had once been, and sometimes he yipped in pain when he couldn't reach them. Together they made a good team. In animal ways and in Ute ways, they supported each other and provided the internal fortitude to push on.

On a crisp late afternoon in September, they reached a rocky ridge overlooking a river to their left and a lake in front of them. Awol checked his map, found the lake, and estimated the Canadian border at no more than fourteen miles ahead. Tomorrow he would complete his trek.

That night, he and Blazer camped at the far end of the ridge, and Awol experienced an unusual but most welcome epiphany. Under a bright full moon, he imagined how tiny and insignificant humans looked inching along in the valleys below. This segued into thoughts about the petty but obstreperous, ridiculous but mighty confrontations in the troubled species of man. Greed and wealth had no place in the further evolution of humankind. Arguments, flustered red faces, feuds, and wars were as asinine as they were futile. Awol realized it and was embarrassed for his species. What in the hell was all the fuss about?

Awol thought of Gregory and Kenny. Linda. Animal and Ute ways. His thoughts compounded, and Awol vowed, yet again, to resurrect himself and begin anew—one day at a time.

The last day on the Continental Divide Trail did not show great promise. Awol had gotten up to void, and on the way back to his tent, he stubbed his toe on a rock near the fire ring. He smothered it with both hands and squeezed gently. Blazer scuttled over, sniffed, and licked the injured toe. The sun peeked into the eastern horizon with the first light of day. The morning beams gave Awol wonderment and hope. He studied the signs. He was lucky to be alive and felt blessed that he had less than fourteen miles to go to accomplish his quest. Blazer sat beside him, also looking to the sun, and the dog seemed satisfied as he sniffed the morning air. Awol reread the signs. All was right with him and his world. And, for the record, Awol and Blazer finished in Waterton Lakes National Park, Alberta, that blustery and overcast afternoon.

BRUCE HENDRICKS WAS SUED by his former clients, all except for Senator Rodriguez. Hendricks avoided prison by cooperating with the FBI and exposing his college friend at Wharton and their inside scheme as well as fraud details in the Cayman Islands. It cost him every cent of his US and foreign funds and savings. In a final stroke of irony, he had to sell every one of his properties and all of his remaining acres on the Front Range to pay his bank loans and the clients he owed in lawsuits. But he didn't pay back Rodriguez. Hendricks fell short. He was flat broke but managed to eat his way to an additional forty pounds.

Ginger stood by him. She read about Butane's body being discovered and was mortified and outraged that the reservation wanted nothing to do with him. She took over and arranged his burial in a potter's lot outside of Denver. No one came to the service except for her and her father, who said nothing during the brief ceremony. Ginger bought a Kawasaki "crotch rocket" and graced each forearm with tattoos, a rose on one, a butterfly on the other. She went on to operate her own Jiffy Lube franchise and made a switch to bubblegum, which she chews constantly.

Senator Rodriguez regained nothing of his investments to Hendricks's FRE. He had gambled everything he had and lost. His relation to Hendricks was hush-hush. He was no longer accepted by the reservation and felt that they would plot against him at the right opportunity. But worse than that, his colleagues and government were suspicious of him. Diana and Avery had nothing solid with which to incriminate him. His fingerprints were on everything, but his signatures were on nothing. The government didn't buy the senator's story. He was told to get his resume on the street. His reelection campaign and government career were over. He remained separated from his wife and gambled at every opportunity.

Chief Running Waters and the reservation continued to request more water. Water Conservation Chairman Anderson maintained that due to unpredictable wildfires and droughts, his request would remain on hold. Expansion plans for the Moffat Tunnel, however, continued unabated.

AWOL WAS VISITING LINDA in his former house. He was sober and stayed busy with his kitchen-bath remodeling business. He'd told his partner, Tommy, to take some well-deserved time off. Blazer napped by the kitchen table where they sat. The spot Blazer picked was closer to Awol.

After reanswering questions and describing details of his CDT hike, Linda was silent for several minutes.

"You deserved more from the FBI after what they put you through. Why should they get all the credit? The papers, that reporter you told me about, why didn't she write a big story, get you on national news?"

Awol smiled. "It's political, I'm sure. National security wants to look strong. They don't want some unknown hiker like me as a national hero. Let them get the credit. Don't forget, Diana rescued me in that tunnel. I wouldn't be here now if she hadn't."

"Who defused the bomb?"

"It doesn't bother me. It was a fifty-fifty chance that I would pull the right wire. Fate was good to me. It was Diana who found Butane dead. She searched the cabin and discovered Reardon's diary and binders. The bureau paid my doctor bills and lodging, the flights, and all that."

"Oh, and don't forget that letter of accommodation from the governor of Colorado." She fluttered her eyes.

Awol smiled and put his glass of iced tea back on the table. He stood and stepped over to pat Blazer. "Guess I should be going."

"Want some supper?"

Awol turned to her, hands on hips. He glanced at his watch. "If you like." He walked to the kitchen window and looked at her bird feeders, which he'd made for her several years ago. Two wrens were scarfing up seed.

Awol didn't say much during the meal. Linda filled in the gaps by discussing this and that. They quieted as Blazer continued to nap.

"Seeing anybody?" Awol said as he swabbed extra cheese on canapés, for him a favorite dessert.

"No. Are you?"

"Not really." He moved the tiny toast to his mouth and looked at her.

"Which means?"

Awol put his hands behind his neck, relaxed his posture, and eyed her after he chewed. "It was a one-time thing, Linda."

"Planning on doing it again?"

"I hope not to. And I won't ask anymore about that stuff."

He cleared the dishes and brought them to the sink. He took out her favorite coffee cup—*Same Shit, Different Day*—and poured her a cup of fresh brew. He placed it in front of her and sat back down. Blazer, smelling the coffee, twitched his nostrils and rolled to his other side.

Awol placed his hands behind his neck again and looked over the kitchen, which in his spare time he'd remodeled several years ago. He rested his eyes on hers.

Linda blew into her cup and took a sip. She started to smile as she held her cup in front of her with both hands. "Oh, Karl, what am I going to do with you?"

He grinned. The night was young. The night was theirs.

A NOTE FROM THE AUTHOR

(4/11/2009)

"DENVER WATER IS PROPOSING to send an additional 5 billion gallons of water to the Front Range through the expansion of its Moffat Collection System." (This involves the Bureau of Reclamation, Moffat Tunnel district commissioners, Colorado Department of Local Affairs, House Interior and Committee on Insular Affairs, Colorado Supreme Court . . .)

LIKE AWOL, I DID NOT COMPLETE a thru-hike of the CDT. At this point in my life, being consumed with writing and promoting the "Awol" series, I doubt that I will go back to finish it. I need to add that it was a rough trail for me to navigate; I got lost a lot. At over 3,100 miles, the CDT is the longest of the triple-crown hiking trails, and I fell behind expectations. This is a disappointment because I did complete the AT and the PCT, the other legs of the triple crown. My advice for the CDT hiker: Go out there with a hiker friend. Two heads are always better than one, and you can share responsibilities.

For the benefit of my readers, I placed all the novel's major scenes in areas that I hiked. I spent most of my time in New Mexico and Colorado and, in particular, Rocky Mountain National Park. I did some hiking in Wyoming and less in Montana. The Continental Divide Trail is an awesome experience for any hiker. Had I the chance to try again for the triple crown, I would—*Go West, young man*—begin with the AT, next the CDT, and save the PCT for last. The PCT was, for me, the most scenic hike and the easiest of the three. Carry on, fellow hikers!